UNTIL WE WEREN'T:

A STORY OF DESTINY AND FAITH

JAMEY MOODY

Until We Weren't: A Story of Destiny and Faith

©2024 by Jamey Moody. All rights reserved

Edited: Kat Jackson

Cover: Anita Hallam

This is a work of fiction. Names, characters, places, and incidents are the product of the author's imagination or are used fictitiously. Any resemblance to an actual person, living or dead, business establishments, events, or locales is entirely coincidental. This book, or part thereof, may not be reproduced in any form without permission.

Visit my website or sign up for my mailing list here: www.jameymoodyauthor.com.

I'd love to hear from you! Email me at jameymoodyauthor@gmail.com.

As an independent author a review is always appreciated.

꽃 Created with Vellum

CONTENTS

Also by Jamey Moody   v

Chapter 1	1
Chapter 2	10
Chapter 3	18
Chapter 4	27
Chapter 5	36
Chapter 6	44
Chapter 7	52
Chapter 8	61
Chapter 9	70
Chapter 10	79
Chapter 11	87
Chapter 12	96
Chapter 13	104
Chapter 14	112
Chapter 15	121
Chapter 16	129
Chapter 17	137
Chapter 18	146
Chapter 19	154
Chapter 20	163
Chapter 21	172
Chapter 22	180
Chapter 23	188
Chapter 24	196
Chapter 25	205
Chapter 26	214
Chapter 27	223
Chapter 28	232
Chapter 29	241
Chapter 30	250

Chapter 31	258
Chapter 32	267
Chapter 33	275
Chapter 34	283
Ten Years Later	289
About the Author	295
Also by Jamey Moody	297
See You Next Month	299
Chapter 2	308

ALSO BY JAMEY MOODY

Stand Alones

Live This Love

One Little Yes

Who I Believe

* What Now

*See You Next Month

Until We Weren't: A Story of Destiny and Faith

The Your Way Series:

* Finding Home

*Finding Family

*Finding Forever

The Lovers Landing Series

*Where Secrets Are Safe

*No More Secrets

*And The Truth Is …

*Instead Of Happy

The Second Chance Series

*The Woman at the Top of the Stairs

*The Woman Who Climbed A Mountain

*The Woman I Found In Me

Sloan Sisters' Romance Series

*CeCe Sloan is Swooning

*Cory Sloan is Swearing

*Cat Sloan is Swirling

Christmas Novellas

*It Takes A Miracle

The Great Christmas Tree Mystery

With One Look

*Also available as an audiobook

1

"Those are doing well despite this heat."

Faith looked up and smiled. "Hi, Mrs. Baker. How are you?"

"Oh honey, I'm just out enjoying this sunshine," Mrs. Baker replied. "I'm glad to see you. I've told the boy who cuts the grass he'd better take care of these plants or you'll be after him."

Faith Fields was the owner of Lush Fields Landscaping. She had planted the grass and created the flower beds for this retirement home several years ago when she was working for another company, but she still stopped by occasionally to check on the plants and shrubs.

Faith chuckled. "Sometimes plants die, Mrs. Baker."

"It's been years since you've planted these and not one has died. The way you lovingly tend to the delicate plants to make sure they thrive makes me wonder if you give that kind of attention to other parts of your life," Mrs. Baker said.

Faith was on her knees and stopped to look up at the older woman and smirk. "You know this was one of the first projects I was able to create and put in. It's special to me and that's why I come by to make sure I chose the right plants for this area. I want you to have something beautiful to look at on your daily walks. Besides, I get to see you."

Mrs. Baker smiled. "Your friend from The Green Thumb came by earlier this week and checked on that very flower bed."

Faith bristled and paused for a moment then she stabbed her small shovel into the earth around the vinca plant she was tending to.

"I still don't understand why you two don't come by together anymore," Mrs. Baker said. "It seems to me you'd be finished a lot quicker with two of you."

Faith pushed the dirt around the tender plants then looked up at Mrs. Baker. "You know why. We both have our own companies now and don't work together any longer."

"Yet you both still come by and check on these plants," Mrs. Baker said, raising one eyebrow.

Faith sighed and tried to push down the knot that had formed in her stomach.

"Why is it again that you two opened separate companies? You did everything together to make this place beautiful," Mrs. Baker said.

"Now, Mrs. Baker, it's been years," Faith said, standing up and dusting off her pants. "You know we had our own ideas about things and decided to go off on our own. Some things don't flourish no matter how much attention you give them."

"Mmhmm," Mrs. Baker muttered, staring at Faith. "It seems to me that sometimes these plants get a little brown or wilt and you think they're gone, but lo and behold there are still little shoots of green at the base. There's still life."

Faith put her hands on her hips and tilted her head. "When did you become a horticulturist?"

"I've watched these plants grow since you put them in, dear," Mrs. Baker said.

Faith reached down to pick up her other tools.

"Some of them have withered, but you haven't had to replace them because they keep coming back," Mrs. Baker continued.

Faith looked into Mrs. Baker's eyes and knew she wasn't just referring to the plants.

"Sometimes plants aren't the only things that wither," Mrs. Baker said. "I live in a place where I see that happen every day. Hell, I experience it because of my age."

"But you're not," Faith said with a smile. "You're thriving."

Mrs. Baker scoffed. "And your business is thriving, but are you?"

Faith smirked. "I'll see you again soon, Mrs. Baker."

"Think about it, Faith," Mrs. Baker said. "It hurts my heart to see my friends wither away before their time."

Faith smiled and walked back to her truck. The last thing she wanted to do was think about *her friend* as Mrs. Baker had called her. Destiny Green was the furthest thing from a friend. It made Faith's stomach queasy that she ever let that woman touch her, much less trust her with her heart.

Mrs. Baker was right that they did work well together. As time passed they became more than co-workers and led their own teams within the company. Faith trusted Destiny with her ideas of how they could turn a piece of ground into something beautiful.

In turn Destiny befriended Faith and they began to spend time together outside of work. They had fun and Faith felt like she'd found a true friend. As their friendship evolved into more, Faith was hesitant at first. Her past was full of people who were supposed to care for her, yet always let her down.

But Destiny could see past Faith's walls and had been patient as well as caring. When Faith moved in with Destiny, she finally relaxed and let herself be loved.

"You were such a fucking idiot," she muttered. She shook her head, put the truck in gear and sped out of the parking lot.

* * *

"They aren't supposed to award the contract until tomorrow. I don't know why you keep checking for an email."

Destiny Green looked up from her computer and smirked at her assistant, Monica. They were friends long before Destiny started The Green Thumb, so when Destiny needed someone to run the office, Monica asked for the job. She was tired of the long hours and stress as a paralegal. Destiny welcomed her to The Green Thumb; they worked well together and had remained friends.

"I know." Destiny sighed. "I was hoping maybe if we won the bid they'd let us know today."

"Mmhmm," Monica murmured. "I know what you're doing."

Destiny met her eyes and raised her eyebrows.

"You're making sure Lush Fields Landscaping doesn't get it."

"I didn't say that," Destiny said defensively.

"You didn't have to," Monica said. "I'm not sure what you hope for more. That we get the job or Faith doesn't."

Destiny scoffed. "Of course I want us to get the job."

"Come on, how long have we been working together?" Monica said. "Who knew the landscaping business was so

Until We Weren't:

cutthroat? I think I need to pitch a reality show. We could call it Landscape Wars."

"What!" Destiny exclaimed.

"You and Faith are the perfect enemies."

"That's not funny."

"It's not supposed to be funny," Monica said. "As much as y'all hate each other it'd make for great TV and probably put both our companies on the map. You'd be turning jobs down."

"I don't hate Faith," Destiny stated.

"Okay, whatever you say." Monica grinned. "I've only known you for ten years and we've worked together for three. It's not like you and Faith weren't both my friends at one time."

Destiny stared at Monica. She could feel her cheeks getting warm.

"You know, they say there's a fine line between love and hate," Monica said.

Destiny looked back at her computer. "I'm actually doing a little research. Do you know that new construction off Interstate 35? It's going to be a huge business complex."

"No comment and a subject change," Monica said. "Okay, that conversation is closed. Yes, I know the area you're talking about."

"They plan to take bids to do the landscaping for the entire complex, but they're also looking at breaking it into different sections and tying them all together in some way. If I can come up with something creative and different, this job could boost The Green Thumb's exposure and make it one of the top landscaping businesses in the state."

"But that place is huge. Can we pull off something like that?"

"We'd have to put everyone on it, but I think we can," Destiny said.

"Is that where you were this afternoon? I wondered why you had dirt on your pants when you came in. You rarely have time to work in the field anymore."

"Uh, no," Destiny replied. "I had to check on something else."

"Don't tell me you were at the retirement home again." Monica shook her head. "What is it with that place? The Green Thumb does not get a penny from that establishment."

When Destiny didn't say anything, Monica continued. "Before starting your own company, you were working for the Galloways at Landscape Artists, right?"

Destiny nodded. "Yes, and they taught me to not only take pride in my work, but also to be attentive. The land can change over time and sometimes your design needs to change with it. Going back and checking on projects I did when I worked for them is valuable in how I bid on jobs now."

"I wonder if Faith does the same thing. She worked there, too, right?" Monica said.

Destiny sat back in her chair and stared at Monica. "If you must know, I go back there not only to check the grounds, but also to visit with one of the residents." She smiled just thinking about Mrs. Baker. "When Faith and I were putting in the flower beds we made a friend. Every time I go back, Mrs. Baker appears while I'm tending to the plants and we have a nice visit."

"Maybe I should ask her what happened between you and Faith because no matter how many times I ask, you won't enlighten me," Monica said.

Until We Weren't: 7

"Maybe because it's none of your business," Destiny said.

"Oh, but it is. I'm concerned with your well-being and I know Faith has a lot to do with that."

Destiny laughed sarcastically. "How so? It's been three years since Faith and I were together."

"Three long years since you've been on a date or smiled when talking about another woman," Monica said. "I've tried to set you up several times."

"If you haven't noticed, I'm trying to run a company," Destiny said defensively. "That leaves no time for dating or much else."

"Oh, you could make time. That's what I'm for. As your assistant, I'm supposed to take some of the burden off of you."

"And you do," Destiny said.

"Why did you and Faith break up again? I forget," Monica said. "Was it because you worked all the time? Because that's all you've done since you two broke up. Come to think of it, you and Faith didn't do much with us or our friend group when you were together."

Destiny looked back to her computer. "You'd have to ask her," she muttered.

"What was that? I should ask her? Come on, Destiny. This is the closest you've come to telling me what happened," Monica pleaded.

Exasperated, Destiny sighed. "I said, you'd have to ask her. She never told me why she left."

Monica stood in front of Destiny's desk with her mouth hanging open. "Really?"

"Yes, really."

"All this time, she has never told you why she left?"

Monica said, unbelieving. "I thought you'd eventually open up about it, but you really don't know?"

Destiny shook her head. "Please don't ask me about this again, Monica." She could feel the familiar stab of loss in her stomach. It was accompanied by sadness now that the anger had washed away.

"Okay, Des," Monica said softly.

"It's time to close up for the day. You go ahead," Destiny said, still staring at her computer screen. "I'm going to stay for a little longer."

"Don't stay too long. We'll be busy in the morning starting that new job we're going to win."

Destiny smiled. "That's right."

"See you tomorrow," Monica said, walking out of the office.

Destiny sat back in her chair and sighed. It had been three long years since her life imploded. She knew that was a little dramatic, but that's how it felt. She had to work late one night and when she'd gotten home, Faith was gone along with most of her things. When she tried to call her, she discovered Faith had blocked her number.

She tried to find her at work the next day, but Faith had cleaned out her locker and quit. Destiny began to call their friends including Monica and her wife, Kim, but they didn't know what was going on either. She finally cornered a worker on Faith's crew who was also a friend. Destiny could still remember the sad look on Mark's face and the hurt in her heart was just as sharp today as it was back then.

"She said to tell you that you know what you did," Mark said.
Destiny looked at him with such confusion, but he shrugged.
"That's all she told me," he said.
"But what did I do?" Destiny pleaded.

"I don't know," Mark said. *"She just said, 'she'll know what she did.'"*

Three years later and Destiny still didn't know what Faith was talking about. She had tried over and over to get Faith to talk to her and even asked their friends to help, but Faith only told them the same thing she told Mark.

Destiny had run into Faith a few times since their breakup because they both had their own landscaping businesses now and bid on some of the same projects. The first time she saw Faith after she'd left, Destiny remembered the pain then the anger flashing in Faith's beautiful blue eyes, the same eyes that used to light up whenever they met Destiny's. But now Faith avoided her and wouldn't meet her gaze.

Destiny could feel tears burn the back of her eyes. "Oh no you don't, Faith Fields," Destiny whispered. "I'm done crying unanswered tears for you."

2

Faith yawned then took a sip of her coffee as she waited for the light to change. It had been a long evening followed by a fitful night of sleep littered with snippets of dreams.

Sometimes after she'd had a visit with Mrs. Baker, thoughts of Destiny Green would not leave her head. No matter how many times Faith pushed them away another memory would surface. How long does it take to get past the hurt of betrayal? She may never get over it, but surely it would eventually go away so she could live her life in peace.

Faith took another sip of her coffee and scoffed. "What life?" she muttered. All she did was work, but that's what it took to run a small, yet successful, landscaping business. Lush Fields Landscaping didn't just maintain outdoor spaces, Faith also created concepts with beauty in mind for this sprawling urban area she served.

Her company provided more than just mowing and trimming the grass. She designed areas with color that were uplifting and others with subdued plants inviting calm and relaxation. The landscape around a building could set the tone for the business inside. It was more than just grass and shrubs.

Faith pulled into the parking lot and drove around to the loading area of her favorite wholesale nursery. She was meeting Mark, her longtime friend who ran the installation crew for Lush Fields. Faith dreamed up the designs, went over them with Mark, and he and his team made them come to life at the project site.

When she'd quit her previous job and decided to start her own business, Mark was the first person she asked to come with her. He believed in her vision and took the leap. They had built a thriving company with a steady client base, but Faith was ready to go after bigger jobs.

"Hey, where were you last night?" Mark asked, walking up to the truck. "I thought you were going to come by and have a beer with us."

"I was, but I heard about a big job off I-35 at that new office park," Faith said. "I started looking at the area on the internet and—"

"The next thing you knew it was midnight. Is that why you look so tired? I know you couldn't possibly be out with anyone." Mark said, giving her a pointed look.

Faith smirked. "It wasn't quite that late, but it was too late for a beer."

"Faith, it's never too late for a beer," Mark said seriously. "One of these days I'm going to convince you that it's okay to smile and have a good time."

Faith shook her head and rolled her eyes.

Mark leaned in and lowered his voice. "There are beautiful women out there who would love to show you a good time."

"I can show myself a good time and these flowers, plants, and shrubs are all the beauty I need."

Mark sighed. "You have a big birthday coming up. I refuse to let you turn forty without some kind of fun. Prepare yourself because I'm not taking no for an answer."

"It's not a big deal."

"Oh yes it is. We'll talk more as it gets closer," Mark said. "Check out these butterfly shrubs."

"Oh, those are nice," Faith said. "I texted Abel and asked him to pull the Black Knights. These dark purple blooms will be beautiful."

"Yeah, he had them waiting when I got here. I'll start loading them," he said. "I've already loaded the rest of our order into my truck."

"I want to look at his gardenias," Faith said. "I really want to try a few of them sprinkled throughout that bed against the building. They smell so good, but can be finicky."

"Not with your green thumb." Mark grinned as he began to put the shrubs in Faith's truck.

Faith chuckled and walked into the nursery. She wandered through the rows of shrubs until she found the gardenias.

"Those would look nice with the butterflies Mark's loading," Abel said, walking up beside Faith.

"They would, but..." Faith said, turning one of the plants around to examine it.

"You can get them to thrive," Abel said. "Everything grows for you."

Faith shrugged. "Most of the time."

"How many do you want?"

"Let me have these," Faith said, pulling four pots into the aisle.

"Come sign for your order and I'll get a cart to load these," Abel said.

Faith followed him over to the counter and looked over her order as Abel loaded the gardenias. She signed the receipt, turned around, and looked straight into the dark brown eyes that once made her melt with the slightest glance. For a moment everything stopped and she was whisked back to a happier time.

"I'll be with you in a minute, Destiny," Abel called from behind them.

Faith's heart started to pound in her chest and she was instantly irate at her body's betrayal.

Where was it, she wondered. She couldn't see the slightest hint of guilt which should be shimmering in Destiny's eyes. Instead, for just a flash, she saw softness, but then Destiny took a shaky breath and stood a little taller. The corner of Faith's mouth slightly turned up from seeing Destiny falter somewhat before regaining her composure.

"I don't guess you're buying supplies for that Sims job," Faith said with a smirk.

Destiny scoffed. "You didn't get it either."

Faith smiled. Lush Fields Landscaping may not have won the job, but knowing The Green Thumb didn't get it either had eased the sting a little.

"At least they gave me a reason why they went with the other company," Destiny said, looking into Faith's eyes.

Faith could feel the heat of Destiny's stare. Was that sadness in her eyes? Surely not.

"We've got plenty to do," Destiny continued, looking away and shuffling her feet. "Besides, I've got my eye on something bigger."

"Surely you don't mean the business complex up the Interstate," Faith said. "That's more my size."

Destiny huffed. "Oh yeah? Because you're such a big player in the landscaping business in the Austin area?"

Faith furrowed her brow, set her feet and folded her arms across her chest. Destiny was a couple inches taller than Faith and heavier. Where Faith's frame was slight and willowy, Destiny was muscular and athletic. Years of moving dirt and planting shrubs and flowers had made both women strong.

Faith remembered how Destiny once marveled at her body.

"You are such an enigma," Destiny said. "Your beautiful, lithe body is so strong and powerful. People don't see that by simply looking at you, but I know. I've felt your strength. I've experienced your power." She ran her fingers through Faith's light golden strands of brown hair.

They were naked in bed when Destiny had told her that. Faith had proceeded to give Destiny another taste of her strength and they'd made love late into the night.

But here they were about to face off—in what, Faith wasn't sure.

"Oh, stop!" Destiny exclaimed. "You don't have to get all big and bold with me, Faith."

"You'll find out how big and bold I can be if you fuck with my company, Green," Faith said, venom in her voice.

"I'm not fucking with you or your company. Why would I do that?" Destiny shrugged and furrowed her brow.

"Why wouldn't you?" Faith said. "It's not like you haven't done it before."

"What?" Destiny exclaimed with a confused look on her face.

"Hey," Mark said, walking up looking from one woman to the other. "Everything is loaded, Faith." He looked at Destiny and smiled. "Abel is taking your order to your truck, Destiny."

"Fine," Faith said, walking past Destiny giving her shoulder the slightest nudge with her own.

* * *

Destiny closed her eyes and fisted her hands where they hung at her side. She tried to calm her pounding heart before she talked to Mark. It wasn't his fault that his boss was such a bitch.

"You okay?" Mark asked quietly.

Destiny opened her eyes and smiled. "Hi, Mark. How's it going?"

Mark grinned. "Oh, you know. Just watching two people that could've had the most amazing life together totally fuck it all up."

Destiny looked at him with shock on her face.

"The air crackles with electricity when you two are near one another. I used to wonder if you were going to tear each other's clothes off and now I'm wondering if you're about to get into a fist fight."

"I would never hit her," Destiny exclaimed with shock in her voice.

Mark smiled and nodded. "She wouldn't hit you either."

"I don't know." Destiny blew out a deep breath. "What the fuck," she said, frustrated.

"Have you ever considered apologizing?" Mark asked.

Destiny's brows flew up her forehead. "For what? Breathing the same air?"

"Uh, no," Mark said slowly. "That's not what I meant."

Destiny tilted her head then realization covered her face. "Oh, you mean..." She sighed. "Don't you think I've thought of that? I don't know what I have to fucking apologize for, Mark!"

Mark winced and led them over to a bench at the side of the counter. "You really don't know?"

"That was probably the longest conversation I've had with her in three years. She never told me what she thinks I did. If I knew what it was and could apologize, I don't know how I'd even do it." Destiny threw up her hands in defeat. "If she saw me come into your shop, I'm quite sure she'd either leave or throw me out."

"Man, what could you have done that's unforgivable?" Mark said.

"I know you don't believe me and you, like everyone else, think I'm hiding something, but I swear, I don't know what I could've done. I was head over heels in love with Faith. I wanted to spend my life with her."

"Was?"

Destiny glanced over at him. "It doesn't matter if I love her or not," she said with a sad smile.

Mark sighed. "All she does is work. I can't even get her to have a beer with the crew. She rarely smiles. Micromanages everything. She trusts no one and if it wasn't for her assistant, Amy, I'm not sure anyone would work for us."

"It's hard starting then running a business," Destiny said, in Faith's defense. "It takes all your time and energy. When you're not at the office or a job site you're thinking about the next job."

Mark gave her a sarcastic smile and chuckled. "You're defending her?"

Destiny shrugged. "Like it matters."

"This morning she was talking about the big office complex over on Interstate 35," Mark said.

"Yeah, I'm going to have a look and work up a bid on it," Destiny said. She whipped her head towards Mark, wondering if she should've told him that.

He chuckled. "It's okay. I'm your friend, too, Destiny, and I would never give up your plans. I'm sure Faith is doing the same thing. It won't be the first time the both of you have bid on the same job."

Destiny nodded. "I've missed you, but I'm afraid if Faith knew we were talking to each other she might fire you."

Mark chuckled. "No she wouldn't. You don't worry about me. And I have a feeling you've been doing the same thing she has. All work and no play."

Destiny grimaced. "I have no desire to give my heart to anyone. When Faith up and left like that I was devastated and it still hurts. That's just the way it is. Believe me, I wish I could get past it all. One of these days, I'll wake up and decide I don't have to stay busy for the next sixteen hours in order to take a deep breath."

"Aww, Des," Mark said, putting his arm around her. "I'm so sorry."

As good as it felt to have Mark's sympathy, Destiny knew she'd burst into tears if she didn't get up.

"Thanks," she said, jumping up and swiping under her eyes. "My mom keeps telling me it will all work out."

"Your mom is a pretty smart lady," Mark said. "You should listen to her."

Destiny shrugged. "What choice do I have?"

3

Faith grabbed a cart and walked into the produce section of the store. She usually either had groceries delivered or picked them up. But lately the avocados and fruit she'd received hadn't lasted very long. Faith knew she could be considered picky, but why do something halfway instead of doing it right? She was that way with her work and expected the same of the people who worked with her.

She squeezed an avocado then another as she put them in a bag.

"Faith?" a woman said, pushing a cart up beside her.

Faith looked up into a kind face with a loving smile. Gretchen Green was one of Faith's favorite people and she didn't have many. The problem was that Gretchen also happened to be Destiny's mother. She hadn't seen her in a long time, but she'd talked to her once briefly on the phone and texted with her a handful of times since leaving Destiny.

One advantage of living in an urban area is that you didn't just run into people like you might in a smaller town.

Until We Weren't:

But Faith missed Gretchen almost as much as she did Destiny. Gretchen was always kind to Faith and genuinely cared about her well being.

Faith hadn't grown up in the best of circumstances and her trust issues had begun at a young age. Her parents hadn't been around much when she was growing up. They provided basic necessities but were never interested in what she, her brother, or her sister were doing. Faith was a decent athlete and managed to get a scholarship at a small college, working her way through school. The only time she heard from her family was when they needed money.

The first time Destiny took her home to meet her parents, Faith immediately liked Gretchen and Michael Green. But somehow Gretchen knew that Faith hadn't had the nurturing influence of a mother and she took her in and restored that part of her wounded soul. Faith truly felt like part of the Green family.

"Gretchen," Faith said with a genuine smile.

The woman held her arms open and Faith walked into them. She couldn't remember the last time she'd hugged another person.

"It's so good to see you," Gretchen said, letting her go.

Faith nodded and smiled at her. She guessed Gretchen knew not to ask how she was doing or could tell by looking at her.

"I've been thinking about you," Gretchen said.

"You have?" Faith replied, furrowing her brow.

"You sound surprised. Don't you occasionally think about the people you love?"

Faith nodded. There weren't too many people Faith could say she loved, but Gretchen Green was definitely one of them.

Gretchen took Faith's hands and inspected her fingernails. "I see you've been out playing in the dirt." She ran her thumb across a faint scar on Faith's index finger.

Faith chuckled. When she and Destiny would visit, Gretchen would send them to the sink to wash their hands. She loved to tease them and said their jobs were "playing in the dirt." But she was their biggest supporter and proud of the beautiful expanses they created.

"I stopped by for a few things on my way home from a job," Faith explained.

"Well, it's good to see you're going home before dark. I'm aware of the long hours you work along with someone else I know." Gretchen raised a brow.

Faith smiled and rested her hands on her cart.

"You know, scars are a kind of blessing. You had to learn that at such a young age," Gretchen said with a compassionate smile. "They can not only make us stronger, but also enable us to look at things again when it might not be as painful."

Faith tilted her head. She knew what Gretchen was trying to say. Maybe enough time had passed for her and Destiny to be able to talk about what happened between them.

"They certainly make us stronger, but..." Faith sighed. "Time is supposed to make it not hurt quite so much, right? I'm not sure about that."

Gretchen nodded. "Oh, I don't know that the pain ever eases. Maybe we learn to deal with it and perhaps not be afraid."

Faith felt like Gretchen was seeing straight into her heart. There was a part of her that was afraid to talk to Destiny. She hoped that someday the fear might fade and she could tell Destiny just how much she'd hurt her.

"I love you, Faith," Gretchen said, hugging her again.

"I love you, too," Faith said around the lump in her throat.

Gretchen pushed her cart past Faith and continued down the aisle.

After several deep breaths, Faith pushed her cart back to the front of the store and walked to her car.

She hadn't seen Destiny or anyone in her family in years and now she'd seen her and her mom on the same day. Faith wasn't sure what the universe was trying to tell her, but she wished it would stop.

Faith pulled into the parking lot in the front of her business. She drove around to the side of the building and through the gate that opened to a large fenced area. The yard held all the various equipment Lush Fields Landscaping owned as well as random plants that hadn't been used. The back of the building was a shop where equipment was repaired, things were stored, and still more unused plants were sprinkled about.

Faith stopped her truck in front of a small tiny house at the rear of the building. Inside was a small kitchen, living area, bathroom, and bedroom that would just fit a queen sized mattress. It was larger than her dorm room in college, but not by much.

There was an area beside the front door with a chair and a small table that served as a makeshift front porch. Faith didn't sit outside very often. Sometimes she'd make it home in time to see a killer sunset this time of year. The summer brought heat, but it also brought beautiful evening vistas. In the winter months the sun disappeared behind the buildings across the street, but this time of year the sun would go down in a small field, lighting up the sky as darkness descended like a soft blanket.

Before she walked up the two steps to her front door she

turned in time to see that the sun was already gone, but the sky was a dark orange fading into a deep purple. When she and Destiny worked together they would always stop, no matter what job they were working or if they were already home, to watch the sunset together.

She remembered one of the first days after they had each been given their own crews at Landscape Artists. Their crews were both working at an apartment complex. Faith and Destiny were on opposite ends of the large complex, each planting flower beds. Faith's phone vibrated in her pocket and when she looked at the screen Destiny was calling her.

"Hey, look at the sun," Destiny said softly.

Faith walked to the end of the building where she was working and saw the sun slipping beneath the horizon.

"That sunset was almost as beautiful as you," Destiny said. "Look to your left."

Faith turned away from the sun and looked to her left. On the sidewalk, two buildings over, she could see Destiny staring her way with her phone to her ear.

Faith chuckled. "You can't see how much dirt is on my face from there."

"I see you with my heart," Destiny said. "And you are beautiful."

Faith smiled and was pretty sure Destiny could see how her face lit up from where she stood.

The orange had disappeared from the sky and Faith sighed. Had the love she and Destiny shared disappeared just as easily? *How could she say she loved me and do what she did?*

Faith walked into the house and could feel the sting of tears in her eyes. Scars may make you stronger, but they still hurt.

Until We Weren't:

* * *

Destiny backed her truck into her parents' driveway. She got out, opened the tailgate, and took out a flat of marigolds.

"Hi, honey," Michael Green said, walking out from the garage.

Destiny got her love of working with her hands from her father. He had a nicely equipped shop built on one side of the garage.

"Hi, Dad," Destiny replied, walking to the flower bed at the front of the house.

"Whatcha got there?"

"Oh, I know how much Mom likes marigolds and I had a few left over from a project I finished today. I thought I'd surprise her and give her flower bed a pop of color." Destiny plopped down on her knees and began to take the bright gold plants out of the plastic carrier.

She reached in her back pocket for the small garden trowel and began to dig holes in the front of the flower bed to evenly space the flowers along the edge.

"She'll love those," Michael said.

"Love what?" Gretchen said, walking out of the front door. When she saw what Destiny was doing, she clapped her hands and exclaimed, "I love marigolds!"

Destiny chuckled. "I know. That's why I'm planting them for you."

"Thank you," Gretchen said, walking over and squeezing Destiny's shoulder.

"These will brighten up your flower bed," Destiny said.

"They'll make me smile every time I pull into the driveway."

Destiny grinned. "Good."

"You'll never guess who I just ran into at the grocery store," Gretchen said.

Destiny continued to plant the flowers then she stopped and looked up at her mom. "Oh, am I really supposed to guess? Uh, I have no idea."

"I talked to Faith," Gretchen said matter-of-factly.

Destiny's hands stopped and she sat back as her butt rested on her heels. "Hmm."

"That's it? Hmm?" Gretchen said.

"What do you want me to say, Mom? Faith wants nothing to do with me. And if I wondered before, she made it abundantly clear this morning when I ran into her at the nursery. She bumped her shoulder against mine, knowing I wouldn't do anything, yet hoping I would," Destiny said, her voice rising with anger.

"That's a lot of information from a brush of the shoulder," Gretchen said.

Destiny looked up at her mom and groaned in frustration. "Just because we broke up doesn't mean I don't know who she is. Well, I thought I did."

Gretchen kneeled down next to her daughter and put her arm around her shoulder. "You do know her," she said softly.

"Mom," Destiny said, carefully pulling away and standing up. "I can't. I'll fall apart." She took a couple of steps away and went back to planting the remaining marigolds.

"She's scared of something, honey," Gretchen said. "I could see it in her eyes."

Destiny sighed loudly. "I know she is. But she will not take, nor does she want, help from me. If you only knew how many times I've seen that frightened look in her eyes

Until We Weren't:

and convinced her to trust me. It worked and we were happy, until we weren't," Destiny said. "I don't know what she thinks I did, but she'll never trust me again and I'm the last person she'd ask for help."

"Maybe not," Gretchen said. "Something seemed different about her."

Destiny stood up and her shoulders slumped. "Not with me. She was just as angry and venomous as ever when I ran into her this morning. We've been over this, Mom. It's been three years."

"Yet neither one of you have moved on. All you do is work," Gretchen said.

Destiny let out another deep breath and looked into her mother's eyes. "Enjoy the marigolds." She gave her mom a sad smile and walked to her truck. "Bye, Dad," she said, opening the door.

"I love you, honey," Michael said, walking over to her.

Destiny paused and smiled.

"You know I don't like to butt into your life," he continued.

Destiny raised her brows. "That's why we get along so well."

Michael chuckled. "I don't think your story with Faith is over."

Destiny nodded. *No*, she thought. *As long as we're both in the landscaping business and occasionally run into each other, Faith will continue to be the nemesis in my story.*

She started her truck and drove away. Destiny used to believe that someday Faith would tell her what she did, but she was beginning to think she'd never know. After seeing her this morning it seemed that Faith was even further away. Maybe that's what seemed different to her mom. Destiny knew she had to stop hoping or she'd end up a sad, lonely old woman.

A bitter laugh escaped her throat as she pulled into her parking space at her apartment. "You're forty-two years old and you're already a sad, lonely woman. Great," she groaned.

4

"Have we received payment for the Collins job yet?" Faith asked as she walked in from the shop after getting the crews lined out for the day.

"Yep," Amy replied. "We received payment yesterday."

Amy's job was to take care of the office and do the payroll. Faith was slow to trust her with much in the beginning, but as the business grew and Faith needed to be out in the field, someone had to be in the office.

As the years passed, Amy had become the closest thing Faith had to a friend. She explained to Faith that her trust issues came across in a very negative way to her other workers. There had been times when Amy smoothed things over to keep a good worker from quitting.

"Were you nice this morning?" Amy asked, looking up from her computer.

Faith smirked. "Yes. I even told them to take several breaks during the day and quit early because it's going to be hot today."

"Look at you," Amy said. "They'll think you actually care."

"I do care," Faith replied.

"Uh huh." Amy raised a brow. "Because you want the job finished."

Faith huffed and opened the laptop on her desk. "That's not the only reason."

"You could smile every now and then, you know," Amy said.

"When I have something to smile about I will."

"I have you set up to tour the new business park so you can prepare a bid," Amy said. "That should make you smile."

Faith gave her a fake smile.

Amy chuckled. "You can do better."

"When?"

"At the end of the week," Amy replied. "They're letting landscape companies tour the grounds at the end of the day so they won't be in the workers' way."

"Even getting part of that contract would be such a big deal for us," Faith said.

"Mark said you ran into your best friend the other day," Amy said. "I'm sure she'll be bidding on this project, too."

Faith groaned at the memory of seeing Destiny at the nursery. Sometimes when she saw Destiny, a pain would slice through her heart. That day when she stared into Destiny's eyes, her heart melted the same way it once had. Faith knew that she unnerved Destiny and could always see it in her eyes. It gave her a little satisfaction, but not that day.

"It seems I can't get away from her lately," Faith muttered, tapping the keyboard. "It's like we're still together."

"What?" Amy asked.

Faith shrugged and busied herself by staring at her computer.

"You mean you were once *with* her, with her?"

"Don't look so surprised," Faith said. "She's the smartest person I know and she's not bad to look at. And there's her —" Faith shook her head, letting those thoughts go. Most of the time when she thought of Destiny she couldn't believe she'd ever let that woman's hands on her, but seeing her the other day had brought up so many feelings that Faith thought were long buried.

"How'd it go wrong?" Amy asked.

"It doesn't matter." Faith said, ending the conversation.

"Come on!" Amy exclaimed. "I've worked here for over two years and the very first day I learned that The Green Thumb was our enemy. How did I not know you and Destiny Green used to be together?"

"Because it's not anyone's business," Faith said sharply.

"She must have really hurt you," Amy said softly.

Faith looked up from her computer. "Why do you say that?"

"Because you're so angry," Amy replied. "I once read that anger is an emotion caused by hurt or fear."

Faith furrowed her brow as she gathered her things to leave.

"Where are you going?"

"I have to take a trailer full of those butterfly shrubs to the Hutto housing development," Faith said.

"I'm sorry she hurt you," Amy said.

Faith stopped at the back door. "Me too," she said sadly.

She hooked the trailer up to her truck and drove through North Austin and into the suburb of Hutto. Lush

Fields had won the contract to do the landscaping for the model homes in this subdivision. The builder was pleased and as the homes were built then sold, they continued the landscaping. It had become one of Faith's best accounts.

As she weaved through traffic she couldn't keep from thinking about what Amy said about anger and the emotions that caused it. Faith was definitely hurt by Destiny's actions, but she knew fear was what fueled her anger.

It had been months since she'd run into Destiny and this always happened whenever she did. A jumble of feelings resurfaced and the hurt came back just as intense.

It had been a little over five years since she'd first laid eyes on Destiny Green. Her dark brown hair was pulled back in a ponytail with little curly wisps framing her face. Those warm brown eyes held a sense of wonder and fascination, but also passion for what she was doing. Faith thought she was the most beautiful woman she'd ever seen.

When Destiny smiled at her, Faith's heart would speed up in her chest and her stomach would do flips. There was something about Destiny that made her so easy to talk to. Faith slowly told her about her past and Destiny seemed to understand why Faith was cautious and slow to trust. She never pushed Faith, she simply reassured her with her words and mainly with her actions.

When they moved in together Faith thought she'd spend the rest of her life with Destiny Green. They were so happy and in love, until they weren't.

She parked and hopped out of the truck with hot tears pooling in her eyes. It was time to plant these shrubs and bury these feelings once again.

* * *

Until We Weren't:

It had been a long, hot day. Destiny was ready to be home and couldn't wait to get in the shower to wash the day away. There had been problems at two sites today and with the added heat it made them seem even worse.

She had taken a back road home to avoid the traffic on the main highways in hopes of stripping off these dirty, sweaty clothes sooner rather than later. Several cars slowed in front of her and she noticed a pickup with a trailer pulled over on the side of the road. They were out of the way, but it still slowed the flow of cars that apparently had the same idea Destiny had of missing the evening traffic.

Destiny thought about stopping, but surely someone was coming to the truck's aid. As she got closer, she recognized the woman standing at the back of the trailer staring at one of the tires.

She sighed loudly. "Well, fuck," she murmured.

Destiny pulled her truck behind the trailer and watched in her side mirror for an opportunity to get out. When the flow of cars cleared she opened her door and walked over to help.

"Hey," she said.

"Oh, you've got to be kidding me," Faith groaned.

"Yep, it's your favorite person," Destiny replied.

"I've already called Mark," Faith said. "He's on the way."

Destiny nodded. "It's not safe to stand out here where these people not paying attention can run over you."

"I know that," Faith replied.

"Call Mark back and tell him you have help. I've got an air compressor in the back of my truck and we can air the tire up. I'll follow you to your shop. It's not that far away."

Faith sighed and to both of their surprise, she pulled her phone out and called Mark.

Destiny got the air compressor out of her truck and began to inflate the flat tire. "Hopefully it'll hold enough air to get to your shop."

"I saw a nail in it," Faith said. "I was at a construction site today and must have picked it up there."

Destiny nodded. "Were you at the housing development in Hutto?"

Faith nodded warily.

"You've done a really nice job over there," Destiny said as she kept her eyes on the tire. "It's beautiful."

"Thanks," Faith said. "What are you doing in this area?"

"Oh." Destiny sighed. "Everything that could go wrong did today. We're doing an apartment building right at the border of Hutto and Round Rock."

"You didn't have to stop," Faith said.

Destiny finished with the tire, stood up, and looked at Faith. "Are you kidding *me*? Of course I did," she said, picking up the air compressor. She looked back at Faith and tilted her head. "You would've stopped for me, right?"

Faith scoffed. "Yes," she said impatiently.

Destiny couldn't stop a hint of a smile crossing her face. "I'll follow you."

Faith nodded and went back to her truck.

Destiny put the air compressor away and got back in her truck. She put her blinker on, signaling that she was pulling back on the road. Once there were no cars coming, Faith eased out on the road with Destiny behind her.

The air held in the tire as they made their way down the road. Faith turned onto a street with less traffic that took them towards her building. A few minutes later they turned into the parking lot of Lush Fields Landscaping.

Destiny followed Faith's truck around the side of the

building into the fenced area at the rear. She slowed to give Faith plenty of room to park the truck and trailer so they could easily get to it to change the tire.

Once Faith stopped and got out of her truck, Destiny pulled up next to her and parked. She walked over to the trailer and checked the tire.

"You could probably fill it up in the morning and take it somewhere to get it fixed," Destiny said.

"I'll take care of it," Faith said.

Destiny looked up at her and her face softened. "Faith, turn around," she said.

Faith slowly turned around and saw the sun was about to disappear in the field across from her business.

"Look at that," Destiny said. "Isn't it beautiful."

Faith watched as the bright red sky began to turn dark orange.

"What happened to us?" Destiny asked softly.

Faith stared at the sky but didn't say anything.

"I'm sorry," Destiny said.

Faith turned around and looked at Destiny. "What did you say?"

"I'm sorry, Faith," Destiny said again. "I apologize for everything I ever did to you. But I will never apologize for loving you." She swallowed the lump that had formed in her throat. "We were happy."

"We were," Faith said with anguish in her voice. "Until—"

Just then another pickup pulled into the yard and parked next to Destiny's truck.

"Hey," Mark said, getting out of the pickup. "I thought I'd better make sure you made it back okay."

Destiny stared at Faith and could see the pain in her

eyes. It broke Destiny's heart to think she dimmed those vibrant blue eyes.

When Faith looked away Destiny knew the moment had passed. For a second, she thought Faith was finally going to tell her what she did.

"I'd better go," Destiny said, walking by Mark and trying to smile.

"Thanks for following her back here," Mark said.

When Destiny opened her truck door Faith called to her. "Thanks."

Destiny turned to look at her one more time. "I miss you," she said, just loud enough for Faith to hear. "I miss us."

Once Destiny was back on the road, she let out a deep breath. There were times when Destiny truly thought she could get past Faith. She'd try to convince herself to give up then a memory would float through her head or she'd catch a glimpse of her. But the last few times she'd seen Faith she could feel her heart open like a flower. It was reaching for Faith. It wanted to pull her back inside where she belonged.

She smiled as a memory forced its way in front of her.

They were driving to a job site and George Michael's song "Faith" came on the radio.

Destiny turned up the radio. "Listen babe, that's me," she giggled. "I've gotta have faith."

"Oh you do?" Faith asked with amusement in her voice.

Destiny scooted over as close as she could and reached across the console to squeeze Faith's thigh. They listened to the words for a moment and Destiny said, "You're not going to throw my heart back on the floor. I've got faith, in you, in us."

Faith chuckled. "Does that mean you're my destiny?" she said in a faux dreamy voice.

They both laughed and sang along with the radio.

Until We Weren't:

Destiny found herself smiling at the memory as she stopped the truck. They had laughed so much and had silly fun like that often.

She walked into her apartment, starting to take her clothes off as she walked towards the shower. *Do I still have faith*, she wondered.

5

"That was nice of Destiny," Mark said. "Of all people to be coming by on that back road."

"She has a job at an apartment complex not far from the housing development," Faith explained.

"You know, when we ran into her at the nursery I thought I was about to break up a fight between the two of you, but today it felt more like I was interrupting something."

"I'm glad the trailer was empty when that tire decided to go," Faith said, ignoring his comment. "I'll take it by tomorrow and get the tire fixed."

"Do you believe in coincidence?"

"What?" Faith said, looking over at Mark.

"You haven't seen Destiny in a long time and now you've run into her twice in a matter of days," Mark said. "I'm not sure I believe in coincidences. I think the universe or fate or whatever you want to call it is stepping in to do something about you two."

Faith rolled her eyes and shook her head. "When did you become so philosophical?"

Until We Weren't:

Mark shrugged. "You used to make fun of her name. Maybe there's something to it."

"Oh, so now you're saying she's my destiny?" Faith asked.

Mark raised his brows. "I've tried to keep my mouth shut about you two, but don't you think it's time you told her what she did?"

"She knows—"

"No, she doesn't, Faith," Mark said firmly. "You may think Destiny knows whatever it is she did to make you leave, but she doesn't."

"Maybe she doesn't want to face it," Faith replied. "Did you ever think of that?"

"What!" Mark exclaimed. "Destiny Green has never been afraid to face anything. You two fed off each other's strength."

He wasn't wrong; they were quite a team when they worked together. Then when they had their own crews, it was fun to try and outdo the other. But Faith liked it best when their crews were working on the same project so she and Destiny could work together.

"I would never choose sides," Mark said, bringing Faith out of her musings.

"I know you and Destiny are friends, Mark. I wouldn't ask something like that of you."

Mark nodded. "You might think about it," he said. "She doesn't know."

Faith sighed, tired of this same conversation. "I'll see you tomorrow."

Mark shook his head and walked back to his truck. "Think about it," he said out the window as he drove off.

"I think about it all the fucking time," Faith muttered.

She had some kind of thought of Destiny every day. And

when she didn't think about her, Destiny would show up in her dreams.

Faith went inside her tiny house and got a beer from the minifridge. She went back outside and sat in the chair on her little porch. The sun had set but the sky was still a dark red with streaks of orange.

She took a long drink of the beer and her thoughts wandered back to when she and Destiny first met. Faith had worked her way through college and graduated with a degree in horticulture. Her family had let her down for the last time when no one showed up for her graduation. A month before that she'd found out her girlfriend was sleeping with someone else on the nights they weren't together.

Faith had vowed to herself then that this was her chance to start over. She wouldn't depend on anyone for anything ever again. She worked as a florist for several years then became interested in landscaping. At thirty-four she'd started to work at Landscape Artists and loved her job. Not long after that Destiny came to work there as well.

They eventually worked on the same crew and there was something about Destiny that made Faith let her guard down. She was friendly, but she had a passion for the job that Faith could relate to. Destiny came from a corporate background and was used to being the boss, but not with Faith. She wanted to learn and had taken classes, but she was genuinely interested in Faith's knowledge, her expertise, and her ideas.

A smile played at the corner of Faith's mouth as she remembered Destiny's excitement when they talked about how they would design a project if given the chance. Faith could feel the respect Destiny had for her work and her ideas, but it was more than that. In reality, they were falling more in love every day.

Destiny had an ease about her, and persistence. She asked Faith out several times before she finally said yes. Faith knew Destiny could see the pain in her heart, but it didn't scare her away. She simply kept asking in her sweet gentle way until Faith could no longer refuse.

After that it didn't take long until they were spending every evening together after work and most weekends.

Faith remembered one particular night when she knew Destiny would always be in her heart. They were lying in bed and Faith had her arms wrapped around Destiny. They had just made love and Faith's hand was gently moving up and down Destiny's back.

"I was drawn to you the first day I saw you," Destiny said. "It wasn't love at first sight or anything like that, but you had something that pulled me to you." She raised her head and looked into Faith's eyes.

Faith smiled and let her continue.

"That's not completely true," Destiny said, running her finger down Faith's cheek. "I couldn't stop staring at your eyes." She smiled. "I love how they change color with the sun or when I kiss you like this."

Faith felt her heart flutter then quickly reach a staccato beat as Destiny's lips nibbled, pressed, and sucked hers. It felt like Destiny's lips were making love to Faith's just as their bodies had moments earlier. God, how she loved Destiny's kisses.

Destiny pulled away and Faith groaned. "Please don't tell me you kissed me like that just to see my eyes turn dark blue."

Destiny smiled. "I kissed you like that because that's when you let me into your heart. I can feel my love rush into your heart and you let it stay there."

Faith sighed at the memory. Little did Destiny know, her

love was still in Faith's heart. Destiny saw past the hurt that lived in Faith's heart. It had taken Faith a while to let Destiny in, but when she couldn't keep her out any longer Destiny's love did indeed rush into Faith's heart. Once Faith stopped fighting it she found that Destiny's love helped to soften the scars. The pain didn't go away, it would always be a part of her, but Destiny's love changed it somehow. It wasn't as sharp, it didn't cut quite so deep.

Faith once thought of her heart like dry cracked earth that needed water. Destiny's love filled those spaces. It was the water that enabled Faith's heart to love again. Years later, Destiny's love was still there. It somehow survived in the desolate fractured expanse that was once again Faith's heart.

Faith finished her beer and thought back to what Mark said. "Come on," she said out loud. "She knows." She took out her phone and scrolled through her pictures and videos. "I have proof."

* * *

Destiny stared at her computer screen then scribbled into a notebook on her desk.

"What are you working on?" Monica asked.

"I'm making some notes about the office complex," Destiny replied.

"Oh, that's right," Monica said. "You're getting a tour this afternoon."

"Yep," Destiny said. "I want to get an idea of the layout of the buildings. It will seem much larger once I get there."

"Are you taking Jake or Claire with you?" Monica asked.

"No, Jake is busy finishing up our lawn clients in east Austin. The rain a couple of days ago pushed him behind.

Claire's team is putting in flower beds at the apartment complex in Round Rock."

"I could go with you if you need someone," Monica offered.

Destiny looked up from her notes and smiled. "Thanks, Mon, but I can handle this myself."

"Hey, Jake told me the other day that you used to work at an office complex like that one," Monica said. "I'd forgotten all about your corporate life."

Destiny sat back in her chair. "That seems like a lifetime ago, but yes, I did work at a big business park like that. My degree is in business and I worked as an analyst for ten years before I couldn't stand the corporate grind any longer."

"How'd you get into landscaping?"

Destiny chuckled. "Jake and I were in high school together. He had a lawn mowing business in the summers and I worked for him."

"No way," Monica exclaimed. "How have I not heard this before now?"

Destiny laughed. "Several of our clients came from Jake's mowing business. When I decided to open my own landscaping company he's the first person I called."

"But mowing yards and doing the kind of landscaping we do aren't the same thing," Monica said.

Destiny nodded. "One day I was sitting in my office and looked out my window where a crew was putting in a flower bed. I was so tired of numbers and spreadsheets and it hit me that the job I really enjoyed was working outside in those yards. I did a little research, took a few classes in landscape architecture, and started a new career."

"Wow," Monica said. "So you got into this business because you love it."

"That's right," Destiny said. "I don't make near as much money, but I quickly learned money isn't everything."

"So now you're happy to come to work every day," Monica said.

Destiny smiled. There was a time when she was a lot happier to come to work every day than she was now. When she and Faith were working together, those were the best days. Happy days. A shadow of sadness fell over her face as she remembered those days with Faith. If she ever got the chance to work with her again, Destiny vowed she'd cherish each day and appreciate it.

"Hey," Monica said. "What's wrong?"

Destiny looked over at Monica and raised her brows. "Nothing."

"You look really sad."

"I was just thinking about another time," Destiny said, looking back at her computer.

"With Faith?"

Destiny cut her eyes over to Monica and sighed. "Faith and I shared a lot of happy times when we worked together, but that was a long time ago." She stood up. "Now, I'm sure it will take a while to tour the business complex, so I'll see you in the morning."

"I'll lock up the office and check with the crews before I leave," Monica said.

"Thanks, I appreciate it."

"Go win us that big job, boss."

Destiny chuckled. "This is just the beginning."

"You've got to start somewhere," Monica said.

"Okay then," Destiny said, chuckling at her exuberance. She got her things together and went out to her truck.

It was a twenty minute drive to the work site and Destiny couldn't help but think of Faith as she drove near her shop.

She wondered if she got her tire fixed on the trailer and then chided herself.

"What do you care," she muttered. "It's none of your business."

Destiny sighed. Now that Faith was in her head she'd be there the rest of the day.

Her contact at the business complex had said they would give them a tour of the facility so they could prepare bids. Destiny knew Faith would be bidding on the project, but doubted they would be on the same tour. There were landscape companies from all over the state bidding on the large job.

She pulled into the parking area and immediately noticed Faith's truck.

"So much for not being on the same tour," she muttered.

6

Faith walked up the street towards the main building in the complex. There was a parking lot on either side of the street then it wound around to the smaller buildings that made up the office park. Each building would have their own landscaping as well as walkways that connected to the main building.

A smile played at the corner of Faith's mouth. This was a huge job, but she could imagine doing this work. It would be completed in stages just as the buildings were being constructed.

She'd noticed several other landscaping companies' representatives walking around the property, but she preferred to do her appraisal alone. Faith would take in the entire scene and let the property talk to her. That way she could get a feel for what aesthetic fit the property best. Then she could envision the plants, shrubs, trees, and turf she would use.

Faith closed her eyes for a moment but before she could picture the property, a memory of doing this same thing with Destiny filled her head. They used to walk around a potential project and bounce ideas off each other until they came up with the best one.

She figured Destiny would be touring the property, but it was almost as if she could feel her nearby. Faith shuddered and tried to focus on the task at hand.

"Do you see a garden or a prairie," a familiar voice said from behind her, "or some other style?"

Faith turned around feeling like she'd conjured Destiny up from thin air.

Destiny smiled. "It's bigger than I imagined."

Faith nodded. "But it's doable."

"Thank goodness they're doing it in stages," Destiny said. "I'd have to hire extra help otherwise."

"Yeah," Faith agreed. "Did you see who all is here?"

"Yep," Destiny replied. "I knew all the biggies would be here." She turned to look at Faith. "But that doesn't mean you or I couldn't do this job."

"I know," Faith said, staring at the building.

"I want to see around back," Destiny said. "Have you been there yet?"

Faith shook her head. Destiny started to walk away then turned around to look at Faith.

Faith hesitated, trying to decide whether to walk with Destiny or not. "They didn't give us much time to look around," she said. "The guy at the gate said they lock up the entire site at six."

"Maybe we could get a better idea if we walked together," Destiny suggested, raising her brows.

"You go around that way and I'll go to the right," Faith said. "I'll meet you at the back of the main building. We can compare notes." She could see the disappointment on Destiny's face when she suggested they split up, but Faith needed to concentrate on the job. It was hard to do that when Destiny was around.

"Okay," Destiny said, turning and walking away.

Faith took a deep breath and slowly let it out. Maybe Mark was right. The universe seemed to be putting her in Destiny's path more and more lately, but why? She shrugged the thought off and headed to the other side of the massive building.

* * *

Destiny walked around the building and jotted down a few ideas as they came to her. She took her time and tried to visualize how to make the landscaping flow. A few people she knew from the other landscaping companies waved or said hello to her as she walked by them.

Destiny detoured near one of the other buildings, trying to get a better idea of what that walk would be like for the employees. One thing she tried to do with outdoor spaces she created was make a walk like this an experience, not just moving from one building to the next.

Sometimes people need a moment to simply take a breath in the middle of their workday. Destiny remembered when her head would be crammed full of numbers and all she wanted was to take a short walk and let them out.

She meandered along the sidewalk to the side of the main building, taking in the view, then took the path around towards the back. She noticed a cloud of dust off in the distance near where she'd parked her truck. A steady stream of vehicles was leaving the parking lot.

She glanced at her watch and realized it was past six o'clock. It occurred to her that she hadn't seen any of the other landscapers for quite some time. The man at the gate had advised her that they locked everything up at night to deter would-be thieves.

She hurried to the back of the building just in case Faith was waiting for her. Destiny had been pleasantly surprised at Faith's lack of contempt for her when she walked up beside her earlier. She'd expected her typical nasty demeanor, but she was almost friendly.

Time had gotten away from her and she didn't want to get them both in trouble with security or the company she was trying to secure the landscaping contract from.

She saw Faith in the distance just as movement caught her eye.

"Oh shit!" Destiny exclaimed. "Those are guard dogs!"

Destiny took off running towards Faith and as she ran, she looked for a place to get away from the dogs.

Faith looked confused, but Destiny could tell she knew something was wrong. She watched as Faith glanced over her shoulder and saw the dogs.

"Over here!" Destiny yelled, running towards a small shack at the back of the property.

Faith had just about reached Destiny when she turned her head to look behind at the dogs' progress.

Just then Destiny saw Faith's foot land in a hole and she went tumbling to the ground.

Without a thought, Destiny ran over, grabbed Faith by the back of her shirt, and pulled them both into the shack, slamming the door just as the dogs, barking ferociously, jumped against it.

"Holy shit!" Destiny exclaimed, her chest heaving for a breath. "Are you okay?" she asked with concern in her voice.

Faith was on the floor with a dazed look on her face.

Destiny bent down and looked into her eyes. "Faith," she said softly. "Hey, it's okay. We're safe."

Faith met Destiny's eyes and raised her eyebrows.

Destiny could see the fear in her eyes and reached to put her hands on Faith's upper arms. She squeezed them gently. "I've got you."

Faith blinked her eyes and found her voice. "What the hell was that?"

Destiny smiled as she saw the fear fade from Faith's eyes. "I'm guessing they lock everything up and release guard dogs as security."

"Fuck," Faith said, her eyes wide.

"I know," Destiny said. "Is your ankle okay?"

Faith looked down at her foot and wiggled it in a circle. "Yeah, it's okay."

"Are you sure you're all right?" Destiny asked.

Faith let out a deep breath and nodded. "When I was a kid," she began, "a dog chased me on the way home from school one day. It scared the shit out of me." She nervously chuckled. "That's probably why I became such a fast runner." She shrugged. "At least it helped me get through college."

"You never told me that," Destiny said, still kneeling in front of Faith. "I wouldn't have kept asking you for us to get a dog."

Faith looked into Destiny's eyes and smiled. "I'm not afraid of dogs. I just don't like them chasing after me like they want to eat me!"

Destiny dropped her head and chuckled. "Yeah, I don't like it either." She got up and looked out of the window next to the door. One dog was sitting, staring at the door, ready to pounce when it opened. The other was pacing up and down in front of the small shack.

"You're not having us for supper," Destiny said, watching the dogs for a moment.

Until We Weren't:

"What is this place?" Faith stood up and looked around the small building.

"It looks like something they brought in before construction started."

"I think they store things they've forgotten about," Faith said, picking up dusty tools.

"I don't see anyone walking around out there." Destiny peered through the dirty window. "Surely they look around before they lock the place up for the night and release the dogs."

"Obviously not!" Faith exclaimed. "Otherwise those little fuckers wouldn't have been chasing us!"

Destiny laughed.

"Oh, that's funny?"

"No," Destiny said. "I was scared, too."

"Of course," Faith said. "That was your nervous laugh."

"Yeah, I don't know why I do that." Destiny shrugged. "Anyway, let's call someone for help." She reached into her pocket for her phone.

Faith suddenly laughed. "Would you look at us," she said. "We were running for our lives, but neither one of us dropped our notebooks."

Destiny looked at the notebook in her hand and joined her laughter. "Always focused on the job."

"Here's the number for the project manager who was giving the tours," Faith said.

Destiny started to punch in the number and groaned. "Oh, fuck. I don't have any service."

"What!" Faith exclaimed, taking out her own phone. "I don't either. What do we do now?"

Destiny raised her brows. "I'm not going out there."

Faith scoffed. "Duh, I know that. Neither am I."

Destiny walked around the small shack, trying to see if there was service in another area. "Nothing."

Faith sighed. She walked over to the window in the back of the building and stared out. "I don't see another soul."

"Yeah, me either."

"What about our friends?"

"Oh, one is staring menacingly at me while the other is sitting, staring at the door," Destiny replied.

"I don't get how their handlers couldn't have seen them take off after us," Faith said.

"They must have already been gone," Destiny said. "I noticed people leaving and looked at my watch. It was just after six o'clock then. I hurried back here to find you and that's when I saw the dogs."

"That gate guard said they lock up at six on the dot," Faith said. "He wasn't fucking kidding."

Destiny scoffed. "No shit."

"Wait—you hurried back here to find me?"

Destiny turned away from the window to look at Faith. "Yeah, you said you'd meet me in the back of the building. I kind of detoured to the others along the walkway. I didn't mean to take so long. Sorry. Maybe if I'd gotten back here sooner this wouldn't have happened."

Faith smiled. "I did the same thing."

"Did you have plans tonight?"

Faith furrowed her brow and stared at Destiny. "What?"

Destiny sighed, but she was smiling. "Will anyone be wondering where you are and come looking for us?"

"Oh," Faith said. "Sorry." She shrugged. "Nope. Amy was locking up and checking with the crews before she left for the day."

Destiny turned back to the window and gazed at the dogs who were still standing guard outside the shack.

"How about you?" Faith asked.

Destiny shook her head and let out a discouraged breath. "It's going to get hot in here," she said, wrestling with the window.

Faith tried to open the window in the back, but couldn't get it to budge. "This one is stuck."

Destiny looked around on the floor and found a screwdriver. "Do you see anything we could use for a hammer?"

Faith rummaged through the random stuff in the corner and found a flat piece of iron. "How about this?"

Destiny took it and tried to pry the window open by holding the screwdriver under the metal frame of the window and hitting it with the piece of iron. Every time she hit it, the screwdriver slipped. She turned to Faith and looked her in the eye.

"I'll hold the screwdriver with both hands if you'll whack it with this," Destiny said, handing the makeshift hammer to Faith.

"Okay," Faith replied.

Destiny worked the blade of the screwdriver under the window frame and nodded at Faith. But before Faith could hit the handle of the screwdriver, Destiny stopped and pulled it away. She tilted her head and narrowed her eyes at Faith.

"What?" Faith asked. "Oh, come on. I won't hit your hands."

Destiny smirked and once again put the blade of the screwdriver under the window frame.

Faith smacked the end of the handle several times until the window began to move.

"Okay," Destiny said. "I think that's good."

7

"Well," Faith said. "At least we have a little air flowing through here now."

Destiny sighed and looked out the window. She turned around and looked at Faith. "Yeah. So what did you think of the project?"

Faith stared at Destiny for a moment and tried to read her expression.

"We were going to compare notes," Destiny explained. "Remember?"

Faith nodded. "I guess we may as well. It doesn't look like we're going anywhere anytime soon." She sat down on the floor and crossed her legs.

Destiny sat down across from Faith and opened her notebook.

"It would be easy to do wispy grasses that would do well in the heat, but I see more of a garden vibe," Faith said.

Destiny smiled. "I'm not surprised. You love that look."

"I do, but it will complement the architecture of the buildings," Faith said defensively.

Until We Weren't:

"Take it easy, Faith," Destiny said, looking up at her. "I agree with you."

"You do?" Faith remembered when they worked together that oftentimes they had different ideas. They rarely agreed in the beginning, but once they talked out their visions, they would come up with a plan that complemented the space—and a plan they both liked.

"Don't sound so surprised," Destiny said. "We created some very beautiful landscapes together."

"I know that," Faith said. "But we rarely agreed at first."

Destiny chuckled. "That's true. Uh, as I walked along towards the smaller buildings the project seemed to grow before my eyes," she said tentatively.

"Yeah." Faith nodded, looking over her notes. "It's even bigger than I imagined."

"I'm concerned they won't take smaller companies like ours seriously during the bidding process," Destiny said. "But..."

Faith looked up into Destiny's eyes. "But what?"

"I was thinking..." Her voice trailed off.

Faith could see hesitation in Destiny's eyes. This was unusual because she was always so confident. It was one of the things that drew Faith to her from the beginning. However, Faith had seen this look a few times before. Destiny had an idea and wasn't sure Faith would go for it.

"Come on, Des," Faith encouraged her. She could see Destiny soften at the way Faith shortened her name.

"Both of our companies have very good reputations," Destiny began.

"Very good?" Faith said, raising her brows. "I'd say we're excellent."

"Okay." Destiny smiled. "We have excellent reputations.

I think if we worked together on a project this size they would take us seriously."

"Hmm. I don't know. I'd have to think about it."

Destiny nodded. "I know. It's just an idea."

"I didn't say no," Faith said. "Can I see your notes?"

Destiny smiled and handed her notebook to Faith. "I did a quick sketch of the walkway between the buildings and where it connects with the side entrance."

"I like this," Faith said, staring at the page. "Let's talk about plants."

Destiny scooted over next to Faith so they could both see the drawings and notes from their notebooks. They talked about trees, shrubs, plants, flowers, irrigation, and soil. Destiny sketched as they brainstormed ideas for the front of the building.

"I still don't understand how you're able to sketch better than I can," Faith said, shaking her head. "I've been sketching and drawing flowers and plants since I started college twenty years ago. You worked with numbers before you started landscaping."

Destiny laughed. "I don't sketch better than you do. It's easier for me to put what's in my head down on paper."

Faith smiled. They'd had this same discussion several times over the years and Destiny would never laud her talents over Faith. She always claimed they both had their strengths and that's why they were such a force when they worked together.

"See what you think of this," Destiny said, handing the notebook to Faith. "It's so fucking hot in here." She got up and stuck her head in front of the window. "Oh, that's better. There's a breeze."

Faith got up and placed her face in front of the other

window. "Oh wow," she said. "Look, Des. The sun is putting on a show."

Destiny stepped over and gazed out the back window. "Damn! That's gorgeous," she exclaimed.

"Yeah," Faith said, getting out of the way so Destiny could get a better look. "It's too bad we're stuck in here and can't really enjoy it."

Destiny turned around and glanced at Faith. "Do you still stop and watch the sunsets when you can?"

Faith nodded. She could see the affection in Destiny's eyes and had no doubt it was love. She turned toward the other window and let the breeze cool her face. Her stomach had done a flip when her eyes met Destiny's and for a moment she couldn't look away. She closed her eyes and tried to find the anger that usually accompanied her thoughts of Destiny, but it wasn't there.

Faith pulled the hair tie out of her ponytail and let her hair fall for a moment. She ran her fingers through the sweaty strands then pulled it back up. She took a deep breath, willing her emotions to calm down. What was she feeling? Familiarity? Loss? Love? Betrayal? *You can't forget what she did*, Faith said silently to herself.

"Are they still there?" Destiny asked.

"Who?" Faith replied, turning towards her.

"The dogs? Who else?"

"Oh." Faith sighed. "Yeah, one is lying in front of the door. The other is sitting and staring at me." She had no doubt the animal would tear into her if given the chance.

"You'd think they'd get bored with us and go patrol or something," Destiny said.

Faith sat back down and leaned against the wall. She watched Destiny take her phone out and walk around the small space trying to get a signal.

"Are you sure your parents aren't expecting you to drop by or something?" Faith asked.

"Nope," Destiny said gloomily. "Mom did say she ran into you the other day."

"Yeah, it was nice to see her." Faith smiled. "Your mom is the best."

"You could go by and see my parents anytime."

Faith nodded and changed the subject. "You know, Mrs. Baker tells me every time you go by the retirement home to work in the beds."

Destiny chuckled. "Just this week she told me that she has decided our trips to see her are twofold."

"Oh yeah?" Faith said, amused. "How so?"

"The reason we still work on the flower beds is to see her," Destiny said.

"She's not wrong."

"No, but she added that it is also our way to check on each other without the other knowing," Destiny explained.

Faith laughed. "Of course we know. She tells us."

Destiny laughed along with her.

"Well, do you have any other ideas?" she asked as Destiny put her phone back into her pocket.

Destiny sat down on an overturned bucket across from Faith and leaned against the wall. "Yeah, actually I do."

"Let's hear it."

"Tell me why you left," Destiny said. "What did I do, Faith?"

* * *

Destiny stared at Faith and was surprised she didn't look away. She could tell Faith was not expecting her question.

She recognized that look though. Faith was weighing her options.

Destiny was trying to keep her face neutral even though her heart was pounding in her chest. It didn't take long for the light to dim in the space since the sun had set, but she could see and feel Faith's eyes studying her.

"You really don't know," Faith said.

"No!" Destiny said desperately. "I thought we were happy. I was." She was glad shadows had begun to fill the small room and hoped Faith couldn't see the tears that suddenly filled her eyes. Destiny blinked them away and took a shallow breath.

"I was, too," Faith said softly. "Until…"

Destiny waited for Faith to continue, but she simply stared.

"Until what, Faith?"

"Do you remember the competitions between the teams that the Galloways used to come up with?" Faith said. "They were supposed to be in good fun, as they put it."

"Of course I remember them," Destiny replied. "But I didn't think they were necessarily fun."

"Really?"

"They were supposed to make the work crews more productive, but it didn't always feel that way to me," Destiny said. "You didn't particularly like them either."

"Not really."

"It was fun when we were on the same team," Destiny said, remembering how they'd work together to beat the other crews. "But not as much when we had our own teams. At least not for me."

"Then why were we always trying to beat each other?" Faith asked.

Destiny shrugged. "I guess because when we won we could choose the jobs we wanted."

"Do you do competitions with your work crews?"

"Nope. I try to treat everyone the same and assign jobs according to several different factors. Do you?"

"No," Faith said. "I've been accused of supervising too closely because it's hard for me to trust that the job will get done."

"Why?" Destiny asked. "You don't trust your employees? Surely you trust Mark."

"I do, but the job getting done on time and done right is my responsibility."

"I get that."

"Do you remember that doctor's office that had three separate buildings?" Faith said. "Mr. Galloway let us come up with our own designs, but we could only use the plants he had in stock."

"Sure, I remember," Destiny said. "Your crew had the building on one end, mine was in the middle, and the crew Mark was on had the other end. I don't remember who was leading that team. Do you?"

"What I remember is using most of the flowering plants we had on hand and you didn't like that very much," Faith said.

Destiny furrowed her brow and tried to think back to that particular project.

"Destiny?"

"I'm thinking, Faith," she said. "Give me a second." She narrowed her gaze and tried to bring up an image of the doctor's office in her head. "Wait a minute. That was the last project we did."

"It was the last job *I* did," Faith said. "I don't know about you."

Until We Weren't:

"I remember," Destiny said. "I tried to get you to trade plants with me because I thought the flowering plants would look better in the middle."

"That's right. But I wanted them for my section so it would stand out more."

"Right. Your bed was overshadowed by a big tree." Destiny shrugged. "You wouldn't trade with me, so I used something else." She wasn't sure what the significance of this memory was, but she could tell it was important to Faith.

"The next day Mr. Galloway was going to judge the beds," Faith said. "Whoever won that competition was going to get to design, build, and complete that apartment complex bid he'd just won."

"Right."

"But you fixed it so your team would win," Faith stated.

"What?" Destiny said, confused. "I fixed it? No I didn't!"

Faith scoffed. "You didn't move all the flowering plants to your bed so Mr. Galloway would award you the project?"

"Move the plants? What are you talking about, Faith?" Destiny's stomach fell and she could see anger and hurt on Faith's face even in the darkened room.

"I knew you would deny it," Faith said, her voice strained. "That's why I never talked to you about it."

"Deny what?" Destiny said, sitting up on the bucket.

"Just tell the truth, Destiny. I have proof!"

Destiny's brows flew up her forehead. "Proof of what?"

"The night before Mr. Galloway was to judge our beds," Faith said, "you pulled up the flowering plants in my bed and transplanted them to yours."

Destiny wasn't sure she heard Faith correctly. "Transplanted them? No, I didn't." She was trying to think back to what they were doing at that time, but it had been three years ago. Snippets of the doctor's office, planting, and laying mulch were coming back to her. What did they do after work that day? When Destiny couldn't bring up the memory, she looked up at Faith.

"What's this proof you're talking about?" she asked. "I can assure you, I have never taken plants that were in your beds and moved them to mine."

"You not only sabotaged my design, you're a liar as well," Faith said.

Destiny bristled at the accusation. She'd never do anything like that much less to the woman she loved.

"Watch this and try to lie your way out of it," Faith said, holding out her phone.

8

Faith handed Destiny her phone. A video was pulled up on the screen. She watched as Destiny viewed the video. Faith could see confusion on Destiny's face, but not guilt.

"What is this?" Destiny asked, standing up and sitting back down next to Faith.

"Here," Faith said, reaching for her phone. She started the video again. "That's my end of the doctor's office. You are digging up the flowering plants then taking them out of the frame to your part of the project. You'll notice you go back several times until you've taken them all." She let the video continue. "I can't believe you didn't even rake the bed or smooth it out. You just left the gaping holes where the plants had been. But then again, the uglier you make it the better. Right?"

Destiny stared at the phone and shook her head. "I recognize the doctor's office." She looked up into Faith's eyes. "That's not me."

Faith scoffed and smiled sarcastically. "I knew you'd say that. Take a closer look. Do you recognize that hoodie?"

Destiny took the phone from her and replayed the video, staring at the screen.

"That's the hoodie you took from me," Faith explained. "Don't you remember? You said you liked to wear it at work because it felt like—"

"You were hugging me," Destiny said softly.

"Could you feel me hugging you that night?" Faith asked with a bite to her voice.

Destiny sighed. "Faith," she said and paused. "That is not me."

Faith could see the truth in Destiny's eyes, even in the dark. "But that's my hoodie."

"I know it is, but you took that hoodie back from me before you left," Destiny said.

"No, I didn't."

Destiny let out a frustrated breath. She closed her eyes and Faith knew she was trying to recall memories from that time in their lives.

"I didn't have your hoodie for days before this video," Destiny said. "I thought you got tired of me wearing it and took it back."

"No," Faith said. "I liked that you wore it, especially when you told me why."

Destiny gasped. "I kept it in my truck, until one day it wasn't there. Anyone could have taken it."

Faith furrowed her brow as a sinking feeling settled in her stomach. She played the video once again. Faith couldn't count the number of times she'd seen it. This had to be Destiny. This person moved like her, was the same size as her. Surely Faith could tell the difference between her partner and someone else.

"I know it looks like me," Destiny said. "But it's not. I would not do this."

Faith felt like Destiny was hearing her thoughts. "Then who could it be?"

"Where did you get this?" Destiny asked. "Did you go back to the site?"

Faith shook her head as the sick feeling in her stomach intensified. She quickly got up and stepped to the window for a big breath of fresh air. "I'm going to be sick," she said, bending over and resting her hands on her knees.

She could hear Destiny rise to her feet and suddenly she felt wafts of air passing over her face. She closed her eyes and let the feeling of nausea pass. When she stood up she saw that Destiny had closed her notebook and was fanning the air around her.

"It's so hot in here," Destiny said. "I'm taking my shirt off. You should do the same."

They were both dressed in their usual summer uniform of shorts and moisture wicking T-shirts with their companies' logos. Faith followed Destiny's lead and pulled her shirt over her head. The feel of air over her sweat-soaked skin helped somewhat, but the heat had nothing to do with Faith's upset stomach.

If Destiny hadn't sabotaged Faith's landscape project that night then Faith had thrown away everything she loved because of some kind of deception.

"Are you feeling better?" Destiny asked softly.

Faith nodded, but realized Destiny probably couldn't see her in the mostly darkened room. "Yeah, I think so," she said quietly.

"Let's sit down and figure out who in the fuck ruined our lives," Destiny said with anger in her voice.

Faith couldn't yet summon the anger she knew Destiny was feeling. Her heart was full of anguish, regret, and grief. What had she done?

"Can I see your phone?" Destiny asked from where she sat on the floor.

Faith handed it to her then sat down beside her.

"Someone must have wanted to win that job desperately," Destiny said. "But who and why?"

"Were they trying to break us up?"

"Why? We didn't bother anyone. I thought everyone liked us," Destiny said. "Who was on the third crew?"

"Mark," Faith immediately said, "but he wasn't really the boss. Kyle had just quit a week before."

"Oh, that's right," Destiny said. "Someone on that team who was about my size and knew about the hoodie must have done it."

At the same time, they looked at each other and gasped. "Gloria!"

"But why would Gloria do that?" Faith asked.

* * *

Destiny leaned back against the wall and sighed. "Because she wanted her own team." She handed the phone back to Faith. "It all makes sense now."

"How?" Faith asked.

"Do you remember that Mr. Galloway sent me an hour away that day?"

"Oh, yeah," Faith replied. "You went to Bastrop to Lost Pines Resort."

"That's right," Destiny said. "I had to do maintenance on the butterfly garden we planted." In the dim light she looked at Faith. "That sanctuary is one of the best places we ever created together."

Faith nodded.

Until We Weren't:

"Anyway," Destiny said, focusing back on the mystery at hand, "I was gone until late that evening."

"I know," Faith said quietly.

Destiny looked back at Faith in surprise. "That gave you plenty of time to pack your stuff and move out."

Faith didn't say anything.

"Gloria knew I went to Bastrop. She came into the office when Mr. Galloway told me the butterfly garden needed a quick weeding because the resort had a big weekend planned. When did you get this video, Faith?"

"My crew was mowing and trimming over at Camden Place," Faith said. "I got the video not long after we got there."

"Why didn't you call me or text me or something?"

Faith sighed. "I tried to," she said. "I thought you didn't answer my text because you knew I'd found out. If you'll remember, Lost Pines doesn't have the greatest cell service. There are dead zones by the river, near the butterfly garden."

Destiny shook her head and released a deep breath. "Mr. Galloway never judged our projects," she said.

"What?" Faith asked, surprised.

"The next day, he said you had to leave unexpectedly and gave your crew to Gloria."

"That was fast," Faith said.

"He was going to put Mark in charge, but he quit and went to work with you," Destiny said. "I quit a week later."

"Why? You would've had the most senior crew and could've picked your jobs."

"No, I couldn't," Destiny said defensively. "He had those competitions, remember?"

"Yeah, but no one could come close to your creativity and knowledge," Faith said.

"It didn't matter." Destiny stared at her hands. "I couldn't stay there." She swallowed the lump in her throat remembering the debilitating sadness she felt when she realized Faith had gone and wouldn't talk to her.

"I saw Gloria today," Faith said. "She's working for one of the big firms now."

"I'm not surprised. She didn't want to do the hard stuff to own your own company. She wanted to run someone else's."

"She gave me the strangest look when I said hello to her," Faith said. "Now I know why."

"I'm not sure what I'll do the next time I see her." Destiny blew out an exasperated breath. She was angry with Gloria, but it wasn't entirely her fault that all this happened.

Faith reached over and grabbed Destiny's hand. "I'm sorry," she said softly.

Destiny looked over and could see tears swimming in Faith's eyes. Suddenly Destiny jumped up and went to the window. She closed her eyes and tried to make sense of this entire fucked up situation.

She was stuck in a small shack with dogs ready to attack if they opened the door and she'd just found out that the reason the woman she loved had left her was because of a case of mistaken identity. *Are you fucking kidding me!* Destiny wanted to scream, but instead she turned to Faith.

"Why couldn't you tell me!" Destiny exclaimed. "Hell, why couldn't you tell Mark, or tell anybody! If you would have just said something then we'd be together right now."

Faith dropped her head and closed her eyes. "I was afraid."

"Afraid of what?" Destiny asked. When Faith looked at her with desperation in her eyes Destiny knew it was about trust. "Oh no, Faith, I know how hard it is for you to trust people. That's why I showed you over and over you were

Until We Weren't:

safe with me. You fell in love with me and you knew you could trust me."

"Maybe we can fix this, Destiny," Faith implored her in a hopeful voice.

Destiny's eyes widened and her heart sank. "How?" she asked with tears in her eyes. "If this happens again, I won't survive it. I trusted you."

"I messed up," Faith said. "I've always trusted you and knew I could. I can't trust myself because I'm so fucked up, but I'll work on it, Des. Until I can trust myself, I know to trust you. Of course you would have never done anything like that to me, but the video was so real. Why didn't I come to you and ask? Because I was afraid it was true! If you had told me you did that to my face I don't think I'd have made it. That would've been it for me."

"Did you ever think I would've told you it wasn't me?"

"I knew that's what you'd say because that's what any guilty person says. See how fucked up my thinking is?" Faith paced around the small room. "Now I'm devastated again because of what's happened and all I can think about is making it right." She stopped in front of Destiny and took her hands in hers. "All I can think about is giving you all this love I have inside me before it blows me up."

"Faith..."

"I know, it's not on you to save me. You did once before. What if we have the beautiful life we were talking about before I destroyed us? Don't you think we can still get there? I know you still love me. Give me a chance to show you."

Tears were falling down Destiny's cheeks now. "How could you ever think I would do something like that to you? I know you were hurt in the past, Faith, but all I did was love you. My love obviously wasn't enough."

"It was! It is!" Faith yelled. "It's me, Destiny. I'm the

fucked up one. Why you ever wanted to be with me is unimaginable."

"Because I love you!" Destiny screamed back.

The dogs began to bark outside the building and Destiny reached for the doorknob.

Faith grabbed her arm. "Stop! They'll hurt you!"

Destiny groaned and bent over putting her face in her hands. "I can't fucking believe this!" she screamed.

"I know," Faith said, gently placing her hand on Destiny's back.

It would be so easy to take Faith into her arms. She desperately wanted Faith to hold her, but what good would that do? Destiny couldn't believe Faith thought she could do something so terrible.

She remembered one evening as they watched the sunset, Faith talked about her parents. She told Destiny that when her parents would miss important events in her life she would convince herself that they had a good reason. When she got home and found out they simply didn't want to be there for her it would put another wound in her heart. Faith explained to Destiny that that's why her heart was nothing but scars.

"When I met you," Faith said, "the very first time you smiled at me, I felt my heart begin to soften.

Destiny smiled, holding Faith's hand. "The scars may always be there, but there's room in your heart for my love. I can feel it."

"Oh, your love is there, but what's even more amazing is that you made me able to love again. Just as we create beautiful landscapes together, we have made a love like nothing I've ever known."

"You can trust our love, babe," Destiny said.

As Destiny remembered that conversation she could just

imagine the thoughts in Faith's head when she saw that video. She must have felt so betrayed.

Destiny stood up and looked into Faith's eyes. "You couldn't trust our love. What were you so afraid of, Faith?"

9

"Destiny," Faith said. "Sit with me." She took Destiny's hand and eased them down to the floor.

Faith could feel strength building inside her and she knew it was Destiny's love. She had to be brave and believe in herself. In the past Destiny was always willing to do anything to help Faith trust and believe in them. It was Faith's turn to be the strong one, to show Destiny their life together was still possible.

"I can't tell you how many thoughts were flying through my head and still do when I remember that time," Faith said. "I was afraid that you would tell me you didn't do it, but I knew it was you because the video was so real. I figured you would come up with some story and I'd believe you then we'd just act like it didn't happen." She sighed. "I didn't think I was strong enough to leave you when I knew you'd done something like that to me. Or I'd take you back and keep being hurt."

Destiny shook her head. "When have I ever lied to you?"

Faith smiled and stroked the back of Destiny's hand with her thumb. "There's always a first time, right? You know how I think."

Destiny blew out a deep breath. "Have you ever lied to me?"

Faith was surprised by the question. She looked at Destiny and furrowed her brow. "I can't think of one time I've done that. There were a couple of times after work that we were supposed to do something with the others, but I just wanted to be with you, so I said I was tired."

"What else?" Destiny asked.

Faith gave her a puzzled look.

"I know those weren't the only thoughts going through your head when you saw the video," Destiny explained.

Faith nodded. "As I said, I was afraid to face you because I truly thought I'd crumble to pieces inside."

"Oh, Faith," Destiny said. "This is all so incredible because the last thing I would ever do is intentionally hurt you."

"That's what I thought. But you've seen the video."

Destiny nodded. "It does look like me, but..."

"After I moved out, I started Lush Fields and things settled somewhat," Faith said. "I was watching the sunset one evening and tears sprang to my eyes. I couldn't stop thinking about you, but I realized in that moment why I was really afraid."

Destiny looked over at Faith and waited.

"I knew I wasn't good enough for you and somehow thought that maybe I could be someday."

"What!" Destiny exclaimed. "Good enough? You are—"

"Wait, Des." Faith stopped her. "When you've been brought up like I have, scraped enough money together to get an education, been cheated on...I could go on and on. You get the idea you're not good enough. So, I figured you were going to leave me someday anyway."

"Faith," Destiny said.

"I know how fucked up that is," Faith said. "But that's the way my heart knew to protect me."

"Did I do something to make you feel that way?"

"No!" Faith said. "That's all on me."

"If I'd known you felt that way..."

"I know, you would have done what you do to reassure me and love me," Faith said. "I don't think I fully realized those feelings were there until I was without you."

"Do you still believe that?"

Faith smiled. "No."

"Good," Destiny said. "Because you're a successful business owner who happens to be the best landscape artist anywhere."

"Oh, really," Faith said with a smile. "What about that Green Thumb place? I've heard they're not so bad."

"So all this time, you think I destroyed your project to win a job." Destiny shook her head. "Incredible," she muttered.

"It says something that neither one of us has had a relationship in all this time. I broke our hearts, Destiny," Faith said. "I can put them back together again."

"My heart is broken all over again," Destiny said, sounding exhausted. "I didn't think that was possible."

"Now you know what happened and why I did what I did," Faith said. "Please give me the chance to show you how much I still love you."

Destiny narrowed her gaze and stared at Faith. "How can you still love me? Every time I've seen you since that fucked up day you've been an asshole to me."

"At first I was angry and hurt," Faith said. "Then I was so sad and lonely, all I knew to do was work."

"Yeah, I know how that feels," Destiny said. "Can I see your phone again?"

* * *

Destiny played the video again. She tried to see it from Faith's perspective. For so long Faith had built a wall around her heart and Destiny had slowly chipped it away until Faith let her in. She remembered one of the first times Faith told her she loved her. Destiny knew that was hard for her and she wasn't sure she believed her.

Faith smiled. "I love you, Destiny."

She smiled and wanted to believe it was true.

"I'm the one with trust issues," Faith continued. "But not with you. I love you and I'll keep saying it until you believe me."

"I believe you, babe," Destiny said.

"I think I need to do more than say it," Faith said, leaning in until her lips almost touched Destiny's. "I want you to feel it."

Faith scarcely nibbled Destiny's bottom lip, sending a rush of electricity through her body.

Destiny shivered, remembering the heat of that kiss. She handed the phone back to Faith. "I understand why you thought that was me. I know you don't like confrontation, but this was our life. You walked away from us so easily."

"Is that how it looked to you?" Faith asked with shock in her voice. "It was the hardest thing I've ever done!"

Destiny leaned back against the wall and sighed. "I'm so tired."

"Lean on me, Des," Faith said, sitting back next to her.

"Mmm," Destiny murmured. "You have no idea how much I'd like to, but..."

"I'll earn your trust again," Faith said softly.

What a crazy twist to the day, Destiny thought. For months, actually years, she had tried to be the person Faith could count on and trust. Look at them now. She had to admit Faith sounded more determined than she'd ever heard her.

They had shared a connection from the beginning that Destiny couldn't explain. She'd never felt it with anyone else. Destiny knew she had to go slow with Faith, but she felt her heart opening as they fell in love.

Tonight, she heard Faith's words, but she also felt the strength and conviction behind them. She'd never heard Faith sound quite so strong and brave. That's what was different tonight. Faith was brave. Where did that come from and why did it take so long?

Destiny felt her head nod as the exhaustion of it all crept up on her. She was trying to think through it all, but her last thought before giving in to sleep was of Faith. *I still love you, too, but...*

Destiny woke to the sound of a dog growling. She opened her eyes and realized her head was on Faith's shoulder.

Just then Faith moved and yawned. "It's getting light outside," she said.

Destiny rose to her feet and looked out the window. The dogs were still there, but she didn't see any sign of the workers.

"Let's hope they start work early around here," Destiny said.

"We fell asleep."

Destiny turned around and looked down at Faith. "Yeah, there were a lot of emotions flying around here."

Until We Weren't:

"I know you think I gave up on us," Faith said. "But I didn't. I gave up on myself. I won't do that again."

Destiny desperately wanted to believe her. "What happened? Have you found a newfound strength overnight?"

"Something like that," Faith said, stretching her arms over her head.

Destiny could remember those arms wrapped around her neck pulling her in for a kiss. She shook the thought aside and raised her eyebrows. "What gave you this strength?"

"I saw the truth in your eyes," Faith said. "I'm sorry I wasn't strong enough back then to look at you."

"I want to believe in you, Faith, but it's so hard. You have to admit this is such a quick turnaround."

Faith nodded. "You'll see. I'll show you."

Destiny sighed. The desire to let all the doubts go was palpable, but Destiny was wary. She'd meant it last night when she told Faith she wouldn't survive losing her again.

"Someone will be here soon and let us out," Faith said. "Will you still work with me on this project?"

Destiny nodded, knowing that was their only hope to win the bid. She reached down and grabbed both their shirts off the floor.

"Thanks," Faith said, putting her shirt back on. "Do you want to work on ideas for the main building at my shop? It's closer."

Destiny sighed. "I think I'd rather go home and shower. Maybe we could get together later this afternoon."

"Okay," Faith quickly agreed. "Whatever you want."

Destiny turned around and stared at Faith. "Don't be like that," she said.

"Like what?"

"Nice," Destiny replied. "Doing whatever I want. That will last about as long as it takes us to walk to the parking lot. I told you we can work together and I meant it."

Faith chuckled. "Maybe I like being nice to you. It's been a while."

Destiny raised her eyebrows and caught herself before she said something unkind.

"Go ahead," Faith said. "It's my fault it's been so long."

A slow smile crept across Destiny's face. There had been times when she was sure Faith could read her mind. That hadn't seemed to change even though they'd been apart.

"We never had any problems working together," Destiny said.

"Not really," Faith said. "Sometimes it took a little longer for you to see it my way than others, but it all worked out."

"Ha ha," Destiny said. Then she caught herself. "Oh no you don't." She shook her head. They were not going to fall right back into the ease they shared before it all blew up. Too much had happened and Destiny would not let her heart be broken over and over again. She suddenly realized that's how Faith must have felt every time her parents didn't show up for her or when her ex cheated on her.

"Des, listen," Faith said. "I think I heard a vehicle."

They both went to the window and saw that the dogs were still there. A whistle echoed from somewhere towards the parking lot. The dogs looked in that direction, but they stayed at the door to the building. When they began to bark, it didn't take long until Destiny could see a golf cart moving towards them. "Here they come."

"I know you're ready to get out of here, but at least some good came from being trapped with me," Faith said. "You did save me from the dogs, Des."

Until We Weren't:

Destiny looked at Faith and smirked. "I would never intentionally hurt you."

"I know that," Faith said. "I knew it then, but I wouldn't let myself believe it."

Destiny swallowed the lump in her throat. How could two people who loved each other so much hurt each other just as badly? It didn't make sense.

"Hey!" Faith yelled out the window. "We're trapped in here."

Two men got out of the golf cart and one leashed the dogs.

Destiny and Faith explained what happened. One man gave them a ride to the parking lot while the other walked the dogs back to his vehicle. They all agreed it was an unfortunate accident, but the dog handler would now be doing a sweep around the property instead of simply releasing the dogs and leaving.

"Do you want to get a cup of coffee?" Faith asked. "I'll buy."

"How about a beer later this afternoon?" Destiny replied. She needed to get away from Faith and process everything that happened last night.

Faith smiled. "I know you're going to have questions, Des. Please don't do what I did. Ask me. I'll answer everything and try to help you understand."

"Understand?"

Faith nodded. "Yeah, while you were sleeping a lot of things became clear to me."

"Hmm, maybe you'll share them with me this time?" Destiny said, trying to stop the sarcasm in her voice.

"I'm sharing everything with you from now on," Faith said. "Don't be afraid. I'm not."

Destiny didn't know what to think or say.

"I know that sounds absurd coming from me because I let all this happen out of fear," Faith said. "But no more."

Destiny simply nodded. "Okay, I'll text you later."

Faith smiled as Destiny got in her truck.

10

Faith got into her truck and immediately knew where she needed to go. It was too early for anyone to be at the shop yet, so she quickly fired off a text to Amy explaining she would be in later. Then she sent another text to Mark with her directions for the crews for the day. She promised to check in with him later that morning.

Faith looked into her rearview mirror and for the first time in a long time she liked what she saw. Yes, her hair was slick with sweat from being confined to that hot shack all night. She quickly smelled her armpits and decided her odor was not overbearing just yet.

A smile played across her lips as she stared into the mirror. Her eyes were clear, determined, and there was a sparkle that only Destiny could put in them. "Hey, Faith," she said to her reflection. "It's good to see you again."

She took a deep breath and slowly let it out. This felt like the first deep breath she had taken in three years. There was a feeling of hope wafting through the cab of her pickup. No longer did she feel like she was going through the motions to make it another day.

Faith had been to counseling at different times throughout her life. Whether it was a counselor or coach while she was in high school or a mental health specialist provided by her college. She was not a stranger to therapy and processing her feelings.

But last night something happened to her in that small shack that she couldn't explain. Part of her didn't care how it happened, but she felt more sure of herself and confident in her feelings than she'd ever been in her life. How could that be with what had happened between her and Destiny? If anything her life had been torn apart, courtesy of her own doubts, and last night should've been the final blow to any hopes she had of living a happy life.

Instead, she saw a future that she wanted more than anything. She thought back to the last time she'd seen Mrs. Baker at the assisted living home. The woman had told her how she'd watched the plants turn brown and seem to wither away, but there were tiny shoots of green that proved there was still life in them.

That's how Faith thought of her and Destiny. It may have looked like their relationship was withering away, but there was hope and a shred of life because they were still in love. Faith could feel it flowing through her body.

She had to talk to someone about all of this and knew Destiny was not ready to hear her. There was only one other person she knew would understand.

Faith pulled into the driveway, went to the front door, and rang the doorbell.

"Well, what a nice surprise," Gretchen Green said, opening the door.

Faith looked down at her clothes then back at Gretchen.

Until We Weren't:

"You'll have to excuse my appearance, but do I have a story for you," she said with a smile.

"You know I don't care how you look." Gretchen smiled and waved her in. "Get in here."

Faith followed Gretchen into the kitchen where she poured them both a cup of coffee.

"Have a seat," Gretchen said as she sat down at the kitchen table. "I am a little curious why you are so dirty this early in the morning."

Faith chuckled and took a much needed sip of coffee. "Oh, that is so good," she murmured.

"I can see you needed it," Gretchen said.

"I look like this because I haven't been home since yesterday morning," Faith began. "My last job of the day was to tour the big office complex they're building on I-35 in order to put in a bid to do the landscaping."

"I've seen it," Gretchen said. "That is some kind of office park they're building. I heard Destiny talking about it with Michael the other day when she dropped by."

"It seems even more immense up close," Faith said. "I saw Destiny there and we agreed that the builder would not take a small landscaping company like either one of ours seriously with such a huge project."

"Okay," Gretchen said, sipping her coffee.

"So, we decided it might be smart to work together."

Gretchen smiled. "You two always made a good team."

Faith smiled. "The property was so large that I went one way and Des went the other. The plan was to meet at the back of the building to compare notes. But the most amazing thing happened instead."

Gretchen raised her eyebrows in question.

Faith recounted her and Destiny's close call with the dogs.

"That is some story," Gretchen said. She gazed at Faith as a smirk grew on her face. "How did you two get along?"

Faith gave her a sad smile. "I made a terrible mistake and I'm hopeful Destiny can forgive me."

"I thought Destiny was the one who messed up," Gretchen said.

Faith told Gretchen about the video and what happened that day three years ago.

"Last night while we were trapped so many truths were right in front of my face," she continued. "When I showed Destiny the video I looked into her eyes and saw the truth. Destiny would never do anything like that to me. I knew that deep down." Faith took a shaky breath and exhaled. "When I saw the truth in her eyes, I saw my destiny. I know it sounds cliché and out there, but I know what I saw."

Gretchen smiled, reached over, and squeezed Faith's hand.

"You know, Destiny always listened to me and made it easy to talk about my past. She was so patient. It's time for me to let go of my family and all the disappointment and distrust. Back then, I wanted them to reach out and be different. What I did was make Destiny different in my eyes. I knew she would never do something like that to me, but I made myself believe she was like them."

"Oh, Faith," Gretchen said softly.

"She is my constant. My love, my trust, my life. I let my past go while I sat in that little shack. I know my destiny." Faith smiled. "No matter how long it takes, my life is with Destiny Green. I'm going after it because she is my happiness and I'm hers." She paused to control her emotions. "I may need your help."

Gretchen smiled. "I will do whatever I can for you because I believe every word you said and Destiny will too.

You may have to give her a little time to process it all, but she'll get there."

"We're working together on this big project, so I'm going to be with her all the time," Faith said with a grin.

"I'm proud of you, Faith." Gretchen grabbed her hand. "I know it's been hard for you and I'm not saying you won't still experience hard times with Destiny. But you won't be alone. You'll face them and go through them together. That makes all the difference."

"The old me would just take the hurt and hold it in my heart until it scarred over. I went on and tried to do better. But when Destiny reached in and started to smooth those scars, something else happened. I found love I couldn't get over. I couldn't just go on like before. I didn't realize that until last night. I knew this was different because I should've been over it by now. But now I know why." Faith looked into Gretchen's eyes. "I'm fighting for Destiny's love, for our love. I'm not going to let it go. I can't. I know how it feels to truly be loved by the person who you're meant to be with."

"How did you leave things with Destiny?" Gretchen asked.

"She has a lot to think about and process," Faith said. "I did to her what's been done to me all these years." Tears sprang to her eyes and she choked back a sob. "I've broken her trust and I'm going to do everything I can to get it back. I want her to feel and believe in our love again. She did that for me and now I've got to do that for her."

"It may take time, Faith," Gretchen said.

"It doesn't matter how long it takes."

"What a mess," Gretchen said. "But you aren't the only one at fault here. What about the woman who ruined your work and blamed Destiny for it?"

Faith shook her head. "I should've shown the video to Destiny that day."

"You said yourself that it wouldn't have mattered," Gretchen said. "You weren't in a place to believe her."

"But I didn't even give her a chance," Faith said quietly.

"Because no one ever gave you a chance, Faith." Gretchen shook her head. "Unfortunately, that's what you knew; that's what had been done to you."

Faith looked at her hands and could feel the familiar burning in her stomach from being let down once again.

"You have to forgive yourself before you can expect Destiny to forgive you," Gretchen said.

"I don't know if I can," Faith said.

"You have the most wonderful of reasons to find a way."

"Destiny," Faith whispered.

"Your Destiny," Gretchen replied.

Faith leaned back in her chair and could feel the exhaustion wash over her. "You don't hate me for what I did to your daughter?"

Gretchen scoffed. "You have hurt yourself just as much as you've hurt Destiny. But as you said there's hope. You know the truth now, about what happened and about yourself," she said. "You are no longer the person waiting to be let down."

"I'm not," Faith said with confidence. "I'm the person who's going to get her love back. Then I'm going to spend my life making her happy."

Gretchen chuckled. "I have a feeling my daughter isn't going to know what hit her."

Faith smiled. "She won't make it easy and she shouldn't. I have to earn her trust back. It's still so amazing to me. Something happened to me in that shack. Destiny fell asleep and I thought about everything we said. It was all so clear to me, but not back then when it happened. I don't understand, but sometime in the night I became a totally different person. I believe in myself and I believe in Destiny. I know the truth. I could see our future. Now I have to get Destiny there." Faith looked back at Gretchen and knew she'd been rambling, but something came over her in that building and she was pretty sure it was the love in Destiny's heart for her.

"I don't know if I can make Destiny understand, but why would she, after what I did to her?" Faith said.

"You make her understand," Gretchen said. "Let her see this person who now trusts in herself. Introduce yourself. I have a feeling she's going to love you even more."

"I wish I could explain it to you, but I've never been so sure of anything before. Destiny and I belong together and we have this amazing life waiting for us."

"You'll find a way," Gretchen said. "How did Destiny get you to trust her?"

Faith smiled. "She showed me. That's what was so strange about it all. Why couldn't I believe her then?"

"I think you had help because of the video," Gretchen said. "It looks like her."

Faith sighed and nodded. "Forgive myself, huh. Maybe Destiny and I can work on that together."

Gretchen smiled.

Faith got up and took her coffee mug to the sink. "I'd better get going. I'm meeting my destiny later this afternoon."

Gretchen chuckled.

"Thanks for listening to me," Faith said.

Gretchen pulled her into a hug. "Let those scars soften again, Faith. You deserve happiness, too."

Faith hugged her back. Now all she had to do was convince Destiny.

11

It didn't take long for Destiny to reach her apartment and just as she hoped, the shower cleaned both her physical and mental grime away. What she really wanted next was a quick nap, but she knew there was no way she'd fall asleep. Instead, she called Monica and gave her instructions for the morning and explained she'd be in later. Then Destiny got back in her truck and sent a text.

Where are you?

Moments later her phone beeped.

The nursery.

Destiny quickly replied.

Wait for me. I'll be right there.

The one person she felt like she could share this bizarre story with was Mark. They had worked together for several years and he had remained her friend through the breakup. He knew parts of Faith's past and had similar experiences with inattentive parents growing up.

As she drove to the nursery, Destiny sighed. "What a fucking night," she murmured.

The same thought kept running through her head. *How could she think I would do that?*

"Not good enough." Destiny hit the steering wheel with her hand. Faith had explained her fears then dropped that bomb about not being good enough for Destiny.

"What bullshit," she said a little louder. Then she sighed and felt the exhaustion wrap around her like Faith's hoodie. Only this wasn't the sweet feeling of a hug.

Gloria must have really wanted to win that project, Destiny thought, but she had to also be a despicable person to go about it that way. Destiny would see Gloria one of these days and she intended to get answers then.

Destiny pulled into the parking lot and saw Mark sitting on the tailgate of his truck waiting for her.

"You aren't trying to get me in trouble with my boss, are you?" he teased as Destiny walked up.

"I'm sure your boss would be fine with me talking to you today." She sat next to him and swung her legs.

"Oh yeah? She didn't come in this morning which is unusual," Mark said.

"She was with me."

It was almost comical the way Mark's eyebrows flew up his forehead. "Oh really?"

Destiny nodded. She told him the story of how they ended up trapped in the little shack all night.

"Damn!" he exclaimed. "I hope you'll let the big boss know. That's dangerous."

"Yeah," Destiny said. "The handler apologized and explained the changes he would make."

"So?" Mark inquired.

Destiny smiled. "Do you remember when we were working for the Galloways and you were on Kyle's crew?"

Mark nodded.

"Who ran things after he left?"

"Well, Mr. Galloway lined us out in the morning and we did our jobs." He shrugged.

"No one tried to take over or anything?"

Mark gave her a puzzled look. "Gloria was always trying to run things, but no one paid her much mind. They just did their jobs. I quit and went to work with Faith right after Kyle left. I'm sure she ended up with the crew."

"You'll never guess what she did," Destiny said.

"Oh, I don't know," Mark said, raising an eyebrow. "That woman has a mean streak."

Destiny reminded him of the doctor's office and the three flower beds at the job.

"Gloria got the hoodie out of my truck one day and wore it to destroy the flower bed Faith's crew had created at the doctor's office," Destiny said.

"She what?"

"Yeah," Destiny said. "That was a special hoodie because it was Faith's and she knew how much I liked to wear it. Anyway, she videoed herself, in the hoodie, digging up the plants and moving them to the bed my crew had planted. Then she sent the video to Faith—"

Mark gasped. "No fucking way! Faith thought it was you!"

Destiny nodded. "Yep."

"Oh my God," Mark said. "That fucking bitch! I knew she was no good."

"I guess she really wanted to win that project," Destiny said.

"Oh, Des. I'm so sorry."

"That's just the beginning." Destiny sighed. "Faith

thought it was me and chose not to tell me or discuss it with me. She simply moved out and wouldn't talk to me."

"Why?" Mark asked. "You would never do anything like that, especially to her."

Destiny nodded and sighed. "That video looks like me, Mark. I couldn't believe it."

"But still."

"I know. She said it didn't really matter what I said. A guilty person would deny it and if I admitted it, her heart was going to be broken either way," Destiny explained, her voice catching.

"Fuck," Mark muttered.

They both sat and swung their legs for a moment, letting the despair of it all hang in the air.

"This is so fucked up," Mark said. "Does she know now that it wasn't you?"

Destiny nodded. "We figured out it was Gloria, but that doesn't make the hurt go away," she said. "How could she think I'd do something like that?"

"I'm sure she didn't want to believe it, but folks have been hurting her most of her life," Mark said. "But if she'd just said something."

"That's what I thought, too, but I'm not sure she could believe it then," Destiny replied. "It's made me take a look at myself."

"What are you talking about?" Mark asked. "It was Faith's messed up past, not you."

"Maybe things weren't as great for us as it seemed," Destiny said. "If something like this could happen, maybe our love wasn't as strong as we thought."

"Then doesn't that mean you have a chance to make it stronger?"

Destiny looked over at him and smiled. "Maybe... But..."

Until We Weren't:

"But?" Mark asked.

"How do I take that chance?" Destiny shook her head. "When Faith left me before, it was all I could do to get out of bed. I went to work because I didn't have to think about her. I could lay out flower beds, plant shrubs, and work up bids. My head was full of work stuff and had no room for anything else. At night, I was so tired that all I could do was shower and fall into bed exhausted."

"I know someone else who did the exact same thing," Mark said.

Destiny nodded. "You know Faith said it means something that neither one of us has dated anyone in all this time."

"Maybe it means you weren't supposed to get over each other," Mark suggested.

"Maybe," Destiny said. "I just don't know if I'm strong enough."

"Strong enough," Mark scoffed. "You are stronger and more sure of yourself than anyone I know."

"Yeah, I was until I got trapped in a shack with Faith last night," Destiny said. "It's making me question my strength."

"It isn't making you question your love though."

Destiny smiled. "I know we still love each other. We could both feel it. I wonder if we can use that love, make it stronger, and recapture our relationship."

"That sounds like your next project," Mark said with a smile.

"We're going to join forces on the business complex bid," Destiny said. "The company evaluating the bids won't take small landscapers like us seriously, so if we team up surely they'll take notice. No one is more creative in coming up with an eye-catching design than Faith."

"And no one can make it happen better than you," Mark

said. "Faith has some crazy ideas and you're the only one who could make them work."

Destiny looked over at him and chuckled. "She's been doing okay without me for the past three years."

"Oh no she hasn't. Her designs are nothing like what y'all did together. She needs you to make what's in her head work at the site."

"We were a good team," Destiny said.

"Don't let fear stop you from taking this chance, Des," Mark said. "Just imagine what a life you two could have."

Destiny smiled and nodded. "I imagined it once before, but look at how that worked out."

"That wasn't entirely y'all's fault," Mark said.

"I thought we were doing great before. I'm not sure how to make us stronger."

"Maybe you're supposed to figure that out together," Mark replied.

"We're supposed to go over our notes this afternoon and begin working up the bid," Destiny said.

"Good," Mark said. "I'm sure you both needed a minute to process all this."

Destiny sighed. "I still can't believe it."

"It's crazy when you think about it, but hey, you and Faith are worth it," Mark said. "You never gave up before, why would you now?"

Destiny nodded. "Thanks, friend. I'll be seeing more of you if we win this bid."

"Then get to work," Mark said, hopping off the tailgate.

Destiny chuckled. "Yes, sir."

The morning seemed to go by in slow motion. Destiny went by to check on each of her crews before going to the office.

Until We Weren't:

Luckily, Monica was at lunch so Destiny didn't have to go through the story again. She would tell Monica eventually, but what she really wanted now was to go home and take a nap. The loss of sleep combined with the emotional turmoil had caught up with her.

Destiny had promised to meet with Faith that afternoon, but she had to get some rest first. She texted Faith and asked her if they could meet at the end of the day and Faith readily agreed.

"Perfect," Destiny mumbled as she got back in her truck. She would take a nap then go over her notes before she went to Faith's. She was confident they could come up with a plan that was better than the other landscape developers, but she wasn't sure they could do it at a cheaper price plus make a profit for their companies. It was such a fine balance.

Destiny's route to her apartment took her near the retirement home. She smiled thinking about Mrs. Baker. Destiny often went by around lunchtime because she knew Mrs. Baker liked to sit outside on a bench in one of the small flower gardens after she'd eaten.

She may be tired, but it wouldn't take a minute to stop by and say hello to the older woman. Destiny didn't know how many times she'd gone by the retirement home when she was having a bad day and Mrs. Baker always made her smile. After she and Faith broke up, Mrs. Baker made sure Destiny knew whenever Faith had been by and that she was just as unhappy as she was.

Destiny pulled through the front gate and drove around to the garden nearest the dining hall. Sure enough there was Mrs. Baker soaking up the sun. Destiny parked and smiled as she walked up to her.

"It's my lucky day," Mrs. Baker said. "Look who's here."

"I'm the lucky one," Destiny said, sitting down next to her.

"Honey, no offense, but you look tired."

Destiny chuckled. "I am headed home for a nap. I was up all night."

Mrs. Baker raised her eyebrows in question. "I hope you were out with a certain friend of ours."

Destiny laughed. "I was."

A big smile lit up Mrs. Baker's face. "You know how much I care for you and Faith."

"I do."

"I also know that you two are more than friends," Mrs. Baker added. "I may be ninety and my eyesight isn't what it once was, but I can see love and you and Faith are in love whether you want to admit it or not."

Destiny smiled. "I do love Faith, but a lot has happened."

"I've known y'all for over four years now and you've been in love the entire time. Even though you weren't speaking to one another, the love was still there. I saw it."

Destiny nodded, knowing the woman's words were true.

"It seems to me that no matter what's happened, as long as you have love then you have a start," Mrs. Baker said. "I've been around a lot longer than you. Your love for each other can withstand anything. I've seen it."

Destiny smiled. "We'll see."

"Come here, let me show you something," Mrs. Baker said, slowly getting up with the help of her cane.

Destiny followed her over to a section of the flower bed that was bathed in sunlight.

"Look at these two plants," Mrs. Baker said. "The sun zaps them and these pretty little pink flowers fold up to nothing. Then when the sun goes behind the building the flowers open up and smile at me like a friend."

"Those are wood sorrel. That's why we planted them there. They can withstand the sun and still be beautiful," Destiny said.

"They remind me of you, Faith, and your love. It may have gone through some hard times, but it's not done. It's ready to smile again."

Destiny smiled. If only it was that easy, she thought.

12

"You can leave early today, Amy. Thanks for taking care of everything while I took a nap. I haven't been that zapped in a long time."

"I'm sure it wasn't just the lack of sleep," Amy said. "An emotional roller coaster can wear you out. I still can't believe that happened to y'all."

Faith smiled. "Yeah, there were a lot of emotions swirling around that small shack."

"When is Destiny supposed to be here?"

"Anytime," Faith replied, looking at her watch. "I'm sure she needed a nap as well."

"Okay," Amy said, gathering her things. "You probably want me out of here so y'all can talk."

"We need to work on this bid first," Faith said. "I so want to win this project. Working next to Destiny every day would be…"

"Like old times?" Amy suggested.

"Better." Faith smiled. "I'll find a way for her to trust me again."

Amy nodded. "Just be yourself. You've been a totally

Until We Weren't:

different person today. I've never seen you this...hopeful and light."

"Because I am," Faith said. "I haven't felt this hopeful in a very long time."

"I wonder if Destiny feels the same way," Amy mused.

Faith shrugged.

"We're about to find out," Amy said. "Here she comes."

Faith couldn't stop the smile that grew on her face as Destiny opened the front door. She had always been and would always be the most beautiful woman Faith had ever seen. When Destiny met her gaze Faith could tell she was holding back a smile, but she could see it in her eyes. *This is a good start.*

"Hi, Amy. I'm Destiny Green," she said, walking towards Amy and extending her hand. "I don't think we've met, but Mark told me you're the one that keeps this place going."

Amy chuckled and shook Destiny's hand. "That's a nice thing to say, but we all know who runs things." She gestured with her thumb towards Faith.

Destiny grinned and leaned in. "She can be quite the perfectionist."

Faith cleared her throat, getting their attention. She knew Destiny was teasing and it made her heart do this flutter thingy that only Destiny could do.

"Um, I'm right here," Faith said, holding up her hand.

"You two get to work and win us that contract," Amy said, walking towards the door. "It was nice to meet you."

"I hope to see you again, Amy," Destiny said with a smile.

Faith looked on and felt such warmth in her heart. Destiny had a way of making someone feel like they were the only person in the room. She was friendly and so charming. She made it look easy. Faith was always amazed because meeting new people was hard for her. She needed to remember to let Destiny present their bid to the contractor. Her charms would be an advantage.

"Why are you staring at me?" Destiny asked, her brow furrowed. "Do I have something on my face?"

"No." Faith smiled and shook her head. "I was just thinking that you need to present the bid to the contractor."

"Why?"

Faith tilted her head. "You know why." She grinned. "You put people at ease; it's one of your super powers."

Destiny grimaced. "I don't know about that. You can be very passionate and convincing when you present a project."

Faith smiled, pleased that Destiny saw her that way. "I'm glad you wanted to meet later in the day," she said. "Did you go home and take a nap?"

Destiny nodded. "Yeah, I had to rest." She shrugged. "I'm not as young as I used to be."

Faith chuckled. "I know what you mean."

"You're still just a baby," Destiny said. "But not for long. Your birthday is just around the corner."

Faith groaned. She wasn't surprised that Destiny remembered because she loved to make birthdays special, but being the center of attention wasn't Faith's favorite thing.

"This is a big birthday. It ends in a zero," Destiny said, raising her eyebrows.

Faith shrugged. "You know how I am about birthdays."

Destiny tilted her head and studied Faith for a moment.

"What?" Faith asked.

"Let's get our work done then maybe we could talk?" Destiny said cautiously.

"I'd like that." Faith smiled. "You can set your computer up over here." She cleared a space on her desk next to her laptop and pulled a chair over for Destiny. The idea of sitting next to her and working on a project together gave Faith a feeling of delight. Was that joy? She hadn't felt that in such a long time. Faith took a deep breath and slowly let it out, hoping to somewhat calm those feelings.

"I've got the business complex layout uploaded into the landscaping software so we can play around with ideas and see how they look," Destiny said, booting up her computer and opening the program.

Faith got her notebook out and opened it. She wondered if Destiny was feeling the same way. If so she wasn't showing it, but she didn't look unhappy or nervous either. "I've been going over my notes and thinking about different approaches to the property."

"Okay," Destiny said, leaning back in her chair.

Faith could feel Destiny's gaze on her and when she looked up Destiny smirked.

"Let me guess," Destiny said. "You want to do a garden."

Faith raised her brows. "Now why would you think that?"

Destiny smiled. "Because the building itself is rather bland and boring, plus... The people inside need something beautiful to look at and also something pleasing to the senses when they do get to go outside."

Faith couldn't hide her surprise as she stared at Destiny. That's exactly what she was thinking.

Destiny chuckled. "I know you, Faith."

"Yeah, you do." God how Faith had missed this. Why did she ever let Destiny go? Why were her fucked up insecurities so loud back then? Why couldn't she simply trust Destiny?

"I happen to agree with this plan," Destiny continued, clicking on a file. "Besides, we talked about it in the shack."

"You realize it will take more to maintain than some of our other options." Faith smirked. "I know you, too, and you're always thinking of upkeep costs for the customer."

"You're right," Destiny said with a smile. "I do, but in this instance I think we need to go big. The architecture is rather subdued and the landscaping can make it stand out. We simply have to convince the contractors."

"They don't seem to be the type to want to blend in," Faith said. "At least that's not the impression I got."

"Me neither," Destiny said. "Do you have an idea of what plants you want to use?"

Faith nodded.

"Okay." Destiny held her hands over the keyboard. "Tell me what you're thinking and I'll build it in the software."

Faith smiled. They had done this several times when they worked together before and easily fell back into their routine. "I think we need something here that's not as bushy," she said. "More sparse, you know what I mean."

"Like this?"

"Yes! Look at that, Des! When we add the color, that will be the perfect background."

Destiny stopped and looked over at Faith. "You know, I was thinking that we might build into the contract an option for us to come and reassess the property every so often. We could keep the landscape up to date as trends change as well as the seasons."

"That's a great idea," Faith said. "I don't think the big firms offer that."

"I would love to structure the bid so we do the maintenance and they pay us monthly," Destiny said. "A stream of income from a property like this would be huge. Don't you think?"

"Absolutely," Faith agreed. "Maybe we could structure the bid to give them options."

"Hmm," Destiny murmured. "It all begins with the design, but let's be honest. That can be subjective depending on who oversees the project and decides on the landscaping. If we give them options that include with or without maintenance and throw in the option for upgrades as trends change—"

"That's so much more than landscaping!" Faith exclaimed. "No one does that, but we could."

Destiny smiled. "We certainly could."

"You've been thinking about this," Faith said, studying Destiny with a smile.

"I have," Destiny said quietly.

"Come on, Des. You're holding back. What aren't you telling me?"

Destiny put her hands in her lap and released a deep breath.

Faith recognized this behavior. Destiny wanted to share something, but was hesitant. "It's me," Faith said.

Destiny looked up at Faith. "I used to think up things we could offer, for when we started our own company, that would be different from the other landscaping companies."

"This was one of those ideas?"

Destiny nodded. "I haven't been able to implement anything like it because The Green Thumb is too small."

Faith raised her brows and her heart skipped a beat. "If we joined forces we could offer something like that."

"Yeah, I think we could."

Faith smiled as her thoughts jumped into the future. If there was hope for her and Destiny then maybe they could live their dream of working side by side and owning their own company, too. That would be too good to be true, she thought.

"I can tell by the look on your face that you like the idea," Destiny said.

Faith chuckled. "I like it very much."

"Then we'd better come up with a landscaping layout that will dazzle the contractor," Destiny said.

"Let's do it."

For the next hour Faith relayed the ideas she could see in her head and Destiny put them in place on their mock-up of the property in the computer. They added shrubs and trees here, then plants there. They took them away or exchanged them for different flowering plants. As they shared ideas, the layout around the main building came together on the screen.

Faith suggested a different variety of flowering plant in one section and when Destiny added it the landscape jumped off the screen.

They both gasped when Destiny clicked the button to show the new changes.

"That's it!" Destiny exclaimed. "My God, Faith. This is your best work," she said, putting her arm around Faith.

Faith stared at the screen. Destiny had once again transformed the ideas in her head and made them real. She felt Destiny's arm around her and closed her eyes, relishing the touch.

"Oh, sorry," Destiny muttered, dropping her arm.

"This is *our* best work," Faith said. "I don't know how you do it, but you see inside my head and make it come to life."

Destiny chuckled. "I just know how to listen to you."

"We get the chance to go look at the property again next week," Faith said.

"We should go together, but this time we'll be mindful of the time," Destiny replied.

Faith chuckled. "I'll set an alarm on my watch."

"We also need to go get prices from the nursery. Abel will make us a good deal."

"We can do that Monday afternoon then go out to the property," Faith said. "That will give us a better idea of what we can use and not use and still make money."

"We should keep this in mind," Destiny said, pointing at the screen. "Then Monday we'll figure out how to tie in the other buildings adjacent to the main structure."

Faith nodded. "That's a good plan."

"Wow," Destiny said, sitting back in her chair. "All the exhaustion I felt earlier is gone."

"Because this is exciting," Faith said. "We have a real shot at this, Destiny."

Destiny nodded and smiled. "I think that's all we can do for today."

13

"Today has become evening," Faith said, looking out the windows at the front of her office.

"Time flies when you're creating something beautiful," Destiny said. She cut her eyes over at Faith. She hadn't meant to put her arm around Faith earlier, but it seemed like the most natural thing in the world to do. Everything seemed natural once they started working on the project. Destiny had felt a flutter or two in her stomach since walking in the front door.

"It's Friday night," Faith said. "Do you have to work in the morning?"

Destiny shook her head. The nap she'd taken this afternoon would get her through the rest of the day, but she planned on sleeping in tomorrow morning.

"How about we go out back?" Faith suggested. "I have beer in my fridge."

Destiny smiled. A beer sounded lovely. "I think we've missed the sunset."

"If we win this bid, we'll be seeing plenty of sunsets together." Faith smiled. "Is that a yes?"

Destiny nodded and closed her computer. "Yes, I would love a beer."

"Come on," Faith said.

Destiny watched as Faith went to the front door and locked it then turned the lights off. She waited at the back of the room and followed Faith into the shop. There was a large garage door open to the back lot where other equipment was stored. Faith's tiny house stood further back.

"This is a lot like my place," Destiny said. "I have an open space to show landscaping options to customers, a couple of offices, and a shop in the back of the building. But I don't have a tiny house."

Faith smiled. "If it's not too hot for you we can sit out here on my fancy front porch."

"It feels nice out here," Destiny said.

"Would you like a tour?" Faith asked.

Destiny grinned. "Heck, yeah. I've always wondered about tiny houses."

Faith walked up a couple of steps and opened the front door. "After you."

Destiny walked into the small living space that held a couch, TV, and bookshelf on one end.

"This is obviously the living room," Faith said. "Excuse me."

Destiny felt Faith's hands on her hips as she squeezed past her to the right. A jolt of electricity shot through her body at the brief touch. *Take it easy.*

"This is kind of the dining area," Faith said, pointing to a small table built into the wall in the back of the space. "And this is the kitchen."

"Wow, you've got everything in here, just smaller," Destiny said, following her a couple of steps to the sink.

"Yeah, it's a two burner cooktop with a small oven," Faith said. "There's a microwave here."

"This is really nice." Destiny could imagine Faith cooking dinner in the small kitchen. She was reminded of when the two of them cooked together in what was now Destiny's apartment. There were times when she thought about moving because of the sadness that loomed in the apartment. But she also had memories of Faith there and just couldn't bring herself to leave.

"Thanks," Faith replied. "These windows are actually like a garage door. I can roll it up and open the space to the outdoors."

"Wow," Destiny exclaimed. "That's cool."

"Yeah, it's not so great this time of year because of the heat and all the bugs," Faith explained. "But it's nice in the spring and fall."

Destiny smiled and looked around the space. It might be small but it was functional and also comfortable.

"Down here is the tiny bathroom and at the end is the bedroom."

Destiny looked down the short hallway.

"Go ahead," Faith said.

Destiny smiled and stopped at the bathroom. "That's bigger than I imagined."

"It's not too bad."

Destiny looked into the bedroom that was big enough to hold a queen-sized bed with just enough room to walk on either side.

"There's storage underneath the bed," Faith said, "and a tiny closet for hanging clothes next to the bathroom."

Destiny paused for a moment to take in the small bedroom. It was neat and tidy just like Faith, but something about the room gave Destiny a feeling of loneliness. She suddenly had an overwhelming urge to grab Faith and hold her to drive out that sensation. Destiny wheeled around and found Faith smiling at her, holding out a beer.

"Here you go," Faith said.

"Thanks." Destiny made sure her fingers grazed Faith's when she took the bottle. For whatever reason she needed Faith to feel her touch. The idea of Faith's loneliness tore at Destiny's heart. She knew there were many times in Faith's life when it had just been her and no one else. Destiny never wanted to be the reason for emptiness in Faith's heart.

"Let's sit out here," Faith said.

Destiny followed her out of the house and tried to shake the feelings swirling around her heart. "Do you like living back here?" she asked as they settled into the chairs.

"Uh, it was the best solution at the time." Faith shrugged. "You know how hard it is to get a business started. I was here all the time anyway."

"Yeah, it is," Destiny said. "I had no idea, but it was better than staying where I was."

"You know, looking back, I loved my job, but I'm not sure the Galloways' competition thing was a good way to encourage employee unity," Faith said.

"Yeah, I don't do anything like that with my teams," Destiny said.

"You were right when you called me a perfectionist, but I couldn't afford not to be," Faith explained.

"Oh, I get it. When it's your money and you don't have any to spare you can't make mistakes."

Faith nodded and sipped her beer.

"I still can't believe everything you told me last night," Destiny began. "There's nothing I'd like more than to erase the last three years, but it makes me wonder if we knew each other as well as we thought."

"Why do you say that?"

"I had no idea you thought you weren't good enough for me. That tells me that I didn't show you just how much I loved you and how truly lucky I felt every day that I got to spend my life with you. I should've known. No wonder you didn't talk to me about the video."

"You can't take the blame, Destiny. I didn't open up. I knew I could trust you. I knew it, but chose not to. That's on me, not you."

"But I knew how hard it was for you," Destiny said, shaking her head. "I thought we were happy. At least I was."

"I was, too, but something inside me kept saying it wouldn't last," Faith said. "It was just a matter of time before you realized I wasn't good enough and moved on."

Destiny groaned. "Stop saying that!" She put her hands over her face then looked over at Faith. "I understand why you don't trust anyone, but why can't you trust yourself, Faith?" Tears sprang to Destiny's eyes and she quickly blinked them back before they could fall. "You knew I loved you," she said with desperation in her voice. "I could see it in your heart. My love was there, you felt it. I could see it in your eyes when you looked at me."

"I can see it now," Faith said softly. "You still love me. We can do this, Des."

Destiny sighed. "We can do it until the doubts creep in again. Then you'll leave me and I won't have a heart left. The only reason I stayed in Austin was because I knew you were here. It hurt, but it also soothed my soul to see you occasionally, even if you couldn't meet my eyes. Even if the things you said were laced with animosity. If we got back together and you did this again, I told you I won't survive, Faith."

Faith got up and knelt in front of Destiny. "I won't do this

Until We Weren't:

again, Des. I promise. I know now! I knew all along, but I believe in myself now. I've always believed in you. That was easy, but I didn't believe I could be the person you needed, the person you should be with."

"It's not for you to decide who I need or should be with," Destiny said, raising her voice.

"I know that." Faith got up and walked a few steps away then turned back to Destiny. "You remember how crazy my thinking can be. How distorted it becomes at times."

"But that stopped when we fell in love," Destiny said. "That's what you told me."

"It did," Faith said. "But then as we began to talk about starting our own business and landscaping our way..."

"The doubts came back," Destiny said.

Faith nodded. "We had dreams, but I couldn't see myself in them," she said. "Until last night."

Destiny looked Faith in the eyes and saw a resolve she'd never seen before. Faith could show confidence when they were talking about landscaping, but this was different. "What do you mean?"

"You'll see," Faith said.

Destiny raised her eyebrows and stared at Faith. The certainty in Faith's eyes and the strength in her voice was new.

"I can tell you I've changed just as you would tell me you loved me," Faith said. "But you also showed me and that's how you won my heart and I came to trust you. So, Destiny Green, I aim to show you that the woman you fell in love with is still here, but she's stronger and worth it."

Destiny shook her head and sighed. "You were always worth it."

Faith smiled. "It's hard to believe being stuck in a hot shack in the dark with guard dogs outside can open someone's eyes. It's dramatic and completely out of character for me." She sat back in her chair. "But Destiny, facing a mistake, seeing love in your eyes, along with the hurt I put there, made everything crystal clear. I'm so sorry I hurt you and that it took me this long to see it. I can't change that, but I can't give up either."

Destiny listened to Faith and knew she was speaking from her heart, but it was Destiny's turn to wonder if she could trust her. The reality that this all started over a work project suddenly flashed in Destiny's mind.

"I'll tell you one thing," Destiny said. "Gloria has not seen the last of me. She did a terrible thing. She ended us."

"No she didn't," Faith said.

Destiny smirked and tilted her head.

"I heard you earlier when you said we didn't know each other as well as we thought," Faith said. "Maybe this would've happened anyway, but I'm not so sure. How about this?"

Destiny looked over at Faith and waited.

"What better way to get to know each other than to go on a date," Faith said.

Destiny scoffed. "A date?"

"Yeah." Faith smiled. "We didn't do that enough."

Destiny shrugged. "I suppose we didn't."

"We loved working together," Faith said.

"We did."

"Let's go look at some of the other business complexes in the area tomorrow then do something we both like," Faith suggested.

Destiny narrowed her gaze, but she felt her heart skip a beat at the thought of spending the day with Faith. "Like what?"

Faith grinned. "You let me worry about that. I'm the one asking you out."

Destiny couldn't keep from smiling. This was different. Faith wasn't usually the one who suggested outings when they were together.

"Well?" Faith asked. "Will you go out with me, Destiny?"

Destiny liked the way Faith was looking at her. There was nothing but hope and love in her eyes and a new kind of swagger in her posture. *Can I trust her? Oh, I want to. It's just a date.*

"Yes, I'll go out with you tomorrow," Destiny replied.

Faith sat back in her chair and grinned. "Good."

14

Faith had gone to sleep thinking about Destiny and her first thought was of her when she woke up. After Destiny agreed to go on a date with Faith they had had another beer and enjoyed the evening.

Faith smiled as she drove to Destiny's apartment. It would feel a little odd picking her up from the same apartment where they'd spent many happy days, but she was happy Destiny wanted to spend time with her. She felt their love in her heart and was sure they could overcome this.

"Hmm," she muttered. "I never knew trust could feel this good."

Most of her life Faith had been afraid of trust. She'd learned at a young age sometimes people didn't do the things they said they would. That caused hurt feelings and as she grew older Faith decided she was the only person she could count on in her life. Then came Destiny.

As she lay in bed last night and thought back over her life with Destiny, she realized they'd actually been apart longer than they were together. There hadn't been many happy times in Faith's life, but the last three years had been the hardest. She should be proud that she'd started her own business and it was successful, but that's not what she wanted.

Faith realized that what she wanted most in this life was to spend it with the woman she loved. Whether it was work, being with friends, or doing something simple like watching TV, Destiny made it better.

It wasn't much of a mystery how she'd let this happen. Her history had set her up for this, but if she'd just listened to her heart...

She sighed and pulled into a parking space next to Destiny's truck. "I'm listening to my heart from now on," she said. "We can do this, Destiny."

Destiny opened the door before Faith could knock.

"Wow, I hope this means you're looking forward to today," Faith said happily.

A nervous smile played across Destiny's lips then she looked down at her feet. "I didn't want you to feel weird picking me up here."

Faith smiled. "I thought about it, I'm okay. Let's go have a fun day. What do you say?"

"I have a question," Destiny said as they walked to Faith's truck.

"Okay," Faith replied, stopping at the curb.

"Are we working first then having a date?"

Faith chuckled. "It's kind of hard for us not to talk about landscaping or notice it when we go anywhere." She walked to the passenger side of her truck and opened the door. "The date starts now."

Destiny raised her eyebrows, smiled, and got into the truck.

"We are headed to Apple's headquarters first," Faith said, pulling out of the parking lot.

"Are you wooing me?" Destiny asked.

"Woo?" Faith chuckled.

"You know how much I like the landscaping out there," Destiny replied.

Faith chuckled. "Is it working? Then yes."

Destiny laughed. "Oh, it feels good to laugh with you again."

They rode in a comfortable silence, simply enjoying being together.

"I thought we might look at how they used fountains," Faith said as she pulled into the property.

"Are you thinking we should try something like that?"

"I don't know," Faith said. "We've got to go big. A small water feature outside each building might be a tranquil place for the workers to take a break or have lunch in nice weather."

"I wish we could find a way to do something different at each building, but tie it together with one theme," Destiny said.

"Oh, that would be cool," Faith said. "Like each building could have their own special area. Maybe one has a water feature, another has—"

"Oh! I've seen these cool rock cairns," Destiny said excitedly.

Faith glanced over at her. "I'm not sure I understand."

"There's this house not far from Mom and Dad's," Destiny explained. "This guy stacks rocks in these neat formations. I thought it might be interesting to try and use something like that in a landscape design."

Faith knew what a rock cairn was but struggled to imagine it at the business complex.

"Here," Destiny said, holding out her phone. "Something like this."

Faith glanced over at the phone. "We could change the rock formations as part of the maintenance plan."

Destiny gasped. "Great idea."

"Are you going to learn how to do that?"

Destiny chuckled. "Maybe I can get the guy to show us how."

"Could we put some kind of examples of how to build it or patterns they could use in the garden?" Faith asked.

"I bet we could," Destiny said. "I'll research it."

"This is a good idea, Des," Faith said. It was her turn to get excited. They often came up with unique ideas like this when they worked together. Faith's heart began to thump a little faster in her chest. She wanted to stop and pull Destiny into her arms and kiss her. Faith chanced a glance towards Destiny and found her staring right at her.

Yep, she feels it, too.

Faith pulled her teeth across her bottom lip and looked back at the road as a grin grew on her face.

They drove over to two other large business complexes and continued to trade ideas.

Destiny sighed and looked over at Faith. "What a nice way to spend an afternoon."

"It's not over," Faith said. "Are you hungry?"

Destiny chuckled. "You know me, I could always eat."

"Some things don't change."

Faith exchanged a look with Destiny and exited the highway. She pulled into an area where several food trucks were in a semicircle and heard Destiny gasp.

"The Pearl Panda!" Destiny exclaimed. "That's my favorite food truck."

"I remember," Faith said, pulling into a parking space. "They joined several other food trucks to park here for the weekend."

While they waited in line, Faith said, "Let's get our food and then I want to show you something."

Destiny nodded. "I'm getting the noodle bowl with shrimp. Will you share an order of sticky dumplings with me?"

"Yes, please," Faith said, gazing at the menu. "I'm getting the noodle bowl with teriyaki chicken."

Destiny laughed. "We get the same thing every time."

"Because we love it." Faith laughed with her.

They placed their orders and Faith paid for the food.

"You didn't have to do that," Destiny said as they sat at a picnic table and waited for their food.

"Yes, I did," Faith said, sitting across from her. "How long has it been since you've been on a date? I invited you."

"The last date I went on was with you," Destiny stated.

"For the record," Faith said, "the last date *I* went on was with *you*. It would be easy to say I didn't have time, but I haven't thought of another woman."

Destiny nodded. "Monica tried to set me up several times, but..."

"Monica probably hates me," Faith said.

"Not at all," Destiny replied. "I told her what happened and how real the video looked. She wasn't surprised by your reaction."

Thankfully the truck attendant called out their number and Faith got up to get their food. Regret burned in her stomach, but she pushed those feelings down, determined to make the most of this day with Destiny.

They got back in the truck and Destiny said, "I hope where we're going isn't too far away. This food smells amazing."

Faith chuckled. "It's right around the corner."

They turned into a subdivision with new homes. Faith

drove down the main street to a common area with a playground for kids and a walking path that disappeared into the neighborhood. She circled around to a small area with a couple of benches.

"We're here," Faith said, getting out of the truck with the food.

"This is nice," Destiny said. "I love the landscaping."

Faith chuckled. "It's definitely your style, isn't it?"

She led them to one of the benches and they sat down. "I completed this project last year," Faith said.

"Oh, Faith." Destiny looked around the area. "It's beautiful."

"The prairie style that you love was the perfect complement to the houses in this part of the subdivision," she said. "I thought of you as I imagined it, planned it, and put it in."

"Last year?" Destiny asked as she opened the container with the dumplings and set it between them. "You hated me last year."

"I never hated you," Faith said, opening her noodle bowl. "I hated myself and as much as I wanted to hate you I couldn't. I don't know how many times I laughed at myself as I planted this particular area. I almost told Mark to bring you by to see it because I knew how much you'd like it."

"You're right, I do."

"I look at it today and remember back to when I created it," Faith said. "It was my way to love you, Des." She turned and waited for Destiny to look at her. "I'll never stop loving you," she said softly.

Tears sprang to Faith's eyes and she quickly reached for her drink. "Sorry about that."

"It's okay," Destiny said. "You didn't notice last night, but tears were in my eyes."

"Yes, I did," Faith said. "We've always been emotional when it comes to our feelings for each other."

"Yeah, we have," Destiny agreed. "You could leave a note in my lunch bag and make me tear up."

Faith chuckled. "You did the same thing to me!"

They sat back against the bench and for several moments they ate in comfortable silence.

"This is so good," Destiny murmured between bites. "I'm glad you thought of the Pearl Panda."

"I'm glad you like it," Faith said, eating the last dumpling.

After a few moments Faith looked over at Destiny and said, "After we got out of the shack, I went to see your mom."

"She told me," Destiny said, taking a sip of her drink.

"Did she tell you what I said?"

Destiny shook her head. "She said it was yours to tell me."

Faith nodded. "I had a lot of things I wanted to tell you that day, but I knew you weren't ready to hear them."

"A lot happened that night."

"I know the things I've told you are hard for you to believe," Faith said. "Especially how quickly and how sure of myself I am now. That's why I suggested dating."

"Dating?" Destiny asked. "This is one date."

Faith smiled. "It's just the first. I hope we keep dating from now on."

"We'll see," Destiny said with a smile.

"One thing that I've figured out is that I'm letting my family go," Faith said.

"What? Why?"

"Let me see if I can explain," Faith said. "I've never been able to trust them and of course that led to my problems today. But I let what they did to me influence how I saw you." She set her bowl aside and moved closer to Destiny. She reached for her hand and was relieved when Destiny didn't pull away. Faith squeezed Destiny's hand and looked into her eyes. "You've never lied to me; you've always done what you said you were going to do. If I would've come to you with that video I'm pretty sure we would've figured out who it was just like we did in the shack that night. But instead I thought you were just like them."

"Faith," Destiny said softly.

"No, please, let me finish," Faith said. "My family only contacts me when they need something. They are never there for me. There is no reason for me to give them another thought." She swallowed the lump in her throat and continued. "Please don't laugh, but you are my destiny. I think I've always known that and maybe the universe had to test us, but I will never lose sight of that again. It's time for me to trust myself, to trust you, and trust our love."

Destiny stared into Faith's eyes and was about to speak when Faith reached up and put her finger over Destiny's lips.

"Don't say anything," Faith said. "I just wanted you to know that I'm standing up for myself. You've had to tiptoe around my issues from the beginning and I'm grateful for that. But I made it hard for you to love me and for that I'm sorry."

"No, Faith," Destiny said. "It was never hard to love you. Most of the time I was angry at your family because I don't understand how they can do that to you."

"You have always supported me," Faith said. "Can we stop?"

"Stop?"

"Yeah, I think that's enough seriousness for today," Faith

said. "This is a date. We've had such a good time so far. At least I have."

Destiny smiled. "I have, too. And by the way, I won't laugh at you."

"No matter how cheesy I sometimes sound?"

"There once was a story about Destiny and Faith," Destiny said with a grin. "Remember?"

15

Faith nodded. "Of course I remember."

"I still have faith," Destiny said, dropping her chin and staring into Faith's eyes. "And it's getting stronger."

The smile on Faith's face told Destiny she'd said what Faith wanted to hear. "I had one more stop planned," Faith said.

"Let's go," Destiny said, gathering their trash.

Faith drove them to their favorite frozen yogurt shop. They sat outside on a bench and enjoyed their dessert. This was so much better than Destiny had imagined. She wanted to spend the day with Faith, but she was afraid things would be awkward. Instead they had a relaxed wonderful time, just as they once did.

"Would you like for me to meet you at the nursery Monday afternoon?" Destiny asked, spooning the last bite of yogurt into her mouth.

"I'd be happy to come get you," Faith said. "I can say hello to Monica."

"Okay."

"Then we can go by the office complex for one more look," Faith said.

"You'll have to bring me all the way back to my shop once we're finished."

"I don't mind," Faith replied.

They threw their trash away and Faith drove them back to Destiny's apartment. The sun was dropping lower and lower in the sky, so she hurriedly pulled into a parking space. She ran around the truck and opened Destiny's door.

"We're just in time," Faith said, holding out her hand.

Destiny took it and chuckled. She let Faith lead them around the corner of the building to a small sitting area. They could just see the sunset through the trees.

"I think we made it," Faith said, pulling Destiny down to sit next to her.

Destiny couldn't help but get caught up in Faith's excitement. This had been one of the best days she'd had in a long time. It's funny how being with someone you love made the simplest things even better.

They hadn't done anything special today. Being with Faith, doing these simple things they both liked, that's what made it special. Destiny couldn't help but squeeze Faith's hand as they enjoyed the sunset like they'd done so many times before.

She sighed and smiled. Faith was definitely showing Destiny that she was not giving up on them. But what would happen if they didn't win the bid? It was such a longshot. What about the doubts? Destiny could feel them at the back of her mind. *Stop!*

Destiny took a deep breath and pushed the doubts away. There would be plenty of time to think about them later. Right now, she wanted to end this date surrounded by the happiness of spending the day with Faith.

Until We Weren't:

"That was a nice sunset to end this day," Faith said. "I was afraid we were going to miss it."

"It wouldn't dare mess up this lovely day you planned for us," Destiny said as they walked back to her apartment.

"I hope you had a good time," Faith said when they stopped outside Destiny's front door.

"I had a wonderful time," Destiny replied. Her heart began to pound a little faster in her chest. "Would you like to come in?"

Faith shook her head. "Not this time." She smiled. "Thank you for today, Des. Will you go out with me again?"

Destiny chuckled. "Yes, but shouldn't it be my turn?"

Faith shrugged. "Not necessarily."

Destiny felt Faith's lips softly touch her cheek. She momentarily closed her eyes and committed the sensation to memory. Oh yeah, she'd be thinking about that later.

"Have a nice weekend," Faith said. "I'll see you on Monday."

Destiny smiled and watched Faith walk back to her truck. She waved as Faith got inside and Destiny opened her front door. Once it was closed she leaned up against it and let out a deep breath.

"What just happened?" she murmured.

There were times throughout the day when the last three years seemed to disappear. It was just the two of them doing what they loved and being together.

Destiny sighed and reached up to touch her cheek where Faith had softly pressed her lips.

"How do we start over?" she whispered.

They couldn't take up where they'd left off because so much had happened, but the love was still there. Destiny felt it and couldn't deny it. She'd tried to tell herself that it didn't matter that they still loved each other, but it did.

Destiny felt like she was falling in love with Faith all over again. She'd met Faith's parents only once, but she understood why Faith gave them chance after chance. They were personable and outgoing, but broke her heart over and over.

She remembered wishing Faith could have parents and a family like she had. She wondered if it would give Faith a sense of relief because it always felt like she was waiting for them to hurt her all over again.

Maybe Faith letting her family go was the next best thing. It was hard to explain but Destiny could feel that hint of underlying tension that was always a part of Faith. It was just there. Sometimes it was stronger and Destiny did everything she could to ease it.

She furrowed her brow as she thought back over their conversations since being trapped in the shack. Faith said she could see everything clearly now and since then she seemed lighter. Come to think of it, Destiny hadn't noticed that unease in Faith since their night in the shack.

It was almost as if Faith's confidence was growing before Destiny's eyes.

"Ahh, this is too much." Destiny fell down on her couch and covered her face with her hands. "You were never easy, my love," she whispered. Her eyes sprang open when she realized she'd just called Faith *my love*.

Her phone beeped with a text, pulling her out of her head.

Thanks for the wonderful day. Let's do it again soon.

Destiny smiled as she read the text from Faith.

Thank you! What do you have in mind? A little flirting wasn't a bad thing, was it? Destiny thought as she replied. The three little dots appeared on the screen then the words.

I'll surprise you. See you Monday.

Destiny chuckled. This was such a role reversal for them. Destiny was the one who usually surprised Faith, but not anymore. Is this what their relationship could be going forward?

Can't wait, Destiny replied.

She sat back against the couch and smiled. "Slow down," she said softly. It would be easy to get caught up in these happy feelings again, but she remembered what happened last time.

* * *

The next day Destiny went over to her parents' house for Sunday lunch. Her dad loved to grill on Sunday afternoons and burgers were on today's menu.

Destiny helped her mom get the rest of the meal ready in the kitchen.

"I talked to your brother this morning," Gretchen said.

"How is Mr. Wonderful?" Destiny replied.

"Very funny," Gretchen replied.

"If you don't believe he's Mr. Wonderful, just ask him," Destiny teased. "I talked to him this morning, too."

"Oh?" Gretchen said with surprise.

Destiny chuckled. "We do talk to one another, Mom. He had a deal on a couple of work trucks for me if I was interested."

Gretchen stopped slicing a tomato to look over at Destiny. "He does give you his price for vehicles, doesn't he?"

Destiny smiled. "He's one of the top car dealers in the state. I'm not sure he did that by giving his sister a vehicle at cost."

"He'd better have given it to you at cost," Gretchen said, pointing the knife at Destiny. "I'll call him back after lunch."

"Mom!" Destiny exclaimed. "I'm kidding. Of course Chase gave me the best price, just as I do for him on landscaping when I can."

"You'd better," Gretchen said. "Y'all are family."

Destiny shook her head and prepared the lettuce for the burgers. "I told him about what happened with Faith. I thought he was going to come up here and hunt Gloria down."

"He's your big brother," Gretchen said. "No one messes with his sister."

Destiny chuckled. "Yeah, Chase is a good brother."

"I wondered how you felt about Gloria."

"I'll see her again someday," Destiny said. "What she did wasn't just unprofessional, it was despicable."

"Faith feels such regret for not talking to you about it," Gretchen said.

"I know. We spent the day together yesterday." She felt a flutter in her stomach thinking back to her time with Faith.

Gretchen smiled and looked over at Destiny. "Good for you. I would think now that you know the truth you wouldn't want to waste any time being apart. You were both hurt and sad for so long."

"Look, Mom. I know you want us to get back together, but it isn't that easy," Destiny said. "First, it's the way we broke up and her trust issues. Now she tells me that she trusts me completely and should have all along. On top of that she wants to give up her family. I don't want her to give up anything for me."

"Honey, she's not giving up her family for you," Gretchen said. "She's giving up her family because she wants a life of trust and love. She wants that life with you!"

"But to give them up?"

Gretchen sighed. "Didn't they give her up long ago?"

Destiny shrugged. "Faith does seem different," she said. "There's a lightness to her that wasn't there before."

Gretchen smiled. "She's letting all the hurt and pain go, but she's also letting go of the responsibility."

"I never thought of it like that," Destiny said. "There was always something hovering around us, like she was waiting for something bad to happen. I didn't realize it then, but I do now. Oh my God!" Realization swept through Destiny.

"What?"

"That's why she didn't feel like she was good enough," Destiny said. "She didn't feel good enough for her parents, so why wouldn't it be the same thing with me. Oh my God, Mom! She tried to explain it to me that night and again on Friday. I didn't get it then, but I do now. My poor baby."

"That's why she's letting them go, Destiny," Gretchen said. "She wants a life with you. She wants to love and be loved. She wants to trust and be trusted."

"That's what I wanted, too, Mom," Destiny said. "How do I know this won't happen again?"

"You don't," Gretchen said. "You have to trust her."

Destiny groaned. "Oh, I want to so badly."

Gretchen walked over and pulled Destiny into a hug.

"Faith is trusting herself," Gretchen said. She stepped back and smiled at Destiny. "You should, too."

"It seems that we're dating," Destiny said, shrugging. "It's Faith's idea."

Gretchen smiled. "She's giving you time."

"I know, but I told her that maybe we didn't know each other as well as we thought," Destiny explained. "She said what better way to get to know each other than going on a date."

"Is that what yesterday was?" Gretchen asked.

Destiny nodded. "We had the best day and we're going to do it again."

"When?"

"I don't know, she's going to surprise me," Destiny said. The thought made a feeling of warmth spread through her body.

"A surprise, huh," Gretchen said with a giggle. "That sounds fun."

"She planned everything yesterday. Who knows what she'll do next."

"You can count on it being something you love, honey," Gretchen said. "Because if there's one thing I know, Faith Fields is still very much in love with you."

I'm still very much in love with her, too, Destiny thought. *What do I do now?*

16

Faith pulled up to Destiny's office and felt her heart skip a beat. She'd had a busy morning, but the clock seemed to stand still. To say she'd been looking forward to working on the bid this afternoon with Destiny was an understatement.

They were going to the nursery first to get prices on supplies, shrubs, trees, and flowers. After that they were headed back to the business complex for one more look. The bids were to be presented next week and they still had a lot of work to do.

"Hi Monica," Faith said, walking up to her desk.

"Faith!" Monica got up and gave Faith a hug. "It's so good to see you. Destiny said you were coming by this afternoon."

"It's nice to see you, too." Faith smiled.

"Hey," Destiny said, walking out of her office.

"Hi." Faith tried to contain her smile, but couldn't help it. She wanted to see Destiny again yesterday, but knew it was too fast. So she settled for a few text messages instead. Was that a sparkle she saw in Destiny's eyes?

"I've heard all about how well you two used to work

together," Monica said, looking from Faith to Destiny. "I hope you're ready to bury those other companies."

Faith chuckled, knowing Monica had noticed them staring at each other. "Oh, we're ready. If only we can convince the contractor."

"Your ideas will convince them," Destiny said. "They're amazing."

Faith shuffled her feet at the praise and smiled. "Only if you present them," she said. "You're the one that makes us look good."

"Oh my God," Monica said, amused. "I'm loving this. No more landscape wars around here."

"What?" Faith furrowed her brow.

"Get Destiny to explain it to you," Monica said. "We need to get together, Faith. It's been too long."

"Yeah," Faith said. "Sorry about that."

"No worries," Monica replied. "What about this weekend? Kim would love to see you both. Drinks? Dinner?"

"Uh—well," Faith stammered.

"We have to work on the bid," Destiny said. "How about next weekend?"

"We can celebrate y'all winning the job," Monica said. "Let's do it."

Faith laughed. "I love your confidence."

"Like I said, I've heard about the great things y'all have done when you work together. It's easy to be confident of that," Monica said.

"Thanks, Mon," Destiny said. "We will do our best."

"Yes we will," Faith agreed. "But we're not the only ones in this."

"Oh, I know," Monica said. "We'll be ready."

"We'd better get going so we'll have plenty of time at the site," Destiny said.

"Please don't get trapped again," Monica said. "Wait...On second thought..."

"No!" Destiny and Faith said in unison.

Monica laughed. "Do I need to text when it's time to leave?"

"No, we'll be watching the clock this time," Faith said. "It was nice to see you, Monica. Please tell Kim hello for me."

"You tell her yourself next weekend," Monica replied.

Faith smiled. "I will."

"See you tomorrow," Destiny said as they turned to leave.

"It's just a matter of time," Monica said with a smile as they walked out the front door.

"That didn't seem too awkward," Faith said as she drove them to the nursery.

"It wasn't awkward at all," Destiny said. "Monica and Kim are our friends. Did you mean it when you said you'd go for drinks or dinner next weekend?"

"Yes," Faith replied. She glanced over at Destiny. "Why? Do you not believe me?"

"No, I do," Destiny said. "It's just that we didn't do a lot of things with our friends before."

"You say that like it's a bad thing," Faith said.

"It's not necessarily bad," Destiny said. "I just wonder if we should have been more social."

Faith glanced over at her and smiled. "Maybe, but you can't blame me if you're so amazing that I don't want to share you with anyone else."

Destiny looked over at Faith with a smirk. "Really?"

"Yes, really." Faith laughed. "Come on, Des. You liked staying home just as much as I did."

Destiny sighed. "Guilty, but this time..."

When Faith looked over at Destiny her eyes were wide and she was staring out the front windshield. *Yes, there's hope.*

"And just like that, here we are," Faith said, pulling into the nursery parking lot. She could've pressed Destiny on what she'd said, but she was just glad they had a chance. Faith knew they couldn't go back to the way things were, but they could go forward and this time things would be even better. She just knew it.

They walked into the nursery and found Abel standing at the counter in the back.

"Well, hello, you two. I heard a rumor," Abel said, looking up at them.

"Rumor?" they both said swiftly in unison.

Abel held up his hands. "Whoa," he said. "Mark said you two were joining forces to take down the big landscaping firms on that business complex. They don't buy from a small wholesaler like me, so I'm here to help. Count me in!"

"Oh," Destiny said, glancing over at Faith.

Abel leaned over the counter. "Is there another rumor I need to know about?"

Faith looked over at Destiny and grinned. "Not yet, but I'm hopeful."

Destiny smirked. "We have a list of things we need prices on."

They opened up their notebooks and explained their vision for the complex. He gave them suggestions, prices, and other options for some of their selections. They walked around the nursery looking at other plants they hadn't considered and made notes.

Faith looked at her watch and gently touched Destiny's

arm. "Hey, we'd better get going if we want to have time to look at everything at the site."

"Okay," Destiny replied. "Thanks for all your help, Abel."

"I'm sure we'll have more questions," Faith added.

"I'm happy to help," Abel said. "By the way, it's nice to see you two working together again. I love the designs you come up with. You make my flowers and plants happy."

Faith gazed over at Destiny and smiled. "It makes us happy, too."

Destiny grinned and nodded. "See you later, Abel."

On the way back to the truck Faith bumped her shoulder against Destiny's. "It was okay for me to say it makes *us* happy just then, wasn't it?"

"Can't you tell I'm happy working with you?" Destiny asked.

Faith raised her eyebrows. She knew Destiny was happy while they worked, but she could also feel her holding back. Faith understood why, but she hoped to earn Destiny's trust once again.

"Yeah, Des," Faith said. "I'm not trying to be a smart ass, but we were really good at this."

Destiny shrugged. "Until we weren't."

"Maybe we're beginning a new chapter of the story of Destiny and Faith," Faith said, bringing up the amusing way they once referred to their relationship. "Because I know we're not done yet."

"I hope the chapter we're writing is about slaying big landscaping dragons," Destiny said.

"Me, too," Faith agreed. "Hey, what was Monica saying about landscape wars?"

"Oh," Destiny groaned. "She wanted to pitch a reality show about warring landscape companies."

"Let me guess," Faith said. "We were the stars because we were always going after the same accounts?"

"Something like that," Destiny said.

"Maybe that's what we're walking into on this project. Except now we're on the same team," Faith said. "I think that makes us hard to beat."

Destiny looked over at her and smiled. "I hope so."

Faith pulled into the parking lot at the office complex. They got out of her truck and checked in with the security guard at the gate. There would be no issues with dogs or the clock this time.

Destiny led them over to the building she had looked over the last time they were there. "This is the area I think we could do the rock cairns in. Imagine several trees placed away from the building providing shade for this area." Destiny spread her arms out. "We put the rocks here, a bench here, and another bench over here," she said, stepping to each location.

"Okay." Faith nodded. "We could make it a triangular space from here at the front, back to where that wing of the building begins." She walked off the area talking as she gestured.

"I like it," Destiny said.

"On the building on the other side of the main structure we can do the same shape because the buildings are identical. Only over there, we can do a water feature," Faith explained.

"This garden will be shielded from the afternoon sun so the rocks should work," Destiny said.

"The other building gets the sun so we could use that to make the water feature glisten in the evenings."

"These people aren't going to want to stay inside to

work," Destiny said with a grin. "They'll want to be outside in our gardens."

Faith laughed. "We still need to tie them together with the landscaping around the main building."

They walked toward the main building and surveyed the area. "We've got to have trees," Destiny said.

"Yeah," Faith agreed. "It is so sparse out here."

"In an area like this sparse is easy to maintain," a voice said from behind them.

Faith and Destiny both wheeled around when they recognized the voice.

"Of course you two probably don't know that," Gloria said with a fake smile.

"Sparse may be easy to maintain, but it isn't much to look at," Faith said.

"We know what you did," Destiny said with a bite to her voice.

Gloria looked from Destiny to Faith as a snide grin grew on her face. "I never dreamed you would both quit, much less break up. Did that ever work out for me! I thought while you were figuring it out, I'd get the project which then led me here, running one of the largest landscaping firms in the country."

"You'd better be careful and not trip on your ego, Gloria," Destiny said. "You might fall off your pedestal and land down here in the dirt with the rest of us."

Gloria laughed. "I think it's sweet how the contractor is entertaining bids from little landscaping companies like yours."

"Watch out," Destiny said. "We have something you don't. It's called creativity. Your *firm* is known for planting flowers in a row and hoping they bloom."

"Wouldn't it be a shame if someone came along and dug them up," Faith said, joining the conversation.

Gloria stood a little straighter and eyed them both. She gave them an evil smile before turning and walking back towards the parking lot.

"Come on," Destiny said, grabbing Faith's hand and walking towards the other building. "There's no way we're going to let that bitch beat us."

A smile crept onto Faith's face as Destiny squeezed her hand even tighter. Faith was usually the one quick to anger, but in this moment she could feel Destiny's need to protect her. She didn't care for that in most instances, but right now, it was Destiny's way to show her love and Faith was all for that.

Destiny was grumbling under her breath when they stopped to look back at the main building.

"Take a breath, Des," Faith said.

Destiny looked at their joined hands and dropped them. "Sorry about that. That smug bitch makes me so mad! She doesn't care who she hurts as long as she gets what she wants."

"She's not getting her way this time," Faith said, catching Destiny's gaze. "They are going to love our trees."

Destiny visibly relaxed and smiled. "Yeah, they are."

17

After walking around the main building in the center of the complex they both stopped to make a few more notes then headed back to Faith's truck. Destiny was much calmer now, but just thinking of Gloria and what she did to them made her angry. Seeing her face to face raised things up a notch.

Destiny sighed loudly. "I'm sorry I lost my temper with Gloria, but she's—"

"Such a bitch," Faith said, finishing Destiny's sentence.

Destiny laughed. "Yeah, that's exactly what I was thinking."

As they reached her truck, Faith stopped and turned to Destiny. "Des, she can't hurt us anymore."

Destiny nodded. "But I can hurt her. Imagine my fists meeting her pronounced cheekbones."

Faith chuckled. "Honey, you've never hit anyone in your life."

"She'd be the perfect person to try it out on," Destiny said with a frown.

Faith opened Destiny's door. "How about we stop by the yogurt shop on our way to your office?"

Destiny got in the truck and waited for Faith to get in on the driver's side. "You weren't angry when you saw her?"

"Yeah, it makes me mad to know what she did to us," Faith said. "But we've got a great vision that I'm sure will beat hers. That's the best way to defeat people like her."

"You've dealt with people like her in the past, haven't you?" Destiny asked. She knew Faith had a couple of teammates in college who were always trying to get her trouble.

Faith nodded. "You have to beat them at their own game. We'll win that contract and send Gloria back to Houston or Dallas or wherever her office is now."

Destiny knew Faith was right and thought back to the new ideas they'd come up with at the office complex. They really could make this space something unique and even groundbreaking if they could convince the contractor.

Destiny looked over at Faith and studied the outline of her profile. She could gaze at Faith for hours, taking in every little curve. Those blue eyes could hold such mischief or turn dark with desire in a flash.

"You're staring at me," Faith said, keeping her eyes on the road.

"I think I'm going to need more than yogurt," Destiny said. "How about a beer?"

Faith glanced over at Destiny. "Okay, there are plenty of bars between here and your shop."

"You mean you don't want to go back to your place?" Destiny asked, amused.

"We can," Faith replied, "but I thought you wanted to be more social."

Destiny furrowed her brow and gazed at Faith. "I'm

having a hard time with this," she said. "It's like you're doing whatever I want."

"No, I'm not." Faith chuckled. "I'm listening. I think you're right, we did stay to ourselves a lot of the time, but we had fun. We like the same things. Why wouldn't we want to be together?"

Destiny knew what Faith said was true, but she also thought there were times they could've celebrated special occasions in ways other than staying at home. "You're not wrong, but..."

Faith smiled. "But it might be nice to get dressed up and go out occasionally."

Destiny looked over at Faith in surprise.

"I know that's not something I liked to do before, but you know, maybe I was wrong," Faith said. "I was wrong about other things and I can see that now."

Before Destiny could say anything Faith pulled into the parking lot of a small bar, turned to her and smiled. "Let's have that beer."

They went inside, ordered beers at the bar, and sat at an empty table. There were only two people at the bar and two others at a table, but it was Monday night and early.

Once they were seated Destiny looked over at Faith. "Since you mentioned dressing up..."

"Yeah?" Faith asked.

"I think we should dress professionally when we present our vision to the contractor next week," Destiny said.

"You don't think our company shirts and shorts are appropriate?" Faith said with a grin. "I get it. We want them to see us as business women, not just the workers who dig the holes and plant the flowers."

"Exactly," Destiny said. "We can talk more about the presentation as we get all the info into the software and make the slides and videos." She grinned and wrinkled her nose. "I'm getting excited."

Faith chuckled. "I can see that. Your eyes are sparkling, Des. You look beautiful."

Destiny smiled and reached for her beer. It had been a long time since anyone had said she was beautiful and she knew Faith meant it. Her heart skipped a beat just as it always did when Faith looked at her that way.

"We're going to kick Gloria's ass in the best way." Faith grinned.

"Seeing her brought up a lot of emotions," Destiny said. "I don't understand people like that. Why would she go to that much trouble to win that project?"

"Some people can't stand it when other people are happy," Faith said. "We were happy and she knew that. We were her competition, only we didn't realize it. At least I didn't."

"I didn't either," Destiny said. "If my team didn't win a project it wasn't the end of the world. We went on to the next thing."

"That's the way it was for my team, too," Faith said. "You can't blame her for our breakup, Des."

Destiny raised her brows. "I certainly can. She set everything in motion. We don't know what would've happened had she not done that."

Faith shrugged. "I know we have to talk about this to get through it, but I can't tell you how much I regret not coming to you with the video."

Destiny could see tears in Faith's eyes. She reached over and took her hand in hers. "I've been thinking about what you said about being good enough." Destiny paused. "I understand what you were trying to tell me. I didn't realize what you meant until later. I'm so sorry you felt like that, Faith."

Faith looked over at her and smiled. "You didn't make me feel that way, Des. But I'm glad you understand now. That's why we're dating. Some things take time to process and understand."

Destiny chuckled and raised an eyebrow. "I think you like saying that."

Faith laughed. "I do. I'm dating Destiny Green."

"It's only been one date." Destiny pointed out.

"I know what I'd like to do for our next date, but you have to be open minded," Faith said with a twinkle in her eye.

Destiny narrowed her gaze at Faith. "Open minded? Hmm," she said with faux skepticism. "Should I? Or not?"

Faith giggled. "Come on, Des. Trust me."

Destiny scoffed. "I'm not the one with trust issues."

"Me neither," Faith assured her. "Not anymore."

Destiny smiled. Did Faith really trust her now? She kept saying the right words, but Destiny was still hesitant. Maybe another date would make things clear for her. Seeing the sparkle in Faith's eyes made it hard to say no. Who was she kidding? She wanted to believe Faith. She wanted them to find a way to be together again. "Okay. When is this date?"

"Um, all I'll say for now is...Friday?" Faith grinned.

Destiny nodded. "I'll be sure and leave Friday open on my busy schedule," she teased.

Faith chuckled. "Actually, we are going to be busy. Do you think we could meet tomorrow evening? I have jobs to complete this week."

"I have jobs, too," Destiny said. "Let's split things up. If I take the rock garden, will you have time to work on the fountain sometime tomorrow? We can meet in the evening and update our progress."

"I can do that," Faith said. "Then we can go from there tomorrow."

"We have all week and the weekend to get it perfect and nail the presentation," Destiny said.

"Agreed," Faith replied.

Destiny took a sip of her beer and looked across the table at Faith. She was smiling at Destiny with amusement. "What?"

"I have an idea," Faith said.

"About the project?"

Faith shook her head. "About us. I think I have a way for us to let go of the anger and hurt of the last three years. Then we can move forward with the story of Destiny and Faith."

Destiny smirked. "You used to think that was kind of silly. Now you're talking about the next chapter and this story."

Faith shrugged. "It may be a bit silly, but it's our story to write."

"Okay," Destiny said. "What's your idea?"

"There's a karaoke system over there and we both can sing," Faith began. "I know a song we could sing to each other. It might be a way to get these feelings out."

Destiny scoffed. "Karaoke? Sing?"

"Yeah," Faith said excitedly. "There's only four people in the entire bar. They're not going to be listening to us."

Destiny looked over her shoulder and noticed the couple at the table were in conversation. The two men at the bar were talking to the bartender. She looked back at Faith and leaned in closer. "We'll never see them again."

Until We Weren't:

"Come on." Faith grinned. "You used to sing to me all the time."

"In the car!" Destiny exclaimed.

Faith giggled. "I have the perfect song. It'll make you feel better."

Destiny narrowed her gaze at Faith. "What song?"

Faith got up, grabbed Destiny's hand, and pulled her over to where the system was set up in the corner.

Destiny looked on as Faith entered the song into the system and handed her a mike. "Wait! You didn't tell me the song."

Faith smiled. "'Stop Draggin' My Heart Around' by Stevie Nicks and Tom Petty."

"Oh, I don't know, Faith," Destiny said hesitantly.

"Yes," Faith replied. "Isn't that what we've both been doing? We're draggin' each other's hearts around and can't let go. I want to let go of the hurt, Destiny. I want to let go of the regret. I want to feel the love. What do you want to let go of?"

Destiny began to understand what Faith was getting at. Maybe belting this song out at each other would give the hurt a place to go. "I feel like I let you down," she said quietly. "I want to let that go."

The music began to play and Faith said, "You didn't let me down." She smiled. "I've got the first verse."

Faith began to sing along with the words on the screen. Destiny couldn't keep from smiling. Part of her couldn't believe they were doing this and another part of her couldn't wait to sing with Faith. It was Destiny's turn and she let the music take her.

So you've had a little trouble in town
now you're keeping some demons down

Then Faith came in and sang the title lines with her.
Stop draggin' my
Stop draggin' my
Stop draggin' my heart around.

They sang with feeling and inspiration as they stared into each other's eyes. At first Destiny felt the anger from when Faith wouldn't talk to her. She did feel like her heart was being torn apart. She could feel the hurt, but she also felt love. There had been a tug-of-war going on inside her since Faith had told her the truth.

Destiny was angry that Faith hadn't told her what happened. She wanted to yell, but what good would that do? Faith now regretted not telling Destiny the truth three years ago. The anger had still been there, but she put it in those words and it was fading.

Destiny had the next verse and she quieted her voice a little as she sang.

It's hard to think about what you've wanted
It's hard to think about what you've lost
This doesn't have to be the big get even
This doesn't have to be anything at all

As Destiny sang the words she felt the truth of them. There was nothing to get even for between them. They had both lost the most important thing to them: each other.

"Sing with me," Faith said.

Baby, you could never look me in the eye
Yeah, you buckle with the weight of the words
Stop draggin' my
Stop draggin' my
Stop draggin' my heart around.

Destiny put all the anger and pain in the chorus. As the words flew into the air the feelings left her heart. The song ended and they stared at each other. Faith was right; she did feel lighter.

The bartender and one of the men at the bar clapped a couple of times. When they looked at each other again, laughter began to bubble up between them.

18

"I think it worked," Destiny said. "The only anger I have left is for Gloria, but even that doesn't feel as intense. When we win that contract I think it will be gone, too."

Faith smiled. She knew Destiny had been holding back her anger. Faith could see it in her eyes and feel it at times. She wanted to gain Destiny's trust again, and she didn't want her to live with that anger and pain if she could help her ease it.

When Faith realized she'd made a huge mistake by not going to Destiny with the video, she could have run away like she'd done before, but something made her stop and look at herself. She chose to believe it was their love that still lived in her heart. It was trying to help her see. That night in the shack with Destiny asleep, her head on Faith's shoulder, it all became clear.

"I have a song for you," Faith said softly. She searched through the songs and hoped the music and lyrics would be there.

Destiny raised her eyebrows.

"You'll know it," Faith assured her. "We used to watch the show."

Faith found what she was looking for and queued up the song. She turned to Destiny and reached for her hand. "Do you remember when we watched *The Fosters*?"

Destiny nodded. "Oh yeah, we loved that show."

"I always loved the theme song," Faith said. "I came across it on my phone the other day and I realized the words are how you make me feel."

Destiny furrowed her brow. "I'm trying to remember."

"You will as soon as you hear it," Faith said. "It's sung by Kari Kimmel."

The soft melody of "Where You Belong" began to play and Faith watched the recognition dawn on Destiny's face.

Faith began to softly sing, "If you're feeling down or weak, you can always count on me, I will always pick you up."

The song continued then Destiny finished the verse, singing, "I will always hold you up."

Faith could feel tears stinging her eyes but she had to sing this next part because these were the lyrics that rang true then and still did now.

"It's not where you come from, it's where you belong," Faith sang softly.

When she couldn't continue, Destiny picked up a few lines later. "You're surrounded by love and you're wanted, so never feel alone. You are home with me right where you belong."

Faith smiled and listened while Destiny continued with the song. She glanced between the words and Faith several times.

Faith tried to join her, but instead listened as Destiny

sang, "Even when you mess up, you always got my love. I'm always right here."

Faith was the one who messed up and she wouldn't let herself believe Destiny would still be there. Instead she'd run, but not anymore.

She knew where she belonged. She knew where Destiny belonged. It may take a little more time, but Destiny knew it, too. Faith just had to help her see.

Karaoke didn't turn out quite as Faith had intended. She wanted to sing the song to Destiny, but when she couldn't get the words out, Destiny could. As the last notes filtered from the speakers they leaned closer and closer to each other.

Faith stared into Destiny's warm brown eyes and saw their love. She hoped Destiny could see it shining in hers. Their lips were so close... Faith leaned in—

The four people in the bar plus the bartender began to applaud.

They both pulled back and their eyes widened like they were in some kind of cartoon.

The moment passed but Faith could still see the love in Destiny's eyes.

"I need another beer," Destiny said.

"I'll get them." Faith quickly went over to the bar and came back to the table with two fresh beers.

"Thanks," Destiny said. "You keep paying for everything. It's my turn."

"It's okay," Faith said, sitting back down.

"I have to admit," Destiny said. "You have surprised me, Faith Fields."

Faith smiled. "I hope that's a good thing."

"Oh, it is," Destiny replied. "While we were singing, I had an idea."

Faith took a sip of her beer. "About the project?"

"No," Destiny replied. "About us."

Faith smiled. *That's a good thing,* she thought. She raised her eyebrows. "Are you going to tell me?"

"Were you serious about being more social?" Destiny asked.

Faith leaned over the table. "I'm sitting in a bar, singing karaoke on a Monday evening," she stated.

Destiny laughed and Faith felt a luscious feeling of warmth pass through her body. God, it had been ages since she felt a rush like that.

"Your birthday is coming up," Destiny said. "I always wanted to throw you a party, but you wouldn't let me. What if we came here and sang karaoke? We could invite Mark and your workers, Monica and Kim, and a few other friends. What do you say?"

Faith sat back and smiled at Destiny. "You want to spend my birthday with me?" she said gently.

Destiny smiled. Faith watched as she took a deep breath and slowly let it out. She recognized this behavior. Destiny always did this when she was gathering her words.

"Yes, I want to spend your birthday with you," Destiny said. "We have a lot to work through and I don't know what's next in our story, but I'm not ready for it to end just yet."

Faith smiled. She'd take that. It wasn't a no and it meant Destiny was willing to at least try. "I was afraid to share some things with you because I've always felt damaged in a way," Faith said. "I had a counselor in college who helped me with that, but I sometimes still feel that way. I wonder why you feel like you let me down?"

Destiny raised her eyebrows. "Okay, we're going from birthdays to…"

"Things we have to work through," Faith explained. "I

have to share things that are scary. It's things that I was afraid would make you leave. In my eyes, you could never let me down, Des."

Destiny looked at Faith and took a drink of her beer. Faith could practically see the thoughts running through Destiny's mind.

"In my eyes," Destiny said, sitting her beer back down, "there's nothing you could've said that would've made me leave."

Faith smiled and nodded. "See there. We have to be brave and share more. How often do the things we're afraid of never happen? We've wasted a chance to know one another better on a deeper level."

Destiny nodded. "I let you down because you didn't feel like you could come to me with the video. It makes me wonder what other things you couldn't share with me. What other things bothered you, scared you? I was the woman you loved—"

"Love," Faith corrected her.

Destiny smiled. "I was the woman you love. I'm supposed to be your safe space. I let you down because I thought I was that person, but I didn't make sure you felt that way."

"I was afraid that you would think I was too much work," Faith said.

"What! Too much work?"

"Yeah," Faith said. "I'm so fucked up with my thinking that we can't have a normal relationship. You always have to be thinking about Faith's messed up background that makes her think fucked up thoughts."

Destiny's face fell. "I have never thought of you that way, Faith." She sat back in her chair. "I thought you were the most interesting, beautiful woman I'd ever known. All I wanted was to know you better, so that way, I could love you more."

Faith smiled and shook her head. "Wow! Listen to us. You're turning my mistake into yours, which is crazy. And the things I hid from you are what you wanted most."

Destiny chuckled. "What is a normal relationship? I'm not sure they exist."

Faith scoffed. "Certainly not my parents, but what about yours? Gretchen and Mike are definitely relationship goals."

Destiny shrugged. "They've had their issues. Everyone does. We aren't special."

"Yes we are," Faith said. "I don't care what you say, we are special."

Destiny laughed.

Faith joined her laughter and held up her glass. "Here's to being brave. You didn't let me down."

Destiny held her glass to Faith's. "You're not too much work."

They both took a big drink and Faith narrowed her gaze at Destiny. "You wouldn't have left me. I think I knew that deep down and that's why—"

"You ran," Destiny said.

Faith nodded. "I'm right here now. As the song says, where I belong."

Destiny took another drink of her beer.

"It's okay, Des," Faith said. "You don't have to say anything. Thank you for singing with me and sharing with me."

"You're welcome," Destiny said.

They finished their beers and Faith drove them back to Destiny's office. She pulled up next to Destiny's truck and got out.

"What are you doing?" Destiny asked.

Faith walked to the back of their trucks and held out her arms. "I think we could both use a hug."

Destiny was hesitant at first, but then pulled Faith into her arms.

Faith nestled her head on Destiny's shoulder and ran her hands up Destiny's back. She had always felt safe in Destiny's arms. Destiny was a few inches taller than Faith, but they fit together perfectly in Faith's opinion. She loved how her nose was in the perfect spot to inhale Destiny's scent and her lips were only millimeters away from Destiny's pulse point. Faith hoped she'd get to kiss that highly sensitive spot again one day. But until then she was content with Destiny's arms holding her close.

Faith didn't want to pull away, but she also didn't want to overwhelm Destiny or seem pushy. Destiny knew what Faith wanted. She'd told her, and she'd also agreed to give Destiny time.

Faith smiled up at Destiny and stepped out of her arms. "See you tomorrow."

"See you tomorrow," Destiny replied. Before Faith got back into her truck Destiny quickly added, "Uh, thanks for this evening. I had a really nice time."

Faith chuckled. "Stop draggin' my heart around," she sang, then got into her truck.

It didn't take Faith long to drive home. She pulled around to the back of the building, stopping to close the gate. Instead of going inside her tiny house she walked into her office. It only took a moment to boot up her computer and get her notebook out. She was beginning to build the garden with a fountain as the centerpiece when her phone pinged with a text.

Get some rest. You'll need it because we'll be working late all week.

Faith read the text and chuckled. She and Destiny may have been apart for three years, but Destiny still knew her. Faith couldn't wait to get started on the project. She felt like if they won the bid then nothing could stop them from rebuilding their relationship. Faith knew one had nothing to do with the other, but right now they were the most important things in her life.

She typed a text back to Destiny and sent it.

I will if you will.

It only took a moment for Destiny's response to appear on the screen.

I have more important things to think about tonight.

"Hmm," Faith mumbled. "I didn't see that coming." She figured Destiny would be excited to get going on the project.

Faith smiled as she typed out her reply.

Could it be Friday?

Destiny quickly replied.

Maybe. See you tomorrow.

Faith knew that was the last she'd hear from Destiny tonight, but what a good day it had turned out to be.

The hope in her heart was growing with every thought of Destiny.

She opened a drawer in her desk and looked down at a framed picture of Destiny. She'd kept it there since she'd opened Lush Fields Landscaping. It was out of sight, but she knew it was there. Maybe it was time to put it on her desk.

"Keep the faith, babe," she whispered to Destiny's picture and smiled.

19

Destiny put her laptop in her computer bag and walked out of her office.

"Are you off to work on the bid with Faith?" Monica asked.

"Yep, we're almost finished," Destiny said. "We have a few final touches to add. I can't wait to see the whole layout this evening."

"After that are y'all going to the karaoke bar? It is Friday night."

Destiny chuckled. "No. We did have a good time there on Monday though."

"I wish I could've seen it."

"Faith surprised me." Destiny smiled. "You'll get to experience it next weekend at her birthday party."

"We're looking forward to it, but we still want to have you both over," Monica said.

"Oh, I know. We're planning on it."

"So." Monica paused. "Are you two back together?"

Destiny huffed. "No, as Faith likes to say, we're dating." She chuckled. "However, we've only had one date."

"You've spent every evening together this week," Monica said. "I think those could be considered dates. You can't tell me you were working the entire time."

"Our second date is tonight," Destiny said.

"Uh huh," Monica replied. "Where are you taking her?"

Destiny shook her head. "It's Faith's idea. She said it's a surprise."

"Wow, she's full of surprises lately. Why are you holding back? I can tell Faith is all in, and she's being very patient with you."

Destiny sighed. "She is being patient. We have a lot to work through in order to keep this from happening again. You know how hard it was when she left. I thought I was going to die."

"I'd say you're being dramatic, but I witnessed it first hand," Monica said. "Kim and I were worried about both of you."

"Besides, this big project is taking up all our time and it's too important," Destiny said.

"It may be important, but it's also the reason you're spending so much time together," Monica pointed out. "Have you thought about what happens after?"

"After?"

"We either get it or we don't," Monica said. "What does that mean for you and Faith then?"

"I haven't really thought about it," Destiny said. "Everything is going into the bid."

"Yeah, but if you win it, you still have to install everything," Monica said.

"I know," Destiny said. "We've talked a little about that. We don't want to get too far ahead of ourselves."

"Do you mean professionally or personally?"

Destiny groaned, plopping down in the chair next to

Monica's desk. "Both, I suppose. It would be so easy to jump right back in with Faith, but every time we're together we find out something else we didn't know or felt from before. It's confusing because we thought we were happy, but we were also holding a lot of things in that neither of us knew about."

"But that's a good thing," Monica said. "You're finding that out now, so it won't happen going forward."

"Yeah, I guess," Destiny said, getting up. "Right now, I have to finish my part of this project so we can see the entire thing."

"Hey, Des," Monica said. "Don't forget that you and Faith have one very important thing going for you."

"What's that?"

"You love each other," Monica said.

Destiny smiled. "Yeah, we loved each other before and look what happened."

"But the love is still there," Monica said, "and look where you are. Neither one of you got very far away from the other."

Destiny nodded. "I'll see you on Monday."

Monica chuckled. "Have fun on your date. I can't wait to hear all about it."

Destiny opened the front door and waved as she walked to her truck. She couldn't help but think about what Monica had said. Faith had come to her office at the end of the day two times this week and Destiny had gone to her office the other day. They were working on the bid, but they also spent time sharing the happenings of their days. Now that she thought about it, they'd been together every day this week.

Destiny smiled as she turned on the street to Faith's shop. She was excited to finish up the project today, but honestly, she was looking forward to this date even more.

Until We Weren't:

Faith wouldn't tell her what they were doing and promised to reveal all once they were finished with work.

Her thoughts drifted back to what Monica said about neither of them getting very far away from each other. Had their love kept them close? Had their hearts found a way to bring them back together?

One thing Destiny knew for sure was that Faith Fields was in her heart to stay. With each passing day, the more they were together, the more Destiny wanted. They worked later and later each night, blaming it on the importance of this bid, but the reality was that they loved being together.

Destiny thought they weren't social enough before, but she was beginning to remember why. She was just as guilty because she liked having Faith to herself.

She chuckled as she pulled around to the back of the shop. Faith had told her to park back there since they had a date tonight.

Before Destiny could get out of the truck she saw Faith come out of the building and into the shop. The smile on her face told Destiny she was just as glad to see her.

"Would you two want to take a break this evening and have a beer with us?" Mark asked as Destiny walked into the shop. She looked at Faith and raised her brows. This was Faith's plan tonight so it was up to her, but Destiny hoped it would be just them this evening.

"We are so close to finishing the layout of the gardens," Faith said. "I promise we'll meet you next time."

"That's what you always say," Mark replied.

"She means it this time," Destiny said. "We found a new bar y'all need to try with us."

"Oh, yeah," Mark said. "Faith told us about the karaoke bar."

"You'll get to see it next Saturday for my birthday party," Faith said.

Mark grinned at both of them. "I'll believe it when I see it."

Destiny held her hands out to her side. "You can trust me on this one, Mark. Just wait until you hear your boss sing."

"Count me in," one of the other workers said. "Can we bring someone with us?"

Destiny had only met the other workers briefly on Wednesday, but if she remembered correctly, the woman's name was Bailey. "Sure," Destiny replied. "The more the merrier."

"Are your teams coming as well?" Mark asked. "What about Jake?"

"Yep, Jake will be there," Destiny replied. "I'm not sure if you know Claire. She runs my other team."

"I know Claire," Bailey said. "That's who I wanted to bring with me."

Mark gasped and stared at Bailey. "Oh, my God!" he exclaimed. "You can't be friends with anyone at The Green Thumb. They're our enemies!"

"Ha ha," Destiny said. "We'll all be working together if we win this bid."

"When," Faith corrected her. "*When* we win this bid."

Mark laughed. "Hell, yeah! You said it, boss."

"Okay, we'd better get to work," Faith said. "I can't wait to see the entire thing."

"Me, too," Destiny said, walking towards the office.

"Hey," Faith said to her team. "Y'all can shut down early today. There's nothing that can't wait until Monday. Enjoy your weekend."

"Thanks," Bailey said, hurriedly getting her things together.

"My, oh my," Mark said. "I love having happy Faith back."

Faith smirked at Mark and Destiny chuckled as she looked on. She had to agree with Mark, having happy Faith back was amazing. Happy Faith was fucking gorgeous. Her blue eyes sparkled and when she glanced over at Destiny, she felt her heart skip a beat. Not trusting her voice, all Destiny could do was smile.

"They act like I never let them leave early," Faith said, walking past Destiny and into the office.

"Hi, Amy," Destiny said, following Faith inside.

"Hi, Destiny. Someone has been watching the front windows anxiously awaiting your arrival," Amy said.

Destiny looked over at Faith and raised her brows. Faith shrugged.

"I couldn't wait to get here," Destiny admitted. "It's probably not for the reason you think," she said quietly to Faith.

"Oh?" Faith asked.

"I'm excited to see the layout, but I'm very curious about our date tonight," Destiny replied.

The biggest smile grew on Faith's face and Destiny thought her heart might just beat out of her chest.

"Get to work, you two," Amy said, "so you can get finished and have fun." She closed her computer and gathered her things to leave. "I'll lock the front door. See you on Monday."

"Thanks, Amy," Faith replied. "See you Monday."

After Amy left, Faith turned to Destiny. "Let's get this done so the date can begin."

Destiny chuckled, got her laptop out, and set it next to

Faith's on her desk. They both went to work tapping their keyboards.

"Okay," Faith said. "I emailed you my garden and finished up the changes we made to the main building."

"Great," Destiny said, staring at her screen. "Let me upload everything into the program and we should be able to view our masterpiece in video format."

"Masterpiece." Faith chuckled. "I know you're kidding, but it may very well be."

"This should give us a view like we're touring the property," Destiny said. "I can pause and zoom in whenever we want." She hit one more key and looked over at Faith. "Are you ready?"

Faith held out her hand and looked up at Destiny. "Let's go."

Destiny slipped her fingers between Faith's and held her hand. Her heart was pounding in her chest at the excitement of what they were about to see, but at the same time, sweet memories of holding hands with Faith flooded her brain. They were never big on public displays of affection, but they did hold hands whenever they were together. It always made Destiny feel closer to Faith and it was a way to show her love.

Destiny took a deep breath and clicked the play button.

The video started as a wide view of the property. It was as if they were walking to the main entrance then veered around on the path to the other buildings. When they went around the back of the main building the little shack came into view.

When they'd started working on the project, whenever Destiny glimpsed the shack, she could feel the emotions of the night they were trapped. The scene would replay in her mind. First came the fear of not getting to Faith before the dogs attacked. It was like a sharp pain in the pit of her stomach. She remembered the heat, the sweat, and the darkness. The hurt from the truth of Faith's story always made it a little darker.

But one day Destiny's view began to change. She smiled when she saw the shack now. It felt like their love had been buried deep in darkness and hurt, but that night it burst through the surface into the light, much like the seeds they sometimes planted. Somehow that night it rose above the darkness and demanded to once again be seen and be felt.

The path wasn't easy, but their love, just like the plants, had survived and it was up to them to tend and nurture it.

"Look, Des," Faith said softly.

Destiny could hear the wonder in her voice.

"It's beautiful," Faith continued. "It makes the building interesting and welcoming. It's definitely unique. I've never seen anything like it. One thing's for sure: it's eye-catching and elicits emotion. They should love that."

Destiny continued to stare and couldn't believe the emotions flying through her mind and body.

"Why aren't you saying anything?" Faith asked. "Des, are you all right?"

Destiny took a breath and found her voice. "Just imagine how we can change the plants for the different seasons, giving a whole new vibe," she said.

"We should do that for the presentation," Faith said.

"Yeah," Destiny agreed. "You're right."

"We did this, babe," Faith whispered.

"Yeah, we did," Destiny said, amazed. She looked over into Faith's eyes and for a moment she saw a glimpse of what could've been. They could have been creating expanses like this for the last three years. Instead they'd been struggling to start their own separate businesses.

A flash of anger shot through her. Destiny dropped Faith's hand. She stood up and began to pace around the office. She ran her hand through her hair as hot tears burned her eyes.

"What's wrong?" Faith asked with concern in her voice.

20

Destiny wheeled around to face Faith. "Look at what we've done," she said, raising her voice. "We could've been doing this all along."

Faith saw tears trickle down Destiny's cheeks. She jumped up and grabbed both of Destiny's hands and held them tightly. "I'm so sorry," Faith said as a lump formed in her throat. Things had been going so well. Faith could feel Destiny's heart opening and they were getting closer every day. The anger in Destiny's voice and the hurt in her eyes broke Faith's heart because she knew she'd put it there. Could they ever get past this?

"I know you're sorry," Destiny said. "I am, too." She looked down at their hands and back up into Faith's eyes. "I'm not mad at you, Faith. I'm mad that this happened to us! Why couldn't Gloria leave us alone? Why weren't we strong enough to get through it? Why couldn't we be honest?"

"Come here," Faith said, wrapping her arms around Destiny. She pulled her close and felt Destiny's arms curl around her shoulders. They stayed like this for several moments. Faith could feel tears in her own eyes. To see Destiny hurting like this was brutal.

Faith pulled away and led them back to their chairs. "Listen to me for a second, Des," she said, holding Destiny's hands once again. "We didn't do anything wrong." She stared into Destiny's eyes. "We were as honest as we could be with each other at that time. We were still learning things about each other."

Destiny sniffed and inhaled a breath. She nodded and looked sadly into Faith's eyes.

"We're different now," Faith said. "It feels like we've wasted three years of our lives being apart. Yes, we are badass landscape artists and we've proved that right here. But I've told you things in the last couple of weeks that I'm not sure I would have ever had the courage to tell you had we stayed together. I know that being without you is worse than anything that has ever happened to me. All the fears from before are gone because they have to be. Those are the things that kept me from you. I won't let anything keep me from you ever again."

Destiny leaned over and rested her forehead against Faith's. "I'm sorry I got so mad," Destiny said. She leaned back and sighed. "It feels a lot easier to tell you things than it did before. How do you know I'm being honest? How do I know..."

Faith smiled. "It's that nasty little trust thing again, isn't it?"

Destiny nodded.

"You trust me now more than you ever did in the past," Faith said. "I can feel it, right here." She put her hand over Destiny's heart. "You may not realize it yet and that's okay."

"Do you trust me?" Destiny asked.

Faith nodded. "I do. I hurt you deeply and that's hard to get past, if you can."

"I can and have," Destiny said. "I understand why you did what you did. That helps to heal the pain."

"Now, we have to go forward."

Destiny nodded. "The story of Destiny and Faith. How they ended the evil landscaper's reign and brought harmony back to the untamed lands."

Faith raised one eyebrow. "Are you planning to bury Gloria?"

Destiny smiled. "That's exactly what we're going to do."

Faith tilted her head. "Please enlighten your partner in planting?"

Destiny laughed. "Partner in planting?"

"That's all I could come up with."

"We're going to bury her by giving the contractor a concept they can't refuse," Destiny said.

Faith smiled at Destiny and gazed at her. "I think that's confidence I'm seeing in your eyes."

"You've had it all along," Destiny said. "It took me a while to get there, but I've finally made it. You're right, Faith, we're going to win this bid."

Faith nodded with a grin. Destiny finally believed in this project the way Faith did. Now if she could just get her to believe in them again.

"Have we done enough work for today?" Destiny asked. "I have a date I'm looking forward to."

This made Faith's smile widen. "No more talking about work?"

"I didn't say that," Destiny said. "You know how ideas pop into our heads."

"That's true," Faith said. "Let's close our laptops and have a drink on my beautiful terrace."

Destiny chuckled as they both closed their laptops. Faith turned off the lights and they went out the back door.

"I have beer and wine," Faith said. "Your choice."

"Hmm, are we going to sit out here and watch the sunset?" Destiny asked.

"We can."

"Then let's have a beer," Destiny replied.

"Coming right up," Faith said. She went into the house, grabbed two beers from the refrigerator, and hurried outside to find Destiny sitting in one of the chairs on her front porch.

"Thanks," Destiny said, taking the beer from Faith.

"To big things coming," Faith said, holding her beer to Destiny's.

"To big things." Destiny clinked her bottle to Faith's.

They both took hearty drinks from their bottles and sighed.

"Faith, I'm sorry I got so upset earlier," Destiny said. "It all hit me at once."

"It's okay."

"No, it's not," Destiny said. "I'm not angry with you. I mean that. I don't want to keep bringing it up because I know it hurts you. The last thing I want is for either one of us to be hurt again."

Faith sighed and put her hand over her chest. "It broke my heart to see the pain in your eyes, especially since I put it there."

"No, Faith, we've worked through that and will continue to do so," Destiny said. "That was all about Gloria. I mean, did you see that presentation? It was incredible."

Faith chuckled. "Yeah, it was."

"Just imagine what all we could've been doing," Destiny said.

Until We Weren't:

"We still can, Des," Faith said.

"Yeah, we can," Destiny said. "Starting next week when we win this bid."

"I'll drink to that."

"Okay," Destiny said. "No more work. What do you have planned for us this evening?"

"Uh," Faith stammered. "Let me tell you a little more about this date."

Destiny leaned forward. "Please do. You've been kind of mysterious about it."

"Well, that's because the surprise part is really early in the morning," Faith explained. "I want you to spend the night with me because it's too early to ask you to come over in the morning."

Destiny furrowed her brow and tilted her head. "Spend the night?"

"I don't mean like that," Faith said. "You can have the bed and I'll sleep on the couch. The surprise is very early in the morning and I'd tell you more but it would ruin it. Will you go along with me on this?"

"So, you want to spend the evening together," Destiny said. "Spend the night and the surprise is in the morning?"

"Early," Faith stressed.

"I'm guessing this has nothing to do with work," Destiny said.

"Absolutely nothing," Faith said. "I've been asking you to trust me all this time. Well, trust me, Des, it's something you're going to love."

Destiny squinted at Faith.

"I do know you," Faith said. "I know things you love."

Destiny chuckled. "I guess we'll find out, won't we?"

"Is that a yes?" Faith asked with hope in her voice.

"Yes," Destiny said. "How could I say no? I've got to find out what it is I love."

"Well, besides me," Faith said, wiggling her eyebrows.

Destiny smirked and took a drink of her beer. "Are you at least going to feed me?"

"Of course I am," Faith said. "The food should be here —" Just then Faith's phone dinged with a message. "Right now." She got up and handed her beer to Destiny. "I'll be right back."

As Faith walked back into the building she was relieved Destiny was going along with her unconventional plan for this date, especially after getting so upset earlier. It felt good to hold Destiny in her arms, even if it was to comfort her. She looked forward to the day she could hold her and kiss her once again.

Faith unlocked the front door and took the food from the delivery driver. She went back through the building to find Destiny patiently waiting while gazing over the field where the sun should set soon.

An overwhelming feeling of love stopped Faith in her tracks. How could she have ever let this incredible woman go? Well, she knew how it happened, but she vowed it would never happen again. Just then Destiny looked over and met Faith's gaze. She smiled and that's when Faith could feel it. Destiny Green was in love with her once again.

Destiny gasped. "You didn't," she said, getting up from her chair. "Is that pizza from DeSano's?"

Faith walked over and set the pizza on the small table between the chairs. "Where else would I order from?"

"Oh, Faith Fields, you do know what I like," Destiny said, inhaling the aroma of the pizza.

Faith couldn't keep from being pleased with herself. "I'll grab plates and wine," she said and went inside.

Until We Weren't:

Destiny filled their plates while Faith opened and poured the wine. It was obvious they'd done this before, but the smiles shared between them said the things they didn't quite have the words for yet. They sat back down to enjoy their dinner.

"Do you eat outside every night?" Destiny asked. "I really like it out here."

"No," Faith said between bites. "It feels special when you're here with me."

After they'd finished eating, Faith suggested they go inside and watch one of their favorite series on HGTV.

"I didn't realize *Restoring Galveston* had new episodes," Destiny said.

"They bought an old boarding house that had been unused for years," Faith explained. "They're restoring the property and making it into an inn. I'd love to stay there once they've finished."

"That is some project," Destiny said.

"I know," Faith said. "It's the largest scale of a restoration they've ever done. It reminds me of what we're taking on."

"Yeah." Destiny nodded. "I guess what we're doing is kind of like that. Maybe we should film our project."

"Are you serious?"

"Why not?" Destiny said excitedly. "Monica was ready to pitch landscape wars to the network. Why not do something like this instead? Our landscape vision will transform that building site."

Faith chuckled. "Wow, when your confidence comes back, it's big and bold."

Destiny raised her eyebrows. "I thought you liked my confidence."

"Oh, I do," Faith assured her. "Let's watch one more episode and then go to bed," she suggested cautiously. "We'll be up early in the morning."

"Are you setting an alarm or..."

"Don't worry, you'll know when to wake up."

"If I wasn't so tired from all the late nights this week," Destiny said, "I might not sleep tonight because of the excitement."

"Oh, God," Faith muttered. "I hope I haven't oversold it."

"Where's that Faith Fields confidence?" Destiny asked. "It came back in the shack that night and it's been with you ever since."

"This is much more important to me than any landscaping project," Faith said. "You're more important to me than anything." She smiled at Destiny and leaned back on the couch next to her.

When the episode was over Destiny leaned forward. "You didn't tell me I'd be spending the night, so I didn't bring anything with me to sleep in."

"I've got something you can sleep in and there's an extra toothbrush on the sink in the bathroom," Faith said, getting up and walking to the bedroom.

She grabbed a T-shirt for Destiny and found her waiting in the kitchen. "Here you go."

Destiny held up the shirt and looked at Faith with surprise. "I wondered where this went," she said. "It's one of my favorite sleep shirts."

Faith shrugged. "It's one of my favorites, too."

Destiny tilted her head and smirked.

"You can have the bathroom first," Faith said, grinning. "I'll change in the bedroom."

After Destiny finished in the bathroom, Faith squeezed

around her and took her turn to brush her teeth. When she came out of the bathroom, Destiny stopped her.

"Hey, it's not right for me to take your bed," Destiny said. "I can sleep on the couch."

"You're my guest," Faith said.

"We're both adults," Destiny said. "It's not like we haven't done this before. Why don't we both sleep in here?"

"Are you sure?" Faith asked.

Destiny nodded. "I'm sure." She walked to one side of the bed.

"Uh, that's the side I usually sleep on," Faith said tentatively.

Destiny chuckled. "Of course it is." She got in the bed and scooted over so Faith could get in on her side.

"Thanks," Faith said. She reached over to turn out the light then rolled onto her back.

They were lying side by side, looking up at the ceiling when Destiny said, "I had a nice time tonight. I don't know if this was part of the date or not, but thank you."

"This has been the best week I've had in a very long time," Faith said. "It's because we spent so much time together. I hope we can keep doing that."

"Me, too," Destiny said softly.

Faith felt Destiny take her hand in the dark then heard her yawn.

"Good night, Faith," Destiny murmured. "See you in the morning."

"Night, Des," Faith replied softly. She closed her eyes, took a deep breath, and thanked the powers above that Destiny was right next to her once again.

21

Destiny had to give Faith credit for remembering the things she liked as well as things they liked to do together. Last night could've been any Friday night for them. They used to order food from a place they both liked because when Friday rolled around neither of them wanted to cook.

Oftentimes they would relax and watch TV together. It wasn't an exciting Friday night necessarily, but it was what they both wanted. The one thing that was missing was the cuddling. They'd seemed to always end up on the couch together cuddling while they watched their latest shows.

Destiny fell asleep holding Faith's hand. Sometime in the middle of the night, she woke up. She and Faith were on their sides and Destiny's arm was wrapped around her middle. Destiny could feel Faith's hand holding hers where it rested against her chest. This was how they'd slept most nights or in the reverse position with Faith holding Destiny.

Destiny took a deep breath. She didn't get angry like she had last night when she thought about all they could've been accomplishing together with work. Right now, she felt thankful and content to savor this moment. Sometimes it felt like they'd wasted so much time being apart, but maybe they needed that time for whatever reason.

Destiny couldn't tell Faith just yet that she was the most important thing to her right now, too. But she was pretty sure Faith could see it in her eyes. Being with her now, holding her close, made Destiny think they could do anything as long as they were together.

Faith gently stirred and squeezed Destiny's hand. Then she sighed and Destiny knew Faith was still asleep. She snuggled a little closer and it wasn't long until her breathing matched Faith's, sending her back to sleep, too.

Destiny rolled over and realized she was alone in the bed. Just then the most tantalizing aroma assaulted her nose. What was that? She sat up in bed, blinked a few times, and saw Faith standing in the kitchen at the stove. From this vantage point, Destiny could see the length of the tiny home and decided it was an interesting perk.

"Good morning," she said to Faith while stretching her arms above her head.

"Good morning," Faith said.

Destiny smiled as Faith stopped what she was doing and gazed at her.

"What? Is my hair sticking out everywhere?" Destiny asked, crawling out of bed.

"No." She turned back to the stove then looked back at Destiny. "You always look so cute when you just wake up."

"Oh please," Destiny scoffed.

"I've told you that many times," Faith said.

"And I haven't believed you even once," Destiny said, walking into the small kitchen.

Faith chuckled and poured Destiny a cup of coffee.

"What's all this?"

"I'm making us breakfast," Faith said. "You come in here." She took the cup of coffee to the couch and waited for Destiny to sit down. She handed her the cup and turned to the TV.

"The game is about to start."

Destiny gasped. She looked from the TV to Faith and exclaimed, "Faith! This is the surprise?"

Faith nodded with joy all over her face. "I know you love to watch the Women's Super League soccer in England. It may be afternoon in London, but it's very early for us. That's why I needed you to spend the night."

"Oh, babe," Destiny murmured. "I can't believe you did this." She caught herself as the word slipped out and glanced up at Faith.

Too late. Faith had heard it and gave her an amused grin.

"Aren't you going to watch with me?" Destiny asked.

"Yes, but first I have to finish breakfast," Faith said. "I'm almost done."

Destiny grinned. "Can I help?"

"Nope." Faith shook her head. "I'll be right back."

Faith went back into the kitchen then turned to Destiny. "Hey, you could get those two snack trays at the end of the couch out and set them up."

"On it," Destiny said. She couldn't believe Faith had not only remembered but gone to so much trouble to get her here for the game. When she and Faith had first gotten together, Destiny explained that she sometimes got up early on weekend mornings to watch soccer. Faith thought it was a little much at first, but once she joined her for a couple of matches she loved it as well. They often made breakfast together, sat in front of the TV, and cheered for their team.

Faith brought their plates over and set them on the TV trays right before the game began.

Destiny looked over at her once she joined her on the couch and smiled. "I didn't watch soccer for a long time after you left," she said. "But this brings back all the joy of those early mornings and how crazy it is to get up on our days off and do this!"

Faith burst out laughing and leaned back on the couch. "Oh, Des, it's not crazy as long as we're together."

Destiny chuckled and nodded. "Look what you've made us." She glanced over at Faith. "Another favorite."

"Waffles and eggs," Faith said. "You like yours over easy on top of your waffle and I like mine scrambled."

"This will go down as one of the best dates in our history," Destiny said, holding out her fork.

They clinked them together much like they would a toast with their glasses.

"I hope we have many more dates that make you smile like that," Faith said.

Destiny grinned and shook her head. How could she not fall in love with this woman over and over again? "It's my turn for our next date."

"It isn't a competition," Faith said, forking a bite into her mouth.

"I remember things we liked to do, too. But maybe our story needs something new."

"Like what?"

"Like your birthday party next Saturday at the bar," Destiny said. "But..."

Faith looked over at her with raised brows. "But?"

"I'd like to do something for just us after the party," Destiny said. "If that's okay with you."

"Are you asking me out?"

Destiny chuckled. "I'm throwing you a birthday party, you'll already be out with me."

"Okay." She laughed. "You know I'm not going to turn you down."

"I'll let you know more, but it may involve a sleepover again to get to the date."

Faith set her fork down and turned to Destiny. "I'm not trying to overwhelm you, but I slept better last night than I have in a very long time."

A smile crept on Destiny's face. "Not trying to overwhelm me? What would you call all this?"

Faith shrugged.

Destiny leaned a little closer to Faith. "I slept better than I have in a long time, too."

Faith grinned. "Oh, the game's about to start."

"It's a match," Destiny corrected her.

"Whatever," Faith said, rolling her eyes.

They both chuckled and dug into their breakfast. The game had them both cheering and their team was ahead at halftime. Destiny got up and took their plates to the sink while Faith put the snack trays away.

"We can do the dishes when the game is over," Faith said.

"Okay, but I'm helping," Destiny said. "Breakfast was delicious. Thanks for making it."

"You can make it next time," Faith said with a sly grin.

Destiny sat down next to her and nodded. Faith scooted an ottoman out in front of them so they could prop their feet up during the second half of the game. As they watched, Faith crossed her legs and Destiny noticed a scar on the back of her leg. It hadn't been there before and it looked substantial.

Until We Weren't:

"What's this?" Destiny asked, touching the puckered skin on Faith's calf.

"Oh, that was an accident," Faith said.

"It looks pretty bad."

"It was," Faith said. "I was in an awkward position and jabbed myself with a sharp shooter."

"Damn!" Destiny exclaimed. "That had to hurt."

"Yeah, it scared me," Faith said. "If Mark hadn't been there I don't know what would've happened."

"What do you mean?"

"I was bleeding pretty bad. He quickly applied a tourniquet and rushed me to the ER," Faith explained. "They were able to stop the bleeding and repair the artery I hit."

Destiny felt a shiver run through her at the thought of anything happening to Faith. She looked up into Faith's eyes and suddenly grabbed her. Destiny pulled Faith into a tight hug and held her close. "If anything ever happened to you..." she whispered. "I could've lost you."

"It's okay, Des," Faith said softly. "I'm right here."

Destiny could feel Faith's warm breath on her neck and held her a little tighter. As if in slow motion, Destiny pulled her head back and stared into Faith's eyes. She glanced down at Faith's lips and without thinking she closed her eyes and softly pressed their lips together. An overwhelming feeling of being right where she belonged wrapped around Destiny like a comforting blanket.

She felt Faith's fingers gently touch her face then Faith slightly pulled away.

"Our team just scored," Faith said softly.

Destiny was aware of the noise and commotion coming from the TV. She smiled and pulled back but didn't let Faith go. "Sorry," she said quietly. "I can't lose you."

Faith smiled. "You won't."

Destiny nodded and leaned back on the couch, letting Faith go, but she took Faith's hand between both of hers and held it there the rest of the match.

The reality that Faith had been in the emergency room, bleeding seriously, and Destiny had no idea sat like a knot in her stomach. What else had she missed?

A smile played at the corners of her mouth as she thought back to their brief kiss. That feeling of certainty and assurance was still with her. She knew why, but wasn't quite ready to accept all that it meant.

As the game ended Destiny asked, "Would you want to work on the presentation this afternoon?"

"Yes," Faith said strongly. "I want to watch the video again."

"How about I go home and take a shower? I'll come back this afternoon, then we can study the video and decide how we want to present it so they can't turn us down."

"You can shower here," Faith said. "The tiny shower isn't so bad."

Destiny tilted her head and smirked. "I don't have any other clothes here. If I would've known I was spending the night I would've brought something with me."

"Maybe you should bring a few things over here," Faith suggested with a smile. "Because we're working so much together," she added.

"I'll put a bag in my truck and be more prepared next time."

Faith nodded. "That sounds like a great idea."

Destiny got up and went to the sink to start the dishes.

"You really don't have to do that," Faith said. "I invited you."

"You cook, I clean up," Destiny said. "I remember."

"Thanks," Faith said.

"Okay," Destiny said a few minutes later, looking around the house. "I think that's everything."

Faith walked her to the door and outside to her truck.

"I'll text you before I come over," Destiny said.

"Okay."

Destiny threw her purse into the front seat and turned around. She reached over and gently cupped the side of Faith's face with her hand.

"I had a really nice time," Destiny said softly.

"I did, too," Faith replied.

Destiny stared into Faith's eyes then slowly closed the distance between them. She gently touched her lips to Faith's. Her heart jumped in her chest and it almost felt like the first time they'd kissed. But she knew Faith's soft pillowy lips and treasured this moment for what it was. This was a kiss of hope. This was a kiss of what was to come. Neither of them knew what that might be, but they were together and it started here.

22

Faith walked back into her house and went to the bedroom. She stopped and inhaled deeply. As she leaned over the bed to make it, there was the slightest hint of Destiny's perfume. She smiled, took a moment to close her eyes, and inhaled again. There was a time when Faith used to tease Destiny about wearing perfume to work.

"I don't know why you spray that on every morning when you know it won't be long until your sweat will be mixing with the scent," Faith said.

Destiny extended her arm and sprayed the bottle near Faith. "I do it for you, babe."

"For me?"

"Yes," Destiny said, taking a couple of steps to pull Faith into her arms. "I may be sweaty and dirty later, but you'll still be able to smell my sweetness."

Faith put her arms around Destiny's shoulders and pressed their lips together in a sweet kiss. "Mmm, you taste sweet, too."

"We're going to be late," Destiny mumbled against Faith's lips.

"Mmm, one more." Faith gently sucked Destiny's bottom lip

into her mouth then deepened the kiss. Their tongues met in a dance of sweetness to match their aroma and taste. Faith slowly pulled away and rested her forehead against Destiny's. "I love you so much," she whispered.

"Even if I smell?" Destiny replied softly.

Faith chuckled. "You will always smell sweet to me."

Faith smiled at the memory and once the bed was made she took a shower. While she washed her hair, thoughts of Destiny's lips against hers sent a shot of desire coursing through her body. The water pelted her now sensitive skin and she longed for Destiny's touch.

When Destiny had grabbed her and kissed her that morning, Faith had to hold back. She wanted to fling her arms around Destiny, hold her tight and never let her go, but she knew it could be too much.

The last thing she wanted to do was rush either of them into something they weren't quite ready for. But then Destiny had kissed her goodbye and that's when Faith felt it. Their hearts reached for each other and held on. Their love wound around them and pulled them closer. Faith could feel them both falling deeper in love and that made this bond even stronger.

She was sure it grew every time they saw each other, thought of each other, and now touched each other. Faith couldn't wait for Destiny to come back over this afternoon.

"I've been thinking about the presentation," Destiny said as they watched the video for the third time.

"Okay," Faith replied. "I'm all ears."

"The contractor doesn't have to know we're two small companies pooling our resources for this bid," Destiny began. "We'll be a united front when we do the presentation. There's no reason to confuse them."

"Hmm," Faith murmured. "I get what you mean, but we have to give them a name for our company."

"What would you think if we did the bid under the name of Fields of Green?" Destiny said tentatively.

A smile grew on Faith's face. She and Destiny had often talked about starting their own landscaping business together and had thrown out names from time to time. Fields of Green had been Faith's favorite. "Seriously?" she asked.

"It's the perfect name," Destiny said with a smile. "It's our names, but also our business."

"You don't mind that my name is first?"

Destiny scoffed. "No! It's the perfect name for a landscaping business."

"You know I always loved that name," Faith said.

"Let's do it then," Destiny said. "We'll use your address for the bid. The formal contract can have both our companies' names on it under the 'doing business as' tag."

"My address?"

"We're here most of the time anyway," Destiny said. "The contact information will be done by email."

Faith narrowed her eyes at Destiny. "So the title of the company for all the slides and on the video will be Fields of Green?"

"Yeah, let me show you," Destiny said excitedly. "I changed a couple of the slides before I came back over." She hit a button on her computer and turned the screen towards Faith. "What do you think?"

Faith stared at the screen and couldn't keep the smile from her face. They had planned to join their two companies together and take on this huge project. Could they possibly pull this off?

"You're not saying anything."

Faith, still smiling, looked over at Destiny. "We always played around with names for this make-believe company." She took a deep breath and slowly let it out. "This is beginning to feel real. We're really doing this."

Destiny nodded. "It's all here, Faith. We've done it."

"Oh no," Faith said, shaking her head. "This is just the beginning. While you've been thinking about the business end of things, I've been thinking about the actual installation."

Destiny chuckled. "That's usually the way we worked." She smiled. "Tell me."

Faith sighed and slowly raised one brow. "We each have two teams."

"Right."

"We put one of your teams on the rock cairns, one of mine on the fountain," Faith said. "The other two teams will be on the largest building working together."

"Okay, what else?"

"We line them out each morning," Faith explained. "Then we do the maintenance for our other clients. We check in with them during the day and make sure things are on schedule. At the end of the day we let the crews off and we take whatever supplies they need for the next day to the site. We'll work the overtime."

"It makes sense," Destiny said. "We don't need to be there watching over them the entire time. Besides, we both have other accounts that have to be maintained." She stared at Faith and smiled. "It'll be like old times. We're finally back on the same crew."

"We always worked better together," Faith said.

"And got more done than any of the other teams," Destiny added.

"Do you still remember how to run a mower and a trimmer?" Faith asked with amusement in her voice.

Destiny laughed. "I should hope so since I was finishing up mowing at an apartment complex yesterday before I came over here."

Faith laughed. "I wasn't sure you still did that since you're the boss and all."

"Oh," Destiny said with a twinkle in her eye. "I know you still mow and trim. There's no way you'd let someone else do it all the time."

"I help where I'm needed," Faith said. "It is my company."

Destiny chuckled. "Okay then. Does this mean I'm on the mower and you'll do the trimming? You know how I hate to trim and you're so much better at it."

"Nice try," Faith said. "Nope, we'll be taking turns."

Destiny laughed. "Okay, it sounds like we have a plan. Now, for the presentation."

"I'm sure you have ideas," Faith said, leaning back in her chair. "Let's hear it."

"You'll stand on one side of the screen and I'll stand on the other," Destiny began. "We introduce ourselves and I'll give them an overview of the project and the vibe we're creating."

"Okay."

"Then you take over at the front of the main building."

Faith nodded. "We walk them around to the right side where the smaller building with the fountain is located. I give them all the advantages of the soothing water vibes then walk them around the back of the main building."

"I'll take it from there—"

"Be sure and point out the little shack," Faith said with a sly look. "Don't be afraid to use it as leverage since we were trapped there."

Destiny chuckled. "Let's hope we don't have to. Anyway, I'll bring them around to the other smaller building with the rock cairns highlighting their benefits then back to the front."

"We should give them our ideas of how the landscape can change with the seasons," Faith said.

"Then we can take questions. Did I leave anything out?"

"We should probably give them a timeline," Faith said. "Contractors are always late and we don't want them to think they'll have to wait on us."

"Oh," Destiny said. "Good point."

Faith watched as Destiny added several notes in her notebook. She had missed times like these. They seemed to always be on the same page when it came to creating beautiful landscapes. Their ideas were different, but they found a way to incorporate them and make the final project even better.

Destiny looked up at her and grinned. "Do you know what you're going to wear to the presentation yet?"

Faith gave her a sexy smile. "Maybe I'll surprise you."

Destiny leaned back in her chair and raised her brows.

Faith watched Destiny's eyes roam up and down her body. That same flash of desire from this morning shot through her. Faith raised her brows in response, challenging Destiny to do more than just look.

Destiny released an audible sigh and shook her head. "If I mess up this presentation it'll be your fault."

Faith chuckled. "You won't mess it up and neither will I."

"Okay, Ms. Confidence," Destiny said. "Let's practice."

They spent the next hour working on what they wanted

to say to the contractor and the group who would be deciding what company won the bid.

"That was the best yet," Faith said after their most recent run-through. "Let's not be tentative when we talk about the costs. This transformation will be worth every penny and we have to make them believe it. Do you want to go through it again?"

"You know," Destiny said, looking over at Faith. "We could practice on my parents." She raised her eyebrows with a hopeful look. "That is, if you'd like to go with me for Sunday lunch tomorrow?"

"I love your parents," Faith said excitedly. "And I love their Sunday get-togethers."

"Is that a yes?"

"Is this a date?" Faith replied with amusement.

"Mmm, I don't think so," Destiny said. "What's special about going to my parents'? We did that a lot."

"It's special to me." Faith shrugged.

Destiny's face lit up. "I have an idea," she said. "Okay, it can be a date."

Faith furrowed her brow. "What's your idea?"

"It's my turn to surprise you," Destiny said.

Faith smiled and tilted her head. "You don't have to surprise me, Des. All I want is to spend time with you."

Destiny reached over and took Faith's hand. They stared into each other's eyes and neither said anything for a moment.

A growl from an empty stomach invaded the peacefulness in the office.

Faith chuckled. "Should we order dinner?"

Destiny nodded and took out her phone. "It's my turn to buy."

"You could stay the night again," Faith said.

Destiny looked up from her phone and smiled.

Faith met her gaze and could see the back and forth in Destiny's eyes. *Too soon?* Faith hoped Destiny could see how much she wanted her to stay. Just having Destiny in bed beside her was enough. Oh, who was she kidding! She wanted Destiny, all of her.

Destiny exhaled and rubbed her lips together. "I want to, but…"

Faith nodded. "It's okay."

"I was wondering," Destiny said.

"Yes?" Faith replied, drawing the word out.

"Could we stay here after your birthday party Saturday night?" Destiny asked tentatively.

Faith smiled and grabbed Destiny's hand. "You can stay here any night and every night. Consider this an open invitation. However…"

Destiny raised her eyebrows. "However?"

Faith sighed and looked down at their hands. "It would be very hard for me to sleep next to you and not…"

"Hold me?" Destiny asked. "Did you not feel me holding you last night?"

"Of course I did," Faith said softly. "I grabbed your hand because I didn't want you to pull away."

Destiny reached up with her other hand and caressed the side of Faith's face. "I didn't want to pull away."

Faith nodded. "What are you ordering us for dinner?"

Destiny leaned over and kissed Faith's cheek then sat back in her chair. "Let's see? Mexican? Italian? Burgers? Ramen?"

Faith smiled and felt their love fill the room. She could be patient until the time was right because she knew Destiny Green loved her.

23

Destiny smiled as she waited for the light to turn green. The kiss she and Faith shared when she left her place last night played over in her head for the thousandth time. Okay, maybe a thousand was a little high, but it had to be close.

It felt easy and almost instinctive for Destiny to lean in and press her lips to Faith's before she got in her truck. What felt unnatural and made her a bit unsteady was leaving Faith at all.

They had spent a lot of time together since they'd raced into that steamy shack days ago. It was funny that Destiny felt closer to Faith now than she ever had. But in the days that followed, Destiny and Faith had talked about the things they were afraid of or uneasy about sharing with each other.

What surprised Destiny the most was how calm and carefree Faith had become. After Faith explained to her that she was letting her family go, it was like a weight had been lifted from her shoulders. She smiled at Destiny every time their eyes met. It might be with amusement or happiness or lately with lust—yeah, it was definitely lust—but also with love.

Faith always had a smile for Destiny. She could see the love in Faith's eyes. It wasn't forlorn or arduous love like whenever they'd run into each other after Faith had left. This was joyous love in Faith's eyes.

Destiny smiled, closed her eyes for a moment, and once again felt Faith's lips against hers. She wanted to stay with Faith last night, but she knew they wouldn't simply be sleeping in the same bed again. The pull to take Faith in her arms and declare her love for all time was greater than it had ever been.

When that happened it would change their lives once again and Destiny wanted to be ready this time. She had already come up with a few ways to make Faith's birthday party special on Saturday night, but it was afterwards, when it was just them, that had Destiny's heart beating double-time.

This project may have been the event that brought them back together, but their future wasn't dependent on a bid. It would be wonderful to create this vision that so far was just computer generated, yet it didn't matter if they lost. They had won the biggest prize of all. A chance to love each other again. This time openly with all the pieces bared and visible so they could support each other.

"Yeah," Destiny said quietly. "Doubts will come and go, but we'll be together to overcome them. I have Faith and I'm your Destiny."

It sounded like sappy humor, but it wasn't a joke. She believed in her heart that she was Faith's destiny. And with Faith in Destiny's heart they'd travel this path together.

"My God, Destiny," she muttered. "Could you be any more syrupy and sentimental?"

She laughed out loud as she pulled around the building to the tiny house where she found Faith standing in the porch area.

"Hey," Faith said as Destiny got out of the truck. "What's so funny?"

"Huh?" Destiny replied.

"You were laughing when you pulled up."

"Oh," Destiny said, her eyes widening. Faith could always read her like a book. "I was just thinking about..."

Faith raised her brows. "Us?"

Destiny grinned. "Maybe."

Faith nodded. "I've been thinking about us, too."

"Oh yeah?"

"Yeah," Faith said. "We've both kind of done a one-eighty compared to the way it was before, but I think it suits us."

"How so?" Destiny wasn't expecting anything serious today. She'd planned a little adventure after lunch that was sure to make them both lighthearted and happy.

"I've never felt so calm and composed," Faith said. "There has always been some kind of push and pull going on inside me, but it's no longer there."

"That's a good thing, isn't it?" Destiny asked.

"That's a better than good thing," Faith said with a smile.

Destiny studied Faith for a moment and smiled. "It looks very good on you."

"Thanks," Faith said. "It feels even better."

"And then there's me," Destiny said. "I was once a confident woman and now I'm wondering if I ever knew anything at all."

"Not true, Des." Faith reached for her hand. "You've become more insightful. I'm not afraid to tell you anything. I know you'll listen and not judge me."

"You thought I'd judge you?" Destiny asked.

Faith shook her head. "That came out wrong. It was more like I was judging myself through your eyes. I know now I need to tell you when something is bothering me or when something is good. It goes both ways. I know you'll listen and together we'll work whatever it is out."

"Or enjoy it together?"

Faith smiled. "I hope so. For example, I'm very excited to see your parents today. We used to have Sunday lunch with them often. The old me would've been nervous about today. I'd be wondering if they're going to be upset with me for what I put us through."

"Oh, Faith, they won't—"

"I know they won't," Faith said. "Your mom tried to help me so many times. Today, they'll be happy to see me and I hope they'll be happy to see us together. That's what I think."

Destiny sighed. "You didn't do this to us." She squeezed Faith's hand. "Let's sit for a minute."

They walked over to the chairs in front of the house. Destiny pulled hers to face Faith's and took her hands in hers. She knew Faith blamed herself for what happened between them, but it wasn't that simple. "We have to look at this for what it is. It was a perfect storm instigated by Gloria."

Faith shook her head. "I don't know, Des—"

"Yes, Faith," Destiny said firmly. "Gloria started it. We found out our relationship wasn't what we thought. You didn't do this. I didn't do this."

"But we can fix it together," Faith added with hope in her voice.

Destiny smiled. "That's what we're trying to do."

Before Destiny knew what was happening, Faith grabbed her face and crushed their lips together. Destiny held on to Faith's wrists then gently ran her hands over Faith's shoulders. She could feel the tension in Faith begin to ease and she softened the kiss.

They didn't pull apart, but instead settled in and basked in this kiss that both of them had longed for since they'd left the shack. Destiny's tongue explored Faith's mouth with pleasure. She remembered how luscious and sweet Faith's kisses could be and now she was right in the middle of all this luxurious joy. Yes! That's what this kiss was. Joy!

Destiny's heart was pounding and she could hear her pulse in her own ears when Faith's arms snaked around her back and pulled her closer. Faith's tongue was now demanding and seeking and Destiny was all for it. She groaned and Faith pulled her even tighter as the kiss flamed in intensity then began to slowly soften.

Destiny caressed Faith's lips with her own, not wanting the kiss to end. "Mmm," she murmured against Faith's lips. "So good."

She felt Faith smile then slowly opened her eyes and pulled away. Faith's fingers feathered down Destiny's cheek then her index finger traced Destiny's lips. "God, I missed you," Faith whispered. "I missed this."

Destiny smiled as she swallowed the emotion caught in her throat. She wanted to jump up and race to Faith's bedroom, but she also wanted to stare into Faith's crystal blue eyes and never look away.

Faith pressed her lips to Destiny's once again and Destiny closed her eyes, imprinting this moment in her memory to savor. This was the kiss of new beginnings mixed with the goodness of the past.

When Faith pulled away Destiny whispered, "I could kiss you all day."

Faith leaned back in and Destiny claimed her lips. She

ran her hand behind Faith's neck and held it there. Her heart was pounding and she was sure Faith could feel it, too.

Faith slowly pulled away and Destiny opened her eyes to the most beautiful smile. "If your parents weren't waiting on us..."

"I know." Destiny sighed.

"Kissing you all day would be a very nice birthday gift," Faith said, raising her brows.

Destiny chuckled. "We have your party."

"There's always the day after," Faith suggested.

Destiny knew her eyes were sparkling because her heart was doing cartwheels. The smile on Faith's face fell and she looked serious. "What is it?" Destiny asked.

"I'm not taking anything for granted, Des," Faith said. "I know we still have things to work through."

Destiny nodded. Faith had made sure not to push Destiny since the truth came out. She was determined not to overwhelm her, but Destiny could see these kisses meant everything to Faith, too.

"Let's go see my folks," Destiny said. "Then I have a little surprise for you." She leaned in and quickly kissed Faith on the lips before getting up and pulling Faith up with her.

Destiny and Faith waved to the Greens as they drove away.

"I can't believe you made us clean out Mom's flower bed before we could leave," Destiny said, glancing over at Faith.

"Come on, it was only a few weeds," Faith said, reaching for Destiny's hand. "You didn't even get dirt under your fingernails. Besides, we always do that for her."

"We used to do that for her," Destiny corrected her. "We can always do new things, Faith."

"I like the sound of that. But we should still keep your mom's flower bed pretty."

Destiny felt Faith squeeze her hand. She couldn't help but smile and shake her head.

"Where are we going now?" Faith asked.

"We are going to see one of our favorite people," Destiny said.

"So much for doing new things," Faith teased.

Destiny chuckled. "Oh, you're going to love this. Trust me." She cut her eyes over to Faith. Trust had always been important to both of them. But now, Faith had willingly put her trust in Destiny. She hadn't wavered a bit. It was Destiny who was slow to trust now, but any doubts she'd had earlier were gone.

Faith gasped. "I know where we're going!"

Destiny could feel Faith's excitement because she was still holding her hand. "I know someone who will be very happy to see us together."

"She may be napping," Faith said as Destiny found a parking space.

"Or watching NASCAR." Destiny chuckled.

"Let's walk by the bench near her room," Faith suggested, reaching for Destiny's hand. "Is this okay?"

Destiny nodded and smiled as their little fingers linked together. "You know how much she likes to sit in the sun."

They stepped off the sidewalk and could see a woman sitting on a bench in a small garden.

"My eyes must be playing tricks on me!" Mrs. Baker exclaimed as Destiny and Faith walked up to her.

"Your eyes are just fine," Faith said.

"They're better than mine." Destiny chuckled.

"Sit down and catch me up," Mrs. Baker said, patting the bench next to her.

Destiny and Faith sat down on either side of the older woman.

"Your hearts have finally won," Mrs. Baker said. "It doesn't matter what happened before. The important thing is that you're together now."

"You don't even want to hear the story?" Destiny asked.

Mrs. Baker slapped them both on the leg. "Some other time. Now, how did I get so lucky to see you girls on a Sunday?"

"We need some of your good luck," Faith said.

"We're giving a presentation this week to win a big job," Destiny said.

Mrs. Baker looked from Destiny to Faith. "Are you working together again?"

"We are on this project," Destiny said.

"We'll see how it goes," Faith said. "You never know what can happen."

"Tell me about this project," Mrs. Baker said.

They took turns telling Mrs. Baker about the gardens they'd designed and how they hoped to tie them together.

"We can show you this one," Faith said. "The computer is in the truck."

"Go get it!" Mrs. Baker exclaimed. "I'd love to see it."

"I'll be right back." Faith jumped up and took off for the truck.

"You always thought that Faith needed you and she did," Mrs. Baker said with a smile. "But I think you've discovered just how much you needed her, too."

Destiny smiled and watched Faith get the computer out of the truck. "I wanted her to know she's loved, but you're exactly right. I had no idea how much I needed her. I think she feels that now too and it hasn't scared her away."

Mrs. Baker chuckled. "She doesn't look scared."

24

"Here we go," Faith said, opening the laptop.

They showed Mrs. Baker the video and both were thrilled when she approved.

"The things you can do with these computers," Mrs. Baker said. "It looks so real."

"We hope it looks like that when we're finished," Faith said.

"Keep trusting each other and you'll win this thing," Mrs. Baker said.

Destiny looked over at Faith. "We've had our problems with trust."

"Problems we didn't even know we had," Faith added.

"But we're working on it," Destiny said. "We're open, supportive, and brave."

Faith met Destiny's gaze and smiled. This wasn't the first time she'd felt like everything was going to be okay, but what Destiny just said certainly gave her confidence.

Mrs. Baker took each of their hands. "Sharing is hard. You're afraid the person you love the most will see you differently if they know your fears. As time goes on your love grows stronger and that fear will shrink, kind of like I have." The older woman chuckled. "You two didn't have time to realize it's okay to be scared. But even more important than that..." She stopped and looked at each of them. "It's okay to let someone be scared with you. That's when you let your love be strong enough for both of you." She squeezed their hands and smiled.

"You don't always have to be the strong one," Mrs. Baker said to Destiny then she turned to Faith. "You don't always have to be the strong one," she repeated.

Faith looked over at Destiny. Their love had grown stronger the more time they'd spent together. She could feel it and from the look on Destiny's face, she felt it, too. Faith knew Destiny wanted to be with her. Those kisses they shared earlier were born of longing and a hint of relief. Faith didn't mean to grab Destiny so forcefully, but she couldn't hold back any longer.

They hadn't made it back to the way they were before and honestly Faith hoped they didn't. She didn't want to be that insecure, somewhat moody person that Destiny somehow fell in love with. That was Destiny's super power. She could see past the parts that Faith wanted to hide and nourish them in her own way.

Faith smiled at Destiny and for a moment gratitude nearly burst her heart wide open. They had the opportunity to fall in love all over again. Yes, the love was still there, but this was falling in love with the parts of each other they hadn't seen. And wow, this was so much better.

"Are you okay?" Destiny asked.

Faith smiled at Destiny and Mrs. Baker. "I'm more than okay. Right now, I'm the luckiest woman in the world. Look who I get to share this bench with!"

Mrs. Baker chuckled. "That's right."

They stayed and visited a little longer and by the time they left, Mrs. Baker had them both believing they would indeed win this bid.

"This was a nice surprise to see Mrs. Baker," Faith said as they headed back to her place.

"I thought she'd be happy to see us together."

Faith chuckled. "I'm happy to see us together."

Destiny smiled. "Do you have plans for the rest of the evening?"

"Nope," Faith said. "It's a lazy Sunday for me." She glanced over at Destiny when she didn't say anything. "Would you want to be lazy with me?"

Destiny quickly looked her way. "I thought you'd never ask."

Faith laughed. "I told you that you're welcome at my place anytime."

"I guess we could go to my place, it's just..." Destiny said.

"There's a lot of history at your place."

"Yeah," Destiny said. "I didn't know if it would upset you."

"It doesn't have to be today, but maybe we should add to that history sometime," Faith suggested.

Destiny smiled. "There are a lot of happy memories still there."

"I know," Faith replied.

"But I really do like your tiny house," Destiny said.

"I wonder why?" Faith asked. "You like your space."

"I thought I did, but there's something about your place."

Faith smiled and reached for Destiny's hand. "I wonder what it could be," she said softly.

"I wonder." Destiny glanced over at her and grinned.

. . .

As afternoon turned into evening, Faith put her arm on the back of the couch and turned to Destiny. "I can't believe you didn't fall asleep and made it through the entire movie."

"What!" Destiny exclaimed, turning towards Faith.

Faith raised her brows and stared.

"Okay, okay," Destiny said. "I usually fall asleep when we watch a movie, but..." She shrugged.

"But..." Faith leaned closer. "You wanted to kiss me and were afraid I'd miss the movie."

"Maybe," Destiny said, moving closer.

Faith leaned even closer until her lips almost brushed Destiny's. "Just so you know, I'd much rather kiss you than watch a movie."

"Yeah?" Destiny said softly with a smile.

"Yeah, I'd rather kiss you than just about anything else," Faith whispered. She gently pressed her lips to Destiny's and felt her heart skip a beat. A soft moan reached her ears and she wasn't sure if it came from her or Destiny.

Faith reached up and buried her fingers in Destiny's hair, pulling her closer.

"Mmm," Destiny moaned.

Faith could feel Destiny's arms tighten around her back as she deepened the kiss. Their tongues met in a slow dance of softness and Faith melted against Destiny. Her heart was once again beating, adding a rhythm to this sexy samba they both knew.

Along with the quiet moans and gasps of breath, Faith could feel her heart reaching for Destiny's. There had been times when they were together that Faith felt like their hearts were so entwined that they beat as one.

What started as velvety delicious kisses intensified until

Faith could feel the significance of this moment. As much as she wanted to keep going, Faith gently pulled away and stared into Destiny's now very dark brown eyes. Until now, Faith had let Destiny initiate any kind of intimacy, aside from taking her hand from time to time. It was clear that she wanted Destiny back, but Faith also knew Destiny needed more time to work through all that had happened.

"I don't want to mess this up," Faith said softly. "Should we talk?"

"Can this be our reward for all the hard work we've been doing?" Destiny offered. "Yes, we do need to talk, but right now, today, it's been so nice. Simply being together with my folks and then with Mrs. Baker, it was so laid-back. It felt like all our cares and concerns could wait, for just a little while."

"I'd say we're getting to know one another again, but I do know you, Des," Faith said. She gently cupped the side of Destiny's face. Faith smiled when Destiny leaned into her hand. "I'm finding out that you're the woman I thought you were all along, but you kept parts of yourself hidden."

Destiny furrowed her brow. "Like what?"

"Like how quickly you wanted to exact revenge for what Gloria did to us."

"I don't want to talk about her today," Destiny said.

"Okay." Faith nodded. "I'm finding out that if I'm more assertive than you expect..."

Destiny raised her brows. "Yeah?"

"Then you'll let me take over."

"You haven't realized you're the one who has been in charge the entire time," Destiny said.

"I don't want that for either of us," Faith said. "We're in this together."

"Of course we are, but I thought you were talking about

something else." Destiny once again raised her eyebrows and pulled Faith on top of her as she slid down the couch.

"Oh, how I want to." Faith's body was pressed against Destiny's. They were both wearing shorts and feeling their skin touch was almost too much for Faith's resolve.

"We'll talk after your birthday party," Destiny said. "But right now, I want more kisses."

Faith raised her brows. "You know where our kisses often take us."

Destiny smiled. "It's okay. Don't you remember, I could kiss you all day."

Faith smiled and brushed a strand of Destiny's hair behind her ear then kissed her with the love that was growing in her heart. They stayed like this for a while, lounging in the luxury of their kisses.

"This has been such a good day," Destiny said.

"It has," Faith replied, holding Destiny's hand as they walked to her truck.

Faith opened the door, but swung Destiny into her arms. She held her close and gazed into her eyes. "I don't think I've ever looked forward to my birthday as much as I am this one."

Destiny smiled, but then her eyes widened. "Oh no, the pressure."

Faith chuckled. "The party will be fun. How can it not be with a bunch of our friends and co-workers singing karaoke? I'm looking forward to you and me, right here, just us."

Destiny nodded. "Me, too," she whispered.

Faith leaned up and gently kissed Destiny's lips. "I'll see you tomorrow."

"Count on it."

Faith stepped back and watched Destiny get in her truck and drive away.

"We're in this together," she said softly with a smile.

* * *

The next morning Faith went over the schedule with her teams and sent them out to their respective jobs. She was reading her emails when she looked up and saw Destiny walk in with a box.

"Good morning," Destiny said with a smile.

"Hey." Faith grinned and got up from her computer.

"Amy, I hope you like donuts," Destiny said, stopping at Amy's desk and opening the box as she winked at Faith.

The things that little wink did to Faith's heart. It was like a blast of sunshine that woke up a flurry of butterflies that were now humming in her stomach.

"I love donuts," Amy said. "It's a requirement to work here." She took two out of the box along with the napkin Destiny offered her.

Faith laughed. "We do love donuts."

"Isn't it remarkable I guessed that," Destiny said with a grin.

"Isn't it though," Faith replied, taking a donut from the box.

"It wouldn't have anything to do with our favorite Sunday donut ritual," Destiny said, leaning against Faith's desk.

"How did we get so lucky to receive this donut delivery?" Faith asked, taking a bite of the breakfast treat.

Destiny shrugged, reaching in the box for a donut. "Did you see the email about the presentations?"

"I just read it."

"Three days of presentations," Destiny said. "We're in the middle."

"Yeah," Faith said, rereading the schedule. "The smaller companies are at the beginning with the big ones at the end."

"Yep," Destiny said. "Gloria is the last to present. If I could figure out some way to go in and fuck that up…"

"Did you notice," Faith said, trying to pull Destiny away from her destructive thoughts, "how good our company name looks on this list?"

Destiny leaned over next to Faith. "It looks like it belongs with those big companies."

Faith nodded. She'd been thinking about what it would be like if they merged their companies not only for this job, but also going forward.

"I have a job for us today," Destiny said, between bites.

"A job?" Faith asked, pulling her attention back to Destiny.

"What if we took rocks with us to the presentation and showed the committee how it works?"

"That's a great idea," Faith exclaimed. "But where do we get the rocks?"

"My dad knows someone who is happy to let us pick up rocks on their land," Destiny said. "Can you go with me today?"

"If it will help us win this bid," Faith said. "Hell yes, I can go today."

Destiny chuckled. "I'll pick you up after lunch."

"Hey wait," Faith said, as Destiny started to walk away. She leaned up and softly kissed Destiny. "You had a little sugar on your lips."

Destiny grinned and walked towards the door.

"Thanks for the donuts," Amy said.

"You're welcome." Destiny stopped at the door and gave Faith a little wave before she left.

"Do you want to tell me what that was?" Amy asked with a brow raised.

"That's hope." Faith smiled as she stared at the front door.

"Well, it goes with faith and destiny, I suppose," Amy said.

25

Destiny looked at herself one more time in the mirror. She smoothed her hands over the front of her black pencil skirt where she'd tucked in a sleeveless ivory silk blouse. A black one-button blazer would complete the power suit. She hoped it gave her a look of professionalism, but also presented her as someone who took care in her work.

A knock at the front door made her heartbeat quicken. That would be Faith. She was picking her up and then they'd go give the biggest presentation of their professional lives.

Destiny quickly grabbed her blazer off the bed and hurried to the living room. She was not prepared for the emotions that ran through her body when she opened the front door.

Faith was standing there in a dark blue suit with the sleeves pushed up revealing her muscled forearms. She wore a pale yellow shirt which highlighted her honey-colored hair where it rested at her shoulders. The pants were tapered at the ankles making Faith's legs look long and lean. The high heels would've made Faith the same height as Destiny if she hadn't been wearing heels as well.

Destiny lost her breath along with the ability to speak and felt her cheeks light up like the Fourth of July. The gorgeous woman standing in front of her didn't have a smirk on her face like Destiny expected. Instead she looked a lot like Destiny was feeling inside right this minute.

"Faith..." Destiny said hoarsely, trying to find her voice. "You look amazing."

"M–m–me?" Faith stammered. "If you put a blazer on over that skirt, I'm going to melt right in front of you."

Destiny smiled and reached for Faith's hand. "Get in here." She closed the front door and felt Faith's hands on her bare upper arms.

"I've always had a thing for your shoulders, babe," Faith said. "You are beautiful."

"Thank you," Destiny said shyly.

Faith leaned in and started to kiss her. "Hold it," Destiny said. "You know what happens when we start kissing. We can't be late."

"You cannot expect me to stand here when you look this incredible and not kiss you," Faith stated.

Destiny smirked and put her hands on Faith's hips. "Okay. You can kiss me, but will you wear this suit after your birthday party so I can take it off of you?"

"Absolutely," Faith said.

Destiny didn't wait and closed the distance between their lips. The kiss was soft, but there was an underlying hint of want and need. When Faith deepened the kiss, Destiny could feel Faith's hands squeeze her shoulders. The strength and power of the entire scene made Destiny once again lose her breath.

Until We Weren't: 207

She pulled away and inhaled deeply. "You're making me dizzy," she said breathlessly.

"I know," Faith replied. "I feel it, too."

A chuckle bubbled up from Destiny's throat. "My God, would you look at us?"

Faith laughed. "Maybe we should dress up more often."

"Would you give us your massive landscaping budget?" Destiny asked with a twinkle in her eye.

"We're beautiful people making beautiful landscapes," Faith replied.

"Yeah, we are," Destiny said. She started to pull away, but Faith stopped her.

"We can do this, Des," Faith said.

Destiny nodded.

"I don't just mean the bid," Faith clarified, staring into Destiny's eyes.

"I know," Destiny said softly. "One thing at a time, babe."

Faith smiled and Destiny could see the recognition in her eyes.

"I'm going to put my coat on now," Destiny said, raising her brows. "Please don't melt. I need you for the presentation."

Faith reached for the blazer and held it out for Destiny to slip her arms into. She turned around and Faith gently settled Destiny's hair on her shoulders.

"Mmm-mmm," Faith enthusiastically murmured. "How could they not want you to complete their project?"

"Us!" Destiny said forcefully. "We're in this together."

"Yes, we are," Faith said. "I just hope we can stack these rocks like we practiced."

Destiny chuckled. "We're going to be great."

Faith reached for the bag of rocks they had collected earlier in the week.

"Wait," Destiny said. She took out her phone and turned to Faith. "We need a picture." She put her arm around Faith's shoulders and pressed their cheeks together then clicked the button.

"Let me see?"

Destiny showed the picture to Faith and they both smiled.

"Fields of Green," Faith said. "At your service."

Destiny stared at the picture and could see happiness in both their eyes. There was also excitement for what was to come and it wasn't just for the presentation.

* * *

They walked up to the main building with confidence in each step. The corporation building the new business campus wanted the presentations done on site. The reception area and lobby of the main building were complete along with several meeting rooms.

A committee made up of representatives from the corporation, the construction company, and the greater Austin community would decide which landscaping company won the bid.

Destiny and Faith walked into the building and were greeted by a woman who was in charge of the schedule for the day. She gave them a packet of information which they'd also received by email and led them to a waiting area.

"Hey," Destiny said to Faith as she looked over the material. "There's David Orr. I wonder if he's on the committee."

Just as Destiny said his name the man looked up and waved. He walked over to where Destiny and Faith were standing.

David Orr was on the City of Austin's Urban Planning

committee. Destiny and Faith had both known him for years. He often came by their new projects to visit and check in with them. Part of his job was to make sure landscapes followed the city codes.

"Hi," he said with a friendly smile. "It's so good to see you both."

"Hi, David," Destiny said. "Are you on the evaluating committee?"

"I am," he replied.

"It will be nice to see a familiar face in there," Faith said.

"I wondered when I saw the list if you two had finally joined forces," David said. "What a good thing for Austin."

"You knew it was us?" Destiny asked.

"Of course," David said. "That's a perfect name for y'all."

Faith chuckled. "This is the first project we've worked on together."

"Yeah, we thought our little companies might get lost in the shuffle, but together," Destiny looked over at Faith, "we're hard to overlook."

"I'll say," David said. "I can't wait to see what you've come up with."

"We've done some things that are out of the box," Faith said, raising her eyebrows at Destiny.

David chuckled. "That's perfect for Austin. I'd better get back inside. It's almost your turn."

"It was good to see you, David," Faith said.

"Good luck, you two." He leaned a little closer. "You know I'll be in your corner."

"Thanks, David." Destiny smiled.

After he'd walked away Destiny felt Faith squeeze her hand. "That's a good sign."

Destiny smiled at her. "Hey, I want you to know, no

matter what happens in there, I wouldn't want to do this with anyone else."

Faith smiled and tilted her head. "Destiny Green," she said softly. "I love you. If they can't see that we're the best people to make their building extraordinary then that's on them. We know who we are."

Destiny nodded. She could feel the love in her heart reaching out and wrapping around Faith. Who cared about the bid and the project? She knew who Faith was. She's the woman Destiny wanted to spend her life with. "I love you, too, Faith."

Faith leaned in and whispered, "We've already won, but let's go win this bid, too."

Destiny chuckled. "Yeah, we have." It might seem like a strange moment for *I love yous*, but it felt like the perfect time. Planning this project had not only brought them together but forced them to take a look at themselves. Here they were, all dressed up, still in love, so why not now.

They turned and walked into the meeting room together. Inside, there was a large screen at the front of the room where they could project their videos, pictures, and information so the committee could see their vision.

Destiny and Faith pulled a small table over to use for their rock demonstration towards the end of the presentation. They stood on either side of the screen while the project manager introduced each member of the committee before turning the meeting over to them.

"I'm Destiny Green," she said with a smile.

"I'm Faith Fields, and we're Fields of Green," Faith said.

Destiny started the presentation by outlining their approach to the site as a whole then went into how they planned to make each building unique.

They took them on a tour of the main building highlighting their ideas with views of the property from a distance and then walking them around the building much like an employee.

Faith took over and led them to the smaller building on the south side of the property. When the triangular garden came into view with the fountain, several pleased sounds echoed around the room.

Destiny glanced at Faith and smiled. This was the reaction they were hoping to hear.

Faith went on to explain the benefits of an outdoor space that employees could use on a daily basis that wouldn't detract from their work, but enhance it.

Destiny watched the committee members as Faith held their attention. There were two members who were in the human resources department and they nodded as Faith explained the benefits. From the looks on the committee members' faces they were interested in what Faith was saying. Destiny felt her heart swell with pride as Faith continued her part of the presentation. She was believable and her passion was apparent as she spoke.

As they made their way over to the other smaller building to the north of the main structure, Destiny continued the presentation. There were several murmurs and comments as the garden with the rock formation filled the screen.

Destiny gave a little history on why she chose this particular feature for the garden as Faith began to set the rocks out on the table. As Destiny continued with the benefits of the garden much like Faith had outlined earlier she saw the committee members nod.

Faith began to stack several rocks and smiled at the committee. Destiny joined her and together they made a small formation in the shape of an arch. They had to hold the rocks just so and slip the last rock into place to make it stand and not collapse.

Several members clapped and Destiny could see they were all interested. She had their attention.

"Now it's your turn," Destiny said. She invited them up to stack a few rocks and give it a try.

After several moments she put different rock formations on the screen that the employees could try during breaks in their day.

While the members were experimenting with the rocks, Faith explained the idea of changing the plants with the seasons. Destiny heard one of the members tell another that no one had mentioned that. They liked the idea.

Finally, Destiny put the all-important cost analysis up on the screen. She explained the project could be done in phases and it was entirely customizable.

Destiny looked over at Faith and raised her brows to see if she'd left anything out. Faith nodded and grinned.

This gave Destiny such a feeling of accomplishment. They had set out to do this together and make it remarkable. Even though they hadn't planted one single shrub or flower yet, they had done this together and it was amazing.

The committee members asked several questions and David spoke up on how well this plan would fit into the city's vision as a whole.

The woman in charge of the schedule knocked on the door indicating it was time for the next presentation. The project manager asked for a little more time as the committee finished with their questions while still stacking rocks.

As Destiny and Faith left the room, David walked out with them.

"That was amazing," he said. "What creativity!"

"Thanks," Destiny and Faith said in unison.

"I don't know how you came up with not one but two unique gardens then tied them together," David said. "Well done."

They walked over to a part of the lobby away from the other people.

"No one has done anything nearly as good," he said. "You've got a real shot at this."

"Yeah, but the big companies have their turn tomorrow," Destiny said.

"It doesn't matter," David replied. "This is on or above their level."

"Thanks," Faith said. "That's good to know."

"I'll keep you updated," he said with a smile. "What are friends for," he added walking back over to the meeting room.

Destiny looked around the lobby then turned to Faith. She grabbed her and pulled her into a tight hug.

26

"Oh my, God," Faith said, beaming Destiny a smile. "That was so much fun!"

"I didn't think you liked to give presentations," Destiny said.

"I don't." Faith grinned. "But it was so much fun with you."

Destiny laughed. "It went well." She looked at Faith. "It did, didn't it?"

"Yes!" Faith laughed. "It went better than we'd practiced. Babe, the rocks were genius! Did you see them? They were stacking and enjoying every minute."

Destiny took a deep breath and slowly let it out. Faith couldn't keep her eyes off of Destiny. The excitement on her face made her glow. She was so beautiful.

"Let's get out of here," Faith said.

"To celebrate?" Destiny said.

"I know just the place." Faith grabbed the bag of rocks and her computer while Destiny fell in step beside her.

Fifteen minutes later they were at the small bar where

they'd sung karaoke. They each got a beer at the bar and sat at the same table.

Faith held up her glass. "To Fields of Green."

Destiny touched her glass to Faith's and drank. "Do you feel like singing?"

"Not yet," Faith replied, setting her beer back on the table. "That was…amazing!"

Destiny grinned. "It was."

"They seemed interested the entire time we were speaking," Faith said.

"I thought so, too."

"I was worried for a second when the construction rep said he wouldn't want to go back to work after his break if he kept stacking rocks," Faith said.

"I was, too," Destiny replied, "until I saw he was kidding."

"It was such a good idea to bring the rocks and let them experience what we were talking about," Faith said, reaching over and squeezing Destiny's forearm.

Both of their phones pinged with a message.

Faith laughed when she saw the text. "It's from Monica," she said. "It's one word in caps: WELL?"

Destiny laughed. "I meant to text her when we finished. I guess she sent it to both of us in hopes of an answer."

"You text Monica back and I'll let Amy and my group know that it went well," Faith said. "I'm not going back to the office today."

They sent their texts and continued to replay the presentation while they drank their beers.

"The excitement on your face after David left us," Faith said, shaking her head. "You were glowing."

Destiny scoffed. "No way."

"So beautiful," Faith said softly.

"I couldn't keep my eyes off of you," Destiny said.

Faith watched Destiny slide her hand over and interlock their little fingers. "It's these suits," Faith said. They stared into each other's eyes for several moments and the desire to get Destiny out of her suit caused Faith to run her teeth over her bottom lip.

"We were in perfect rhythm, sync, or tune. Whatever you want to call it," Destiny said.

Faith covered Destiny's hand with hers. "We were. We are," she said quietly.

"Take me home with you," Destiny said softly.

"Are you sure?"

Destiny nodded.

It only took a few moments for them to finish their beers and get back into the truck.

"Will Amy and your workers still be there?" Destiny asked.

Faith shook her head and squeezed Destiny's hand. "No, they'll be gone."

"Good," Destiny said.

Faith glanced over at Destiny who now had the sexiest look on her face. *Oh my God.*

When Faith closed the front door to her tiny house she turned around and Destiny grabbed the lapels of her jacket and pulled her close.

"I love you, Faith Fields," she said softly, "and I'm going to show you how much."

The softest lips gently touched Faith's. Her heart was already beating wildly in anticipation, but this tender kiss almost brought her to her knees.

Destiny pushed the blazer off Faith's shoulders and tossed it onto the couch.

"Oh, no you don't," Faith said. "I've wanted to undress you all day."

Destiny turned around so Faith could ease the blazer off. Faith kissed her shoulder then her neck and stopped just under her ear. She knew how sensitive this particular spot was on Destiny's body. Who was she kidding, she knew all the most sensitive spots on Destiny's body, but maybe they would discover something new. They had revealed their fears and innermost thoughts since being trapped in the shack. Why wouldn't there be new discoveries here as well.

Destiny turned around and Faith eased the blouse over her head. She saw Destiny take a shuddering breath and waited.

Destiny slowly unbuttoned Faith's shirt, pulled it out of her pants, and eased it off her shoulders. "I don't know how much longer I can wait," Destiny said breathlessly.

"Then don't," Faith said. She reached for the front of her pants and slid the zipper down. She quickly stepped out of her pants. "Wait," she said to Destiny. "Let me do that."

Faith reached around Destiny and unzipped her skirt. She slowly pulled it down Destiny's hips and let her step out of it.

"My God, Destiny," Faith said, her voice hoarse with emotion. "You are even more beautiful."

Destiny's hands cradled Faith's face. "We are in this together, Faith," she said clearly. "From now on."

"Together," Faith replied. "Always."

Destiny pressed her lips to Faith's and this time there was no softness. This kiss was full of want, desire, and need.

Faith deepened the kiss, put her arms around Destiny, and pulled her close until their bodies were pressed together. She could feel the pounding of Destiny's heart where it touched hers. The heat and electricity flying through her body made her weak for a moment.

Faith pulled back and took a deep breath while staring into Destiny's eyes. "I love you so much," she stated.

"Oh, baby," Destiny said. "I love you."

Faith grabbed Destiny's hand and pulled them the short distance to the bedroom. She stopped at the door and reached around Destiny to unclasp her bra. "This bra is beautiful and I will appreciate how good it looks on you another time," Faith said with a sexy smile. "But now..."

"Get it off," Destiny said, raising a brow and unclasping Faith's bra. "Oh, Faith."

It used to unnerve Faith when Destiny would look at her this way, but not anymore. She felt beautiful under Destiny's gaze now. Yes, she was still vulnerable, but she trusted Destiny completely.

"I've missed you so," Destiny murmured.

Faith gently pushed Destiny onto the bed and slid her undies down her legs. She could see Destiny's desire glisten and couldn't wait to taste her love once again. Before joining Destiny on the bed she removed her own undies.

Destiny moved up the bed and Faith placed her hands on either side of her. She slowly lowered her head until their lips met in a searing kiss. Faith felt Destiny's arms wrap around her shoulders, pulling her down until there was nothing between their bodies but love.

Faith groaned and moved her thigh between Destiny's legs. She could feel the wetness from both of them and slowly began to move. Her hand found Destiny's breast and cupped it gently. The moan she heard from Destiny was pure music to Faith's ears. She tweaked Destiny's pebbled nipple between her thumb and finger to another chorus of moans.

Faith nibbled down Destiny's neck and they both panted for breath. "I want to keep kissing you, but..." Faith's lips trailed lower and lower until she took Destiny's nipple into her mouth and sucked gently.

Destiny arched her back and nearly came off the bed. Her fingers were tangled in Faith's hair causing the most delicious tingles throughout Faith's body.

"Mmmm," Faith groaned.

"Babe," Destiny groaned. "I need you."

Faith smiled against Destiny's chest as her hand slid down Destiny's outer thigh then up between her legs.

"Oh, God, yes!" Destiny groaned.

Faith whispered her finger up Destiny's center causing another loud groan as Destiny's hips bucked off the bed.

"Babe!"

"I've got you, Des," Faith said softly. She ran her finger through Destiny's slick folds and could feel her sink back into the bed.

"Mmmm," Destiny moaned.

Faith circled Destiny's swollen clit several times then found her entrance with one then two fingers. She pushed inside and heard the most beautiful moan echo around the room. Destiny raised her legs and dug her heels into the bed.

There was no way Faith was going to tease her in this moment. They'd both waited years to be this in love and this close again. She began to move in and out and it was Faith's turn to groan. Destiny's velvety center grabbed her fingers and Faith never wanted it to end.

Destiny reached for Faith's face and brought her down for a scorching kiss that Faith felt through her entire body.

She closed her eyes and fell into Destiny's love. She could feel it every place their skin touched, but what truly amazed her was the sensation gripping her heart. It felt like their hearts were holding each other. How could that be? Faith didn't have the ability to think about that right now. All she could do was feel.

Faith pushed her fingers in one more time and held them still as Destiny closed around her.

"Oh God, yes," Destiny groaned, staring into Faith's eyes.

Faith could see the orgasm flash in Destiny's eyes then she could feel it racing through her hand and the rest of her body.

Destiny's hands on Faith's face eased and she fell back on the bed. Faith couldn't take her eyes off of Destiny as they both struggled to breathe. How could she be even more beautiful?

"That was..." Destiny said softly.

"I know," Faith said, falling down beside her. She put her arm around Destiny and pulled her into her side. "Did you feel it?"

"Yes," Destiny said. She raised up and looked into Faith's eyes. "It felt like your heart was beating inside me."

Faith nodded. "I could feel your heart. Our love was wrapped around us."

Destiny smiled. "I've felt our love before, babe, but it wasn't anything like this."

Faith gently ran her fingers down Destiny's cheek. "It's new love," she said. "We're seeing those parts we left hidden."

"I'm not hiding anything," Destiny said. "Not anymore."

Faith felt Destiny's lips claim hers with intention. She closed her eyes and let Destiny's body wrap around hers. Faith could feel her everywhere.

Destiny pulled away and looked down at Faith with a sexy smile. She reached for Faith's hands and held them over her head. Faith could feel Destiny slide up her body.

"I've always loved this view," Destiny said.

Faith felt Destiny's thigh push between her legs and then she started to move. "You are so fucking sexy, babe," Destiny said, looking down into Faith's face.

"Mmmm," Faith said as her breathing began to quicken. "That feels so good."

Destiny kissed Faith again then grinned. "This is going to feel even better."

Faith felt Destiny drop her hands as her lips kissed a hot path down her body. Her tongue swirled around Faith's nipples licking from one to the other.

"Good God, babe," Faith moaned.

When Destiny sucked Faith's nipple into her mouth and bit down Faith slammed her hands on the bed.

"I love you," Destiny murmured as she continued to kiss down Faith's stomach.

Faith felt Destiny stop and she opened her eyes. Destiny was staring at her once again and this time Faith only saw love in her eyes. There was no hesitation, no doubt, just love.

Destiny reached under Faith's outstretched legs and Faith bent her knees, spreading wide for her love. Faith reached for one of Destiny's hands and felt her strength. She watched as Destiny dropped her head then Faith felt the most exquisite sensation as Destiny lavished her with pleasure.

Destiny's tongue swirled in and around, up and down, and Faith moaned to the rhythm. This felt so good! She never wanted Destiny to stop.

"Oh, babe," Faith groaned.

Destiny's fingers squeezed Faith's hand just as she sucked Faith into her mouth.

Faith raised up then fell back on the bed as an orgasm raced through her body. Every muscle was tensed and Faith tried to hold this pure feeling of love inside as long as she could. Finally she let go and a sound escaped her throat that she'd never heard before. This had to be the sound of ultimate surrender, trust, and love.

"I'm home," Faith whispered.

27

"What did you say?" Destiny asked as she cuddled against Faith's chest. She could feel Faith's hand lazily stroking up and down her back.

Faith sighed. "I'm home," she repeated. "The few times in my life when I've felt like I was where I was supposed to be were with you. You may be my destiny, but you're also my home."

"Oh, baby," Destiny said softly. "I have felt off balance for so long, but when I saw you at the site that day something inside me changed. This is going to sound so sappy, but I know now our hearts were tired of being apart."

"That's not sappy," Faith replied. "I felt it too. It was such a feeling of anticipation, like something big was about to happen."

"It certainly did," Destiny said.

"Mmm," Faith murmured.

They held each other for several moments as Destiny snuggled in as close as she could get to Faith. They were so relaxed and even though Destiny didn't want to sleep, she was afraid it might sneak up on them. "Are you going to take me back to my apartment before work?"

"What if I don't want you to go?"

"Mmm," Destiny moaned as Faith's arms tightened around her. She started to chuckle then couldn't keep from laughing.

"What's so funny?"

"I've kept a bag in my truck since I spent the night." She giggled. "But my truck is at my apartment."

Faith joined her laughter.

"Are we ever going to get this right?" Destiny asked, raising up and looking into Faith's eyes.

"I love you, Des," Faith said softly. "That's all the right I need."

Destiny leaned down and kissed Faith tenderly. She pulled away slightly. "The other day you said you liked kissing me more than just about anything." Her hand snaked between them and she ran her fingers through Faith's wetness once again. "What's the anything?"

"Mmm," Faith moaned, staring into Destiny's eyes. "Right now it's this." She raised her hips and closed her eyes as Destiny's fingers slipped inside her once again.

"God," Destiny groaned. "This is the best." She began a slow rhythm and Faith's hips moved with her.

"Yeah," Faith moaned. She opened her eyes and looked at Destiny. "You know when we were afraid to tell each other things?" She groaned as Destiny's fingers slid in a little deeper.

"Mmhmm," Destiny replied.

Faith gently pushed Destiny's shoulder and rolled them onto their sides until Faith was on top of her. She grabbed Destiny's shoulders and sat down on her fingers. "I really like this."

Destiny put her other hand on Faith's hip and shifted slightly so she could move with Faith. "God, baby," she murmured as they began to move together. "You should've told me about this a long time ago."

Destiny's thumb found Faith's pulsating clit and she was rewarded with another glorious moan.

Faith threw her head back and the sweetest sound echoed around the room as Destiny pushed up and held her fingers still. She could feel Faith's warmth gush over her fingers as Faith collapsed on top of her.

"Fuck!" Faith exclaimed in a whisper. "That was intense and fast."

"Babe," Destiny said. "Look at me."

Faith raised up just far enough to see Destiny's face.

"I'm never letting you go," Destiny said passionately.

Faith swallowed and stared into her eyes. "I'm never leaving you again."

Destiny raised up so their lips could meet in a soft kiss.

"I'm sor—"

"No!" Destiny said forcefully, putting her fingers over Faith's lips. "We're only looking forward."

Faith smiled and nibbled the end of Destiny's finger.

"I love you," Destiny said.

"Can you feel my love?" Faith asked.

"Mmhmm," Destiny replied as Faith began to kiss down her body.

"I can't stop," Faith said. "There are so many things I want to tell you, but maybe right now it's best if I show you."

Destiny felt Faith's lips and tongue kiss and lick a delicious trail down her body. As much as she wanted to bask in the euphoria they'd created she couldn't wait. "Here it is again," she said breathlessly. "I need you, babe. Now!"

Faith's tongue took over Destiny's body. She reached

down to comb her fingers through Faith's hair and fisted the blanket with her other hand. Faith had always known where Destiny needed her most, but this was so much more. Destiny could feel love with every touch. Faith would take her so close to going over the edge then bring her back just enough for another wave of delicious sensations.

Faith moaned and Destiny knew she was about to explode into their world of love.

Destiny shuddered and took a deep breath. She let their love surround her then reached for Faith. She pulled her up for a soul-melting kiss.

"Together," Destiny whispered.

"Always," Faith replied softly.

* * *

Destiny stirred and found her cheek resting on Faith's chest. She remembered they were about to fall asleep, but couldn't do anything about it. They were too comfortable, too spent, too happy to move.

"Mmm," Faith murmured. "We did something together yesterday that we love."

"We sure did," Destiny said, yawning. "Over and over."

Faith giggled. "We did, but that wasn't what I was talking about."

Destiny raised up and looked into Faith's eyes. "Oh, you mean the presentation."

"Yes," Faith said. "But this was going to happen whether we gave that very successful presentation or not."

Destiny smiled. "It almost happened Sunday afternoon and I planned for it to happen after your birthday party tomorrow. That's one reason I asked to stay with you."

"Oh," Faith said as a delighted look covered her face. "Was this my birthday present?"

Destiny rested her head on her elbow and slowly ran her thumb along Faith's cheek. She'd never imagined her love as a gift, but she certainly considered loving Faith Fields a precious honor she would never take for granted again.

"You've been patient with me since we ended up in that shack," Destiny said.

"Have I thanked you lately for saving me from those dogs?" Faith said with a playful smile.

Destiny chuckled. "I wanted to take you in my arms and never let you go," she said as tears began to burn her eyes. "Thank you for giving me time, but Faith, my love, I want our arms around each other from now on."

"Even when we're scared," Faith said softly. "Because there will be times when we're afraid."

"But we'll be afraid together," Destiny said.

Faith nodded. "We've promised to be together forever before and I meant it when I said it then, but I doubted myself. You know now how I was thinking."

Destiny nodded and continued to caress Faith's cheek.

"I can't imagine not sharing all of myself with you. I knew who you were all along, but now I can trust myself."

"I don't like the idea that we had to go through this to get where we are right now," Destiny said. "I think we would've grown together. You would've seen that we belonged together and I would've given you the space to do that."

"All that matters is that we've made it here together right now," Faith said.

Destiny smiled. "I know you're right, but I still can't stand what Gloria did to us."

"We're stronger than her," Faith said. "Believe me, darling. She'll get hers one of these days."

Destiny nodded. "We've got a happy life to live with absolutely no room for thoughts of her."

"That's my girl," Faith said.

"I like being your girl," Destiny murmured, bringing her lips to Faith's for a sweet kiss.

"I'll take you back to your apartment to get ready for work, but I don't want to be without you ever again."

"You won't," Destiny said. "We'll figure it out."

Faith sighed. "Yes we will. What do you have planned for today?"

"Well," Destiny said, drawing the word out. "I'm going to sit on a mower since I was accused of being more of a CEO type than a hands-on boss."

"I did not accuse you," Faith said, her eyes widening. "I simply asked a question."

Destiny chuckled. "What about you?"

"I may be a hands-on boss, but it's because I expect good work," Faith explained. "However, I compensate my workers fairly. It's Friday and I try to plan things so they get finished early and can enjoy their weekends."

"Imagine that," Destiny said. "I try to do the same thing."

Faith chuckled. "We talked about how we'd run things enough times that I'm sure our companies are very similar."

Destiny nodded. "Maybe we should talk about our companies."

Faith raised her brows. "We don't have to do that right now. How about I show you the benefits of a tiny shower?"

Destiny smirked. "Babe," she said. "I don't have any other clothes to put on."

Faith smiled. "You can wear something of mine. I'm just taking you home."

Destiny smiled. Hearing Faith call the apartment her home didn't feel quite right to Destiny. When Faith left, the apartment no longer felt like a home. There was an emptiness yet Destiny couldn't bring herself to leave. This tiny house had felt much more like home lately and Destiny was pretty sure why. Faith was here.

"What's that look?" Faith asked. "You know, you could put that skirt back on." She wiggled her eyebrows suggestively.

"Just so you can take it off of me again?" Destiny asked with a grin.

"What a great idea."

Destiny leaned down then stopped. "Why did you want to know what I was doing today?"

"I hoped we could have lunch."

"That would be nice," Destiny said. "Where are you working?"

"We are finishing up another house that was sold in the Hutto subdivision," Faith said.

"Oh, that's where you were coming from that day you had a flat on your trailer," Destiny said.

"Yep," Faith replied. "Don't you have something in that area?"

Destiny nodded. "We mow and do maintenance at a couple of apartment complexes on the Round Rock Hutto boundary line."

"Maybe you could try that mower out over there today?" Faith asked with an eyebrow raised.

"Maybe," Destiny said. "But right now, I'd rather try out your shower."

The sweetest smile grew on Faith's face. Destiny thought her heart was going to melt in her chest. "I love you so much," she said and pressed her lips to Faith's.

The kiss may have started softly, but it quickly became a scorching flame as they held each other tightly. Faith pushed up from under Destiny and smiled. "I love you, too."

Destiny watched Faith scoot to the end of the bed, stand up, and offer her hand. She smiled and took it. "I won't let anything come between us again, but it takes both of us."

Faith nodded and took Destiny's other hand. "I've been hiding things all my life to try and keep from getting hurt. When I hid parts of myself from you I ended being hurt more than I could've ever imagined and I hurt you in the process. I showed you the Faith I was afraid you'd run from, but you didn't. You ran to me."

Destiny tilted her head. "I'm here now and here is where I'll always be."

"I don't want to hide anything from you, Des," Faith said. "You don't have to be careful and try so hard with me anymore either. Like I said, I'm home and this is where I'm staying. With you."

Destiny felt tears pool in her eyes. She pulled Faith into a tight hug. Standing at the foot of the bed, both naked, exposing their innermost selves: Destiny had never been happier and felt so loved.

"I didn't mean to make you cry," Faith said.

"They're happy tears," Destiny said, looking into Faith's eyes which were misty as well.

"You believe me? I promise you can trust me, baby."

"I do," Destiny said. "I always have."

Faith let out a big breath and shook her head. "I don't know why you do or how I got so lucky, but I'm holding on this time, for life."

Destiny chuckled. "*We're* holding on."

Faith nodded and led them to the shower.

Destiny knew the hurt and the pain from the past

couldn't be washed away, but this new love was stronger, honest, and true.

28

"It's been nice having you back on the team today," Mark said.

Faith smoothed mulch around a plant in the flower bed they were finishing up. "It's been nice playing in the dirt." She chuckled. "That's what Destiny's mom says we do for a living."

"That's one way to look at it." Mark laughed. "And how about Destiny happening by just in time for lunch? It reminded me of when we all worked together years ago."

Faith looked up at Mark with a smirk. "You know she didn't just happen by."

Mark chuckled. "Does that mean we'll be seeing a lot more of her around here? Are things changing, boss?"

"I've changed," Faith said honestly, rocking back on her knees to sit on her heels. "I let things get in the way of having a happy life. Destiny and I are in this together from now on. I don't know what that means for our companies, but we're waiting to hear from the bid. If we win, we'll all be working together. We'll see how it goes from there."

Until We Weren't:

"That sounds like a solid plan," Mark said. "Hey, I'm really happy for you both. You belong together."

Faith grinned. "Yeah, we do."

Her phone beeped with a message and Mark raised his brows. "Someone must already miss you," he said.

"Ha ha." Faith looked at the message and frowned. "Huh, it's from David Orr."

"The guy from urban planning?" Mark asked.

"Yeah," Faith replied. Before she could say anything else her phone rang. She could see Destiny's smiling face in the caller ID. "Hey, babe."

"Hi," Destiny said. "I just got the strangest text from David Orr."

"I did, too," Faith replied. "He asked if I could meet him at the site. He said it was about our presentation."

"That's what he messaged me," Destiny said.

"Do you want me to come get you?" Faith asked. "I have my truck."

"Yeah, I'm with Claire's team. I'll text you the address," Destiny said.

"Okay, I'll be right there," Faith said, ending the call.

"Good luck," Mark said.

Faith got up and dusted off the dirt from her knees. "Fingers crossed."

As she drove to the apartment complex where Destiny was working, Faith couldn't fight off the bad feeling she got from the text.

Destiny was waiting and jumped into the truck when Faith pulled up. She leaned over the console and kissed Faith on the lips. "I've got to tell you," she said, buckling her seatbelt, "I don't have a good feeling about this."

Faith looked over at her and widened her eyes. "I don't either!"

"I can't imagine why he'd want us back at the site."

"They were doing the last presentations this morning," Faith said. "I figured they'd be meeting to decide on who won the bid."

"Yeah, me too." Destiny reached for Faith's hand and pulled it into her lap.

Faith squeezed Destiny's hand and smiled over at her. At least they were facing this together. "They're about to find out that we lead our companies by working. I hope they don't mind sweat."

"I think you look absolutely beautiful," Destiny said with a big grin. "We were very sweaty last night."

Faith chuckled. "You liked how we got sweaty."

"Yes, I did," Destiny said.

"Me, too," Faith replied. "Mark commented that it felt like old times with the three of us having lunch on site."

"Yeah, it did."

"I told him we were not letting anyone or anything get in the way of our happy life together," Faith said, glancing over at Destiny.

"That's right." Destiny kissed the back of Faith's hand. "Mmm, salty." She grinned at Faith.

Faith chuckled. "He asked me what was going to happen with our companies."

"Yeah, we didn't get around to talking about that last night," Destiny said.

"I explained if we win the bid that we'd all be working together and we'd go from there."

Destiny nodded. "That makes sense."

Faith could feel Destiny's eyes on her and quickly glanced her way. "What?"

"Neither one of us has said it, but we've always wanted to run our company together."

"I'm thinking the same thing, darling." Faith squeezed Destiny's hand and smiled.

"Maybe this will be the first of many jobs for Fields of Green," Destiny said.

"Oh, I hope so," Faith said, pulling off the interstate and onto the road to the construction site.

Faith and Destiny walked into the main building and saw David talking to two other people at the reception desk. He smiled and waved as he excused himself and walked over to greet them.

"Hi," he said. "Sorry to pull you off a job."

"No problem," Destiny replied.

"What's going on?" Faith asked, unable to contain her curiosity.

"Well, the committee would like to ask you a few follow up questions," he said.

"Okay." Destiny shrugged.

"Right this way," David said.

As they followed him into the meeting room, movement caught Faith's eyes. Over by the windows she noticed two people watching them.

"Des," she said softly, reaching for her arm. When Destiny glanced back at her, Faith nodded towards the window.

"You've got to be kidding me," Destiny said, rolling her eyes.

"Yep," Faith said. "Gloria's been watching us since we walked into the building."

"Do you know her?" David asked.

"Oh, yeah," Destiny said. "We're her favorite people."

David furrowed his brow.

"We'll explain it to you another time," Faith said.

They walked into the conference room and sat down at

one end of the large table. It wasn't lost on Faith that just yesterday they had dazzled this same group of people with their presentation. Today the energy in the room was not positive.

"Thank you for coming in," the project manager said.

"It looks like we've brought you in from the field," the construction representative commented.

Destiny smiled. "We not only design and create landscapes—"

"We also make them come to life," Faith added.

The people around the table smiled.

"We were very impressed with your presentation," the project manager began. "Did you share your vision with anyone else before presenting it to us?"

Faith looked at Destiny and furrowed her brow. "I'm not sure what you mean?"

"Did you tell any of the other landscapers bidding on the project what your ideas were?" he replied.

"No," Destiny stated. "When bidding on a project you don't usually share your ideas with your competitors."

"That's what I thought," he said.

"Here's the thing," David said, sharing a look with the project manager. "Your idea to do the rock cairns was unique as well as interesting, but another company also presented the idea."

Faith exchanged a look with Destiny. How Gloria fit into this Faith wasn't sure, but she could feel it and from the look on Destiny's face she did too.

"We thought it was odd," the project manager said.

"Okay," Destiny said. "Are you asking if we took the idea from another company?"

"Destiny gave you the history behind the rock cairns and why we chose to use them," Faith said.

Until We Weren't:

"You gave your presentation before the other one, too," David added.

"Let me put everything out on the table," the project manager said. "Another company—a larger company—mentioned rock cairns in their presentation and offered to do whatever type landscaping we liked best for a better price."

Faith and Destiny looked at each other and shook their heads.

"We gave you a presentation you liked along with the costs," Destiny said.

"We wouldn't have bid on the project if we couldn't deliver," Faith said. "So the size of the company shouldn't matter if you like the vision."

"I'm not sure how this other company can do the fountain or the rock cairns that we laid out for you without our plans," Destiny said. "It would be a substandard copy, if you ask me."

"The fountain you showed us was like nothing I've seen," David said.

Her patience wearing thin, Faith cleared her throat. "Why did you ask us here? Are you accusing us of something?" She felt Destiny's hand gently rest on her thigh in an effort to calm her agitation.

"No," David said. "It's obvious that one of the larger, well-known companies couldn't come up with anything near your creativity. They found out about your ideas for the property and are trying to, dare I say, steal them."

Faith took a moment to look into the eyes of each committee member. She wondered what they saw. Did they see two hard-working landscapers who could be taken advantage of? Or did they see two creative women who loved to bring beauty to buildings?

"We're in a business where size seems to matter," the construction rep said. "Just look at this place. The entire layout is huge, but you made it look welcoming instead of like a giant building trying to impress God knows who."

"The building is big because we have a lot of employees," the project manager said defensively.

"I understand that, but you don't need a huge landscaping company to swoop in with big ideas when they aren't as good as theirs," he said, gesturing towards Faith and Destiny.

"I agree," David said. "That other company is trying to do something deceitful and convince you that's how things are done. Well, I'm here to tell you, that's not true."

A woman who represented the HR department for the corporation stood up. "Would you mind waiting outside for just a moment so the committee can clear up a couple of things? It won't take but a minute."

The woman smiled at them both and Faith felt like she was about to explain to this group of men how things were going to be done.

Faith and Destiny got up and walked out of the room. It was obvious that Gloria had somehow found out about their ideas and offered to implement them at a lower cost.

When the door closed, Faith turned to Destiny and grabbed her hand. "She can't hurt us, babe."

"I know," Destiny said between clenched teeth. "But that doesn't mean I can't hurt her."

Faith grinned. "You are so hot when you're...hot."

Destiny's eyes widened and the corners of her mouth quivered until a small smile crept onto her face. "Stop that!"

Faith chuckled. "Let them give the job to Gloria. I'd love to see her try to stack rocks."

"Rock cairns?" Gloria said, walking up behind them. "Whose idea was that?"

"Have you ever had an original, creative thought in your life?" Destiny asked, dismissing Gloria's question.

Gloria laughed. "When you're the CEO you pay people to be creative."

"I guess you didn't pay them enough this time," Faith said with a smirk.

"That's when you flex your big company muscles and get the job done no matter what," Gloria said brashly.

"No matter who you hurt in the process," Faith said, staring at Gloria.

"When you're playing with the big boys you have to get dirty just like they do," Gloria stated.

"What about the women at the table?" Destiny said. "It would be unwise to overlook them."

"Ha," Gloria replied. "Women stick together."

Faith put a protective arm around Destiny's waist. "Be careful, Gloria. While you're playing dirty with the boys some small company may come along and trip you up when you least expect it."

Gloria scoffed. "You two were meant for each other." She pointed at the closed conference room doors. "If you think a major corporation is going to choose a little company like you've put together with bosses who smell of sweat and dirt over a national leader in the industry, you're both delusional. Why, you're lucky they even entertained your bid. They wouldn't if we weren't in liberal Austin."

"It's called urban planning, Gloria," Destiny said. "It doesn't have anything to do with being liberal or not."

"You never did understand aesthetics," Faith added. "It's always about the numbers and the cost."

"Damn right it is," Gloria said, bristling. "That's how things get done."

Destiny grinned and tilted her head. "Wow, Gloria. You're getting worked up."

"Are you afraid you're going to lose this bid?" Faith asked with a sarcastic grin of her own.

"What would happen to your bottom line then?" Destiny smirked.

The conference room doors opened before Gloria could reply, but Faith felt like they'd won a little battle whether they got the job or not. The look on Gloria's face showed she was worried.

29

"Destiny, Faith?" David said. "Could you come back in?"

They walked back into the room and the negative energy that had greeted them before was now gone. The committee members were all smiles and the project manager explained that their bid had been accepted. The contract would be drawn up and signed next week. He welcomed them to the team and each committee member shook their hands and expressed how excited they were to see Fields of Green's vision come to life.

David walked them to the door. "Gloria's handling of the bid will not go unnoticed," he said quietly. "One perk of working with this particular corporation is that when they break ground on new properties they will reach out to you for input and maybe even offer you upcoming jobs."

Faith and Destiny exchanged a look. "Wow, that would be awesome."

David nodded. "You deserved to win this bid," he said. "But you need to prepare for what that will bring." He smiled. "Fields of Green is going to be busy."

They both returned his smile. "Thanks, David," Destiny said.

As they walked out of the conference room Faith inhaled deeply as they walked by Gloria. "Ah," she said. "I love the smell of dirt and sweat, don't you, babe?"

"It smells like money," Destiny replied, giving Gloria a sarcastic smile.

They walked out of the building and Faith stole a glance at Destiny. "We won the bid," she said, her eyes widening. "Be cool," she mumbled.

Destiny nodded as their steps quickened. "We won!" she squealed quietly. "Stay cool, stay cool."

When they reached the front of the truck, Faith turned to face Destiny. "We won the bid!" she yelled, jumping into Destiny's arms.

They hugged each other tightly as they bounced up and down.

"We have to celebrate," Faith said once they got back into the truck.

"Let's have all our people meet at your shop," Destiny said, taking out her phone. "I'll text Monica to give everyone the location and to lock up."

"I'm texting Amy and Mark to tell them we'll be there soon. We've got to stop by the store and buy a bunch of beer."

Destiny waited for Faith to put down her phone. "We did it, babe," she said, leaning over the console. Their lips met in a fierce yet happy kiss.

"I love you so much," Faith said, breathing heavily.

"You've made me so happy," Destiny said with tears in her eyes. "I get to do all of this with you! You're the love of my life, my soulmate, my everything, and we're doing this together."

Faith chuckled. "That's some list."

"I didn't want to leave anything out."

"You are my destiny," Faith said softly.

Destiny could see tears in Faith's eyes. She leaned in and their lips met in a poignant kiss full of emotion, redemption, and love.

She slowly pulled away and smiled. "I can't wait to get you home."

"Mmm," Faith murmured, raising one eyebrow. "We're getting lucky tonight."

Destiny laughed and buckled her seatbelt. "We already are."

They stopped by the store and bought beer, two bottles of champagne, and a few snacks for their impromptu celebration.

"Wow," Faith said, when her shop came into view. "My parking lot is almost full."

Destiny looked over at Faith and grinned. "Those are my three trucks and Monica's car."

"I love it," Faith said.

"Fields of Green," Destiny said softly. "Is this a dream coming true?"

"Oh, babe." Faith reached for her hand. "We have a lot of dreams that are going to come true."

Destiny didn't know her heart could feel this full. Tears stung her eyes once again.

Faith glanced over at her and stopped the truck before she pulled around to the back of the building. "It's okay, baby. I feel it, too."

Destiny unbuckled her seat belt, leaned over, and embraced Faith. "I love you," she said, pulling back and kissing Faith softly.

"I love you."

Destiny nodded and sat back in her seat as Faith put the truck in gear and pulled around to the back of the building. She backed the truck into the shop where several people were standing around talking.

Faith lowered the tailgate and set the beer down while Destiny brought the champagne and cups with her.

"Let me help," Monica said, walking up from the office.

Once everything was laid out on the tailgate, Destiny gazed around the shop. "Is everyone here?"

"I think so," Amy said. "I locked the front door. Give us the news."

Destiny glanced at Faith and nodded.

"Has everyone introduced themselves?" Faith asked. "I know I haven't met all of Destiny's workers, but I will."

"Monica and I introduced everyone," Mark said.

"Great." Faith looked over at Destiny and smiled. "You are all aware that Destiny and I joined forces and bid on a big project." She paused. "Yeah, well..." she hesitated.

"We won!" Destiny yelled, popping the cork on one of the bottles of champagne.

The crowd cheered as Faith opened the other bottle. Cups were passed around and Destiny and Faith made their way around the space until everyone had a glass.

"You go first," Faith said.

Destiny raised her glass. "We have a new company name for this project. Here's to Fields of Green."

Their co-workers cheered and everyone sipped.

Faith raised her glass. "To dreams coming true." Destiny clinked her glass to Faith's and they both drank.

"Let's celebrate!" Mark said, opening the cases of beer.

"Congrats," Amy said, walking over to where Destiny and Faith stood away from the crowd.

"We celebrate today, but the big work is about to begin," Faith said.

"We can do it," Monica said, joining them. "I guess this is the end of landscape wars."

Destiny laughed. "Well…" She looked over at Faith.

"Maybe landscape wars are alive and well," Faith said. "We definitely have an enemy."

"Let me guess," Amy said. "Gloria."

"I really hope we've seen the last of her," Destiny said. "But I doubt it."

"We're in the big time now," Faith said playfully. "We can handle her."

Everyone laughed as the party began. Destiny and Faith met the workers they didn't know from each of their respective companies as they made their way through the crowd.

"Uh, hey," Faith said, getting everyone's attention. "I know my teams are aware that it's my birthday tomorrow and we're having a party."

Faith's workers whooped and hollered.

"I hope all of you will join us. There's going to be karaoke and all kinds of fun. Don't worry, Destiny is in charge. She's the fun one."

There were several chuckles and Faith continued. "I want to get to know the workers from The Green Thumb," she said. "I hear they have a fantastic boss."

Destiny grinned as Faith put her arm around her.

"Y'all have fun," Destiny said. "We'll have plenty to do on Monday, but now let's celebrate."

* * *

Destiny could feel Faith next to her and smiled. Her eyes fluttered open and she saw the sweetest sight. Faith's face was relaxed in sleep. The corners of her mouth were almost turned up in a smile.

Destiny was on her side with her arm resting on Faith's stomach. She thought back to last night and the celebration after they won the bid. All of their workers came together and seemed to get along. It was a good start.

After everyone left they ordered food, like they had done most Friday nights, and the dinner conversation revolved around the project. They bounced around ideas of which teams should work on what parts of the project, but they stopped to take in the sunset together.

Destiny meant what she said to Faith in the emotional moments after they'd won the bid. Faith was everything to her and they had much to look forward to.

She smiled as she gazed at Faith again. They had celebrated together long into the night, but why not start the day the way yesterday had ended. "Let's make your birthday as special as you are," she whispered.

Destiny slowly moved over Faith and kissed between her breasts. She softly feathered kisses down Faith's stomach as she started to stir.

"Mmm," Faith murmured, her voice heavy with sleep.

Destiny slowly ran her tongue from hip to hip across Faith's lower abs. She knew this was one way to drive Faith wild.

"Oh!" Faith exclaimed. Her hand reached for Destiny and Faith's fingers tangled in her hair.

Destiny continued to kiss lower and smiled as Faith spread her legs wider. She didn't waste any time and ran her tongue from Faith's entrance through her folds and around her clit. "My, oh my," Destiny murmured. "Someone is wet."

Faith moaned, raising her hips.

Destiny continued to explore Faith's wetness with her

tongue. It didn't take long for her to wake up and be present in the moment.

"Oh God, babe," Faith groaned.

Destiny loved these quiet moans and groans almost as much as she loved Faith. At times being together again felt surreal, but Destiny knew how it felt to be without Faith. There was no way she would ever let that happen again.

Another more intense moan from Faith brought Destiny back to this moment. She could hear and feel Faith's now labored breathing and slipped one arm under Faith's leg, reaching for her hand splayed on the bed. Their fingers intertwined and Destiny squeezed Faith's hand as she sucked Faith into her mouth.

Destiny's tongue moved with purpose and brought Faith over the edge. Quick gasps of breath were the only noise in the room until Faith's hips fell back on the bed.

Destiny raised her head and looked into Faith's euphoric face. "Happy birthday, baby."

"God!" Faith groaned loudly. She chuckled as Destiny rested her head on Faith's stomach.

"Good morning," Faith finally said in an almost normal voice.

"Mmm," Destiny murmured. "It is."

"Was that my birthday present?"

Destiny raised up and settled next to Faith, propping her head on her hand. She lazily rested her leg over Faith's and smiled at her. "That was just the start of your birthday."

"It's already the best birthday ever because I woke up with you, well, with you between my legs." Faith giggled.

"I hope that was all right," Destiny said. "If you haven't noticed, I'm having trouble keeping my hands off of you... and my mouth."

"I know the perfect birthday gift you could give me," Faith said with raised eyebrows.

"Oh yeah?" Destiny grinned. "What's that?"

"Move in with me," Faith said with a serious face.

Destiny was not expecting that. Her eyebrows flew up her forehead. "Really?"

Faith nodded. "Move in with me, Des. You're here most of the time anyway."

"I love being here with you," Destiny said. A smile grew on her face. "Do you think the tiny house is big enough for both of us?"

"We can live wherever you want," Faith said. "I just don't want to be without you ever again."

Destiny closed her eyes, barely able to contain her excitement. She opened them and grinned at Faith. "I'd love to move in here with you!"

Faith grabbed Destiny's face and kissed her hard. "Now that's a birthday present. Woo hoo!" she yelled at the ceiling.

Destiny laughed at her enthusiasm. "I do have an actual birthday present for you, but I'm not giving it to you until tomorrow."

"Okay," Faith said, nodding. "Is this part of why you asked to spend tonight with me? Because you had something special for me the next day?"

"That's right," Destiny said. "We have the party tonight, so your special gift has to wait until tomorrow."

"I have my special gift right here," Faith said, caressing Destiny's cheek.

"Okay, birthday girl." Destiny sat up. "What do you want for breakfast? I'm cooking and I made sure we have all of your favorites here."

"Hmm," Faith murmured, raising her brows. "I know

what I want first." She raised up, pushed Destiny down on the bed, and hopped on top of her.

Laughter filled the room, followed by heated kisses and more very pleased moans.

30

"I had so much fun last night," Faith said, reaching over and taking Destiny's hand. "Thank you for my birthday party."

"I think everyone had fun. Thank you for letting me make such a big deal out of your birthday. In case you haven't noticed. You're a very big deal to me."

Faith chuckled. "I'm beginning to get that idea."

"We may have a few singers between both of our companies," Destiny said as she drove out of Faith's parking lot.

"And our friends," Faith added. "Monica and Kim surprised me. They can sing."

"Did you see Bailey and Claire?" Destiny asked. "I didn't know they even knew one another."

"Now they get to work together and I think they are almost as happy about that as we are," Faith said.

Destiny pulled onto the Interstate and sped up.

"Are you going to tell me where we're going?" Faith asked.

"When I take our exit you're going to know where we're

going," Destiny said, "but you don't know what we're going to do."

"Okay, my mysterious girlfriend." Faith grinned and squeezed Destiny's hand. "I loved the song you sang for me last night. Will you sing it again?"

"Now?" Destiny asked, looking over at her.

"Why not?" She reached for Destiny's phone. "I know you have it in your music library."

"I have a playlist with songs for you," Destiny replied shyly.

Faith gasped. "You do?"

"I wasn't sure what song I wanted to sing to you for your birthday, so when I heard a song or remembered one I added it to the list."

"Babe," Faith said softly.

"Come on," Destiny said. "Don't you have songs that remind you of us? You could sing to me."

Faith smiled. "Yeah, I may have a favorite song or two about us."

Destiny took the Highway 71 exit towards Bastrop and Faith gasped again.

"Des!" she exclaimed. "Are you taking me to Lost Pines?"

Destiny laughed. "I knew you'd figure it out."

Faith giggled. "I can't wait to see the butterfly sanctuary. In the meantime, let's sing."

"Okay," Destiny said. "Did you remember the song I sang for you last night?"

"Of course I did," Faith said. "We heard it while watching TV. I can't remember what show, but I remember how it made us feel."

"It's an old song and I don't think anyone else had heard it until I sang it last night," Destiny said.

"But they loved it," Faith replied. "Here goes."

Music filled the truck and Destiny began to sing "How Glad I Am" by Nancy Wilson.

"My love has no beginning, my love has no end, no front or back and my love won't bend," Destiny sang. "I'm in the middle, lost in a spin loving you. And you don't know, you don't know, you don't know, how glad I am."

The music continued to play and Destiny looked over at Faith. "Sing with me."

Together they sang. "My love has no walls on either side, that makes my love wider than wide. I'm in the middle, and I can't hide loving you. And you don't know, you don't know, you don't know, how glad I am."

They sang together until the song ended. "That's our love," Faith said. "It may be an old song and the words are simple, but they're true."

"Okay, it's your turn," Destiny said. "What song are you going to sing for me?"

"Hmm, do I stay nostalgic or go current?" Faith scrolled through her phone. She chuckled and looked over at Destiny. "Okay, since we're talking about our love then I have to do this oldie but goldie because it's what you do to me."

The music began to play and Faith knew Destiny immediately recognized the song. "It's all true, but towards the end is the best part."

Faith began to sing "I Feel the Earth Move" by Carole King. The look on Destiny's face told Faith she loved the song and agreed with its sentiment.

"Here comes the good part," Faith said and sang along. "Ooh, darling, when you're near me and you tenderly call my name. I know that my emotions are something I just can't tame. I just got to have you baby."

Destiny joined in and sang to the end of the song.

"Thanks, babe," Faith said. "That was fun."

"Look at us doing new things," Destiny said.

Faith chuckled as Destiny exited the highway onto the road that led to the resort. "On the way back we'll do current songs."

"I have a few," Destiny said. "How long has it been since you've been out here?"

"Since we left Landscape Artists over three years ago," Faith replied.

"I'm sure it's changed."

"You did get us permission, right?" Faith asked.

"Yes, it's Sunday, so most of the guests are checking out," Destiny said. "They said it was fine to go through the sanctuary and we can walk down to the river if you'd like."

"I knew this was going to be the best birthday."

The Lost Pines resort was a place people could go to get away from city life. It was an oasis of sorts that offered a large pool with a lazy river winding around it, a golf course, tennis courts, spa, and several restaurants. It was built next to the Brazos River that offered trails down by the water.

The butterfly sanctuary was a garden constructed between two wings of the hotel. It featured a canopy of trees with tall native vines that made natural arches along the path made of pea gravel and wood chips. Flowering plants were all along the path that attracted butterflies passing through the region or native to the area. It felt like walking into a fairy land.

"Wow," Faith exclaimed as they walked up to the entrance. "I knew how we constructed it and hoped it would turn out, but I never dreamed it would grow and bloom..."

"Into this," Destiny finished.

Faith nodded and slipped her hand into Destiny's. "It's better than I imagined."

They walked along the path and immersed themselves, letting the garden tantalize their senses. There were beautiful and unusual plants to see and their noses were treated to exotic and sweet scents. As they walked deeper into the garden the world fell away and they were just two people, in love, experiencing something they had created together.

"Let's sit," Destiny said when they came to a bench.

"The bench even blends in with the foliage," Faith said. "I wasn't too sure when we first put it here."

"Things had to grow around it, but it fits," Destiny said.

"Maybe that's what we did," Faith said, turning to Destiny. "We had to grow, but we fit now. We're not perfect, but—"

"We're perfect together," Destiny said. She reached into the bag slung across her shoulder and pulled out a small box with a bow on it.

Faith's eyes widened and she looked from the box to Destiny's eyes. "Uh, babe..."

Destiny grinned. "It's not that kind of ring, but...open it."

Faith chuckled. "What have you done?" She untied the bow and opened the box to reveal a silver band. "Oh, babe, it's beautiful."

"I wanted to get you something you could wear that would remind you of us, but wouldn't get in the way of your work," Destiny explained. "Do you see how the band widens then raises into a little orb?"

Faith nodded.

"It's a droplet," Destiny said. "It can be a little droplet of joy you felt that day or a little droplet of our love, whatever you want it to be."

"When I look down at it or feel it, I'll think of our love wrapped around me," Faith said. "Put it on me."

Destiny slid the ring onto Faith's finger and she held it out to admire it. "I love it, baby." Faith leaned in and cupped the side of Destiny's face. "Thank you." She pressed her lips to Destiny's and felt truly loved. She knew Destiny's love came with no conditions, no agenda; she loved Faith and wanted to live this life together. This might be the most perfect moment of love Faith had ever felt. Here, immersed in this beautiful place they'd created with their own hands, expressing their love in a sweet kiss and their hearts beating as one.

Faith pulled away and looked into Destiny's eyes. "Do you feel it?"

Destiny nodded. "Instead of a droplet, it's a moment."

Faith nodded. *Destiny felt it too!*

They stared at each other, locked in this sweet moment.

"Uh, I've been thinking about something," Faith said.

Destiny raised her eyes and waited.

"Are you sure you don't mind living in the tiny house behind the shop?" Faith asked. "We don't have much of a view." She raised her hand and swept in front of them, gesturing to the beauty.

"I don't care where we live as long as I'm with you," Destiny said.

Faith smiled. "I had a feeling you'd say something like that. We're going to be busy with the project, but I was thinking after that..." Faith trailed off.

"After that?"

"We could look for a bigger place and make Fields of Green a reality, not just a one project thing," Faith said. "We could combine Lush Fields and The Green Thumb."

Destiny smiled. "I'm listening."

Faith shrugged. "We could move the tiny house somewhere that isn't also our business."

"And get a bigger building and yard that would hold all of our equipment and inventory," Destiny added.

Faith nodded, a hopeful look on her face.

"We'd be doing this like we used to talk about?"

"Only better," Faith said, "our businesses have grown, but so have we. I'm a different person, Des. Thank God you still love me."

"You're not an altogether different person," Destiny said. "You're the person I've always had faith in."

Faith could see the twinkle in her eyes. "I'm glad you did, but what's different is that I have faith in myself now, too."

"And you can trust your feelings, babe," Destiny said. "We have so much love and we have to let it make us strong, especially when the doubts creep in."

Faith nodded. "I know things aren't always going to be like this. We'll have challenges, but we have to make room for the happiness."

"I feel like that's what we've been doing," Destiny said. "We put the past behind us. No matter how it happened, we're together now and that's what's important."

"I know what it feels like to be without you and I never want to feel that again. I trust you. I'm not afraid to tell you what's in my heart because I know you won't leave me."

"I'm never letting you go," Destiny said.

"You don't have to because I'm holding on." Faith smiled and leaned in for a gentle kiss. "Let's sit here a little longer then walk down to the river."

"Whatever you want, birthday girl."

"You've made it hard on yourself, babe," Faith said with a playful grin.

"I have?"

"Yep." Faith nodded. "You'll be trying to top this next year on my birthday and I don't know how you can do that."

"You let me worry about it." Destiny put her arm around Faith's shoulders and they sat back on the bench, watching the butterflies, surrounded by their love.

31

The contract was signed and the Fields of Green work crews began preparing the soil around the buildings. While the crews were at the site Destiny and Faith were busy fulfilling their maintenance contracts by mowing and trimming. They stopped in from time to time to be sure the work was progressing and to bring other supplies when needed.

Once the crews had the soil turned and ready for planting, the shrubs and other plants would be delivered along with the material used to create borders around the gardens.

Everything was progressing according to plan. Destiny gave notice at the apartment and moved some of her things to Faith's while storing the rest at her shop. When the project was completed they were going to go through Destiny's stuff and make piles to keep, donate, and throw away.

Destiny was looking forward to the process because she loved living with Faith at the tiny house. She quickly realized she didn't need as much stuff as she thought.

They spent their days working together and making sure

Until We Weren't:

the project was on schedule while also ensuring their other accounts were up to date. In the evenings they would watch the sunset together and recharge for the next day. They thought of that time as their little piece of heaven.

Then it started to rain.

"This is the fourth day in a row," Destiny said, looking out over the mud puddles that surrounded the three buildings.

"It's okay, Des," Faith said, reaching over and squeezing her shoulder. "We've found the places we need to put in drains so water doesn't stand in the beds."

"We figured that out the first day." Destiny sighed. "If this keeps up there's no way we'll finish on time."

"Babe," Faith said. "This isn't the first time a project has been delayed. As soon as things begin to dry out we'll catch up."

Destiny sighed again and continued to stare out the front of the truck.

"Have a little faith," Faith added with a grin.

Destiny looked over at her and smirked then a small smile appeared on her face. "I have you."

"Yes you do," Faith replied. "This reminds me of when we first met." She smiled, raising her eyebrows. "Remember?"

"I remember a muddy woman on her first day of work with the cutest smile who my co-worker wouldn't let in their truck," Destiny said.

"Lucky for me, we were working at your apartment complex."

"And lucky for me, Jonas was being an asshole," Destiny replied.

"I know," Faith said. "I still think he was trying to make sure I knew he was the boss."

"That's why I rescued you and got you added to my crew," Destiny said.

"Oh and here I thought it was because you wanted to work with me." Faith winked at her.

"I hadn't officially met you, but I let you into my apartment so you could shower and I even gave you a shirt to wear since yours was so muddy."

"You were making your move from the start," Faith teased.

Destiny chuckled and glanced over at her. "You were muddy because you fixed the leak he made by breaking a sprinkler head," Destiny added. "I remember that."

"Yeah, I think he was testing me," Faith said.

Destiny smiled at Faith as the memory flashed before her eyes. "You had a smear of mud right here." She reached over and ran her thumb across Faith's cheek.

"You did the same thing back then." Faith smiled.

Destiny's face softened as love fluttered in her chest. "I'm so glad we found each other." She leaned over and pressed her lips to Faith's in a sweet kiss.

"We can't do anything here until the rain stops," Faith said with her hand on Destiny's cheek. "What do you say we go back to the office? No one's there."

Destiny smiled. "Now who's making moves." She put the truck in gear and stepped on the gas, quickly pulling away from the site.

Faith giggled and Destiny reached for her hand. *Let it rain; I've got Faith.*

* * *

A couple days later, the rain stopped, the mud dried up, and the teams began to plant. Just as Faith said, they caught up and were set to have the project completed right on time.

"Let's swing by the site before we go home," Faith said to Destiny as she started the truck.

"Okay." Destiny sniffed her shirt. "Damn, babe. I smell horrible."

Faith chuckled. "It's okay," she said. "I can't smell you over the odor coming from me."

"Tiny shower that's not so tiny," Destiny said, grinning at Faith, "here we come."

Faith laughed and in no time pulled into the site. The landscaping was taking shape. There were trees and shrubs already planted along with a few flowering plants.

"Hey," Mark said, waving at them. "We need more yellow bell shrubs."

"Abel has at least twenty more waiting for us at the nursery," Destiny said. "We were running out of room at the shop."

"We'll go get them and bring them here in the morning," Faith said.

"Thanks," Mark said.

"Anything else?"

"We may need more of those mini pepper plants over by the rock cairn," he replied. "Let me see how it goes then we can always pick up a few more if needed."

"Okay," Faith said. "We'll see you in the morning."

"I'll call Abel and tell him we're on the way," Destiny said.

"I guess our shower will have to wait." Faith glanced over at Destiny with a wink.

Destiny gave Faith a sexy smile. "I hope this honeymoon thing never ends—oh hey, Abel," she said into the phone, her eyes widening.

Faith laughed and could hear Abel say something then laugh through the phone.

"We're on our way to pick up the rest of the esperanzas," Destiny said. She listened for a moment and ended the call.

"Let me guess," Faith said. "He wanted to know when we got married."

Destiny chuckled. "Yep."

Faith exited the interstate and turned down onto the street where Abel's nursery was located. "Is there anything else we need? Oh, we should pick up something for Mrs. Baker," she said. "She needs a new flower next to her favorite bench."

"Let's get something pink," Destiny said. "She loves bright colors."

Faith pulled in parallel to the loading area. She was pulling a trailer with a mower and other equipment on it, but there was room for the shrubs as well.

When they got out of the truck Abel hurried to meet them.

"We have a problem," Abel said. "One of my workers sold your esperanzas. I've called around and there are none in Austin or the surrounding area."

"You're kidding," Faith said. "They're not uncommon. I'm surprised."

"The person who bought them put one over on my worker," Abel explained. "He's new. I explained to everyone that the yellow bells were already sold and whoever this was convinced him that esperanzas weren't yellow bells."

"Isn't it on the tag?" Destiny said.

Abel shrugged. "I'll keep trying to find you replacements. Would anything else work?"

"Not really," Faith said. "We'd have to change out the others."

Until We Weren't:

"Hmm." Destiny took out her phone and pulled up a website. "Would you mind if we talked to your worker? I want to show him a picture."

"Sure," Abel replied. "I'll be right back."

"What are you thinking, babe?" Faith asked.

"I think Gloria came and bought the plants," Destiny said.

"Oh, come on," Faith said. "How would she know we're using them?"

"As you said, they're not uncommon. What better way to get back at us than to delay the project past its completion date?"

Faith furrowed her brow. "That seems extreme."

Destiny stared at her and cleared her throat. "Excuse me," she said. "Look at what she did to us three years ago."

Before Faith could reply, the worker walked up with Abel. After a short conversation, Destiny's theory was proven correct. Gloria had purchased the shrubs.

"That's why there's not any in the area," Destiny said. "Damn! I wonder what she's going to do with them."

"Who cares!" Abel exclaimed. "You're the ones that need them."

"I have an idea," Faith said. "Abel, can you check further away, maybe as far south as San Antonio?"

"Sure, let me make a couple of calls," he said. "I'll be right back."

"We can go pick them up and still make the deadline," Faith said.

"That's a great idea, but when do we have time?" Destiny asked. "We're already behind with our other accounts and we need every person at the site."

Faith narrowed her eyes then smiled. "I know someone who will bring them to us."

"Who?"

"Chase!" Faith exclaimed.

"You think my brother would bring us twenty yellow bells?"

"He would if I asked," Faith said with a cocky smile. "He loves me."

Destiny chuckled. "You're not wrong."

"He'd do it for you, too," Faith said.

Abel came back and had located enough of the plants at a nursery in San Antonio. Destiny got on the phone and called Chase. He eagerly agreed to pick up the plants and drive them the hour and a half to Austin in the morning.

Once they were back in the truck and Faith had them headed towards home, she glanced at Destiny and smiled. "Look at us, solving problems," she said.

"Together," Destiny said, reaching for her hand.

"What are we going to do about Gloria?" Faith asked. She knew Destiny wanted revenge from the video and with this latest round of disruption, Faith was afraid it would fuel that even more.

"We're going to keep solving the problems she throws at us," Destiny said. "The easiest way to get revenge is to live happily ever after."

Faith widened her eyes and stared over at Destiny. "Who are you and what did you do with my girlfriend?"

Destiny chuckled. "Gloria can't hurt us. That's what you told me when we walked out of that conference room. I'm not going to waste any of my energy even thinking about her when I can spend it doing things I love," she said. "Like taking a shower with you."

Faith gave Destiny the biggest smile. Gloria might still try to make things hard for them, but she also had a lot of yellow bell shrubs to do something with and that wouldn't be easy.

She pulled up to the tiny house and took Destiny's hand as she walked around the truck.

"I hope that's the last problem we have to solve today," Destiny said.

Faith opened the front door pulling Destiny through it. "Your only problem is deciding what you want to have for dinner." She captured Destiny's lips in a hungry kiss as she pulled her shirt over her head.

"Who needs dinner," Destiny mumbled, taking her sports bra off and shimmying out of her shorts.

Faith laughed, undressing as she walked through the kitchen to the bathroom. She reached into the shower and turned the water on, letting it warm up. Destiny's arms wrapped around Faith from behind. Faith moaned, leaning back against her. "Be careful where your lips touch me. All you'll taste is dirt and sweat."

"I don't care," Destiny said, pushing them under the water.

Faith turned in Destiny's arms and kissed her with passion and desire. How quickly Destiny could light a fire inside her. "I love you," she said breathlessly.

Faith reached for the body wash and poured a generous amount in her hand. She rubbed her hands together and placed them on Destiny's shoulders. Her hands slid down Destiny's arms then back up and around her neck. She smiled and looked into Destiny's eyes. They were dark with desire, but were also shining with love.

Faith ran her hands down Destiny's chest and cupped her breasts. Her nipples were already hard and Faith gave them a gentle pinch.

"You look at my body with such wonder," Destiny said. "Can you see how much I love and want your touch?"

"Can you feel how much I love you in each touch?" Faith knew the answer to her question and let her hand slide lower until she cupped Destiny's sex.

Destiny moaned and widened her legs as she leaned against the shower wall.

Faith slowly ran her fingers through Destiny's slick folds, keeping her eyes on Destiny's.

"Babe," Destiny moaned, her eyes fluttering closed.

Faith slowly pushed one finger then another inside Destiny and felt her muscles almost relax with relief. Destiny's hands were on her shoulders holding on and Faith wasn't about to make her wait.

She began a slow rhythm to the music of Destiny's moans. Faith could feel Destiny's fingers squeezing her shoulders as she got closer to the edge. "Let me see your beautiful eyes, babe," Faith whispered. She wanted Destiny to see her love as the orgasm swept through her body.

Faith pushed in deeper one more time and curled her fingers. She saw the flash of pleasure light up Destiny's eyes as her fingers dug into Faith's shoulders.

"Good God, babe," Destiny groaned, resting her head against the shower wall.

Faith kissed Destiny's neck and giggled. "Oh, how I love to hear you make that sound."

"Mmm," Destiny mumbled. "It's my heart talking to you."

Faith pulled back and kissed Destiny softly. Their hearts had been talking all along. That's why they were together now and would be from now on.

32

Faith and Destiny had split up that morning, each meeting with their own customers. They planned to go rock hunting this afternoon. Anytime they came across a rock that would be suitable for their purpose in the rock garden they grabbed it. But now they needed flat smaller rocks that could be stacked in creative formations.

The landscaping around the main building was almost complete and the garden with the fountain only needed mulch added to the flower bed floor. Everything was coming together.

Faith was on her way back from the Hutto housing development to pick up Destiny when a *For Sale* sign caught her eye. It was in front of a commercial building with a fenced area around the perimeter. She quickly exited the highway and pulled into the parking lot in front of the building.

"This might work," she mumbled. She pulled up to the sign and took a picture so she'd have the contact information for the realtor, then continued on her way.

. . .

"Hi, honey." Destiny greeted Faith as soon as she walked into the office.

Faith smiled, leaned up, and kissed Destiny on the lips. "Hey, babe."

"I've gotten used to working with you every morning," Destiny said, kissing Faith back. "I missed you."

Faith chuckled. "We've got it bad."

"Yes, you do!" Monica exclaimed from her desk. "But it's cute," she added, wrinkling her nose. "I've seen a change in both of you. Kim and I were talking the other day, we thought you were perfect for each other before, but things happened. Don't mess this up. We were right from the get-go."

"We're not going to mess this up," Destiny said.

"You mean, *I'm* not going to mess this up," Faith stated.

"Let it go, Faith," Monica said. "What happened wasn't your fault."

"It doesn't matter because we've made it through," Faith said, putting her arm around Destiny's waist.

Destiny smirked. "She says that because she's worried I'm planning a revenge plot to get Gloria back."

Faith smiled. "We're stronger and closer than ever."

"Yes we are," Destiny said. "Our best revenge is living happily ever after."

"Would you listen to that," Monica said. "I almost believe you."

Faith chuckled. "We'd better get going. I have something to show you before our rock hunt."

"I'm all yours," Destiny said.

"Lucky me." Faith took Destiny's hand and led them to the door. "See you later, Monica."

"Bye, y'all."

"So what do you have to show me?" Destiny asked.

Faith left the shop and drove them back towards the building that was for sale. "I came across a place that might be perfect for Fields of Green," she said, glancing over at Destiny.

"Oh really?"

"Come on," Faith said. "I know you've thought about combining our businesses into one. It's our dream, remember?"

"Of course I've thought about it," Destiny replied. "I'm always thinking about our dream."

Faith smiled and reached for Destiny's hand. "I know we've been busy and stretched thin. We agreed to get the project done before we did anything else. But..."

"I'm getting the idea you like this place," Destiny said.

"I haven't really looked at it," Faith replied. "I wanted you to see it with me." She squeezed Destiny's hand. "We're at our best when we're together."

Destiny grinned. "We are one helluva team. Gloria is finding that out."

Faith raised her brows and glanced over at Destiny.

"I didn't do anything," Destiny said, holding up her hand. "I heard she was trying to sell those shrubs to anyone who would take them."

Faith chuckled. "She'll leave us alone now that we've cost her money. She's all about the profit."

"Still..."

"Un huh," Faith said warily. "We are not the revenge type of people."

"Well," Destiny said, drawing the word out.

"Des."

"I'm kidding, babe." Destiny laughed. "I was serious about living happily ever after."

Faith smiled. "That's what we're doing." Faith pulled off

the highway and into the parking lot of the building. "It looks big enough," she said. She drove around to the back of the building and they got out of the truck.

"Those bay doors in the back will open up into the shop," Destiny said.

"We could fit all of our equipment inside," Faith said.

Destiny stopped and scanned the property from one end to the other. "Where do you want to put the tiny house?"

"Well," Faith said, walking over and standing next to her. "Do you see how the property borders that residential area?"

Destiny nodded as she looked to her left.

Faith rested her hand on Destiny's shoulder. "I thought we might build a house over at the property line. We'd be away from the business, but still nearby."

Destiny looked at Faith and furrowed her brow. "You want to move out of the tiny house?"

Faith smiled. "Someday."

Destiny looked back over to where Faith envisioned the house.

"Do you remember why we stayed in the apartment after I moved in instead of getting a house together?"

"Yeah," Destiny replied. "We didn't want to come home and work in our own yard after working in other people's yards all day."

"What if we built the house so we could have our own private garden in the back?" Faith said. "Designed by us."

Destiny looked over at her and Faith could see the delight shining in her eyes.

"I like that idea," Destiny said. "Once we get it the way we want it then there wouldn't be much maintenance to it. All we'd have to do is enjoy it."

"Together," Faith added.

Until We Weren't:

"You've been thinking about this haven't you?" Destiny said, turning to face Faith.

"I couldn't help dreaming, babe. We've jumped into this project together and even though there have been struggles, we've made it through them together. Just like we're doing with our lives."

"What about the tiny house?" Destiny asked. "You know I love it."

Faith nodded and smiled. "We won't be able to build a house for some time. That's our future. We'll move the tiny house over here and keep living in it until we're ready for the rest."

Destiny smiled. "When did you become such a thinker and planner? That was my thing."

Faith chuckled. "I had to when you became so creative, suggesting things like rock gardens with cairns."

Destiny laughed. "We really have changed."

"I don't think so," Faith said, putting her arms around Destiny's neck. "We've become more open and with that all kinds of ideas and possibilities can flow."

"God, I love you," Destiny said.

Faith was smiling when Destiny's lips crashed into hers. She expected Destiny to be open to the idea, but her excitement was suddenly intoxicating. The intensity and passion with how their lips and tongues melded together left Faith breathless.

"Mmmm," Faith mumbled. "We have to go find rocks, but we're going to continue this later."

Destiny smiled. "I'm going to have Monica call and find out the info on the property while we gather rocks. Then we can discuss what she finds out tonight."

"I'll text her," Faith said. "I have the realtor's info."

"You were pretty sure of yourself," Destiny said.

"I was sure of us," Faith replied, sending the text. She put her phone back in her pocket and looked up at Destiny. "I could see us here."

"Don't get too far ahead," Destiny warned. "Let's see if we can afford it."

Faith nodded. "Come on, babe. We have rocks waiting for us." She took Destiny's hand and they walked back to the truck. "I'm going to build you a special cairn. You'll see."

Later that night Faith was still awake with Destiny pressed into her side. Her rhythmic breathing and quiet snore made Faith smile. They had an appointment with the realtor to tour the property tomorrow. She was confident they could make it work by combining their companies, consolidating their equipment, and moving into one place.

The thought of their dream becoming a reality made it hard for Faith to fall asleep. She'd been thinking about all they'd been through and how they'd gotten to this point.

When they were together before, Faith always had a sliver of doubt living in the back of her mind. It would remind her from time to time that she couldn't trust anyone. Sooner or later the people she loved always let her down. Her love for Destiny was stronger than this ingrained doubt and she could usually push it away when it decided to come to the surface.

Living with something that picked away at the scars around her heart was exhausting. That's why the video of Gloria had devastated her so. But the night the truth came out in that little shack, Faith's mistrust and doubt disappeared. All along her heart knew she could trust Destiny and it won that night.

It crushed her to know she'd hurt Destiny so badly, but it

also made her realize she could trust her heart. Since then her heart had been opened to imagine and believe the dreams they shared could really come true.

Faith wondered if Destiny had extinguished all her doubts. A smile grew on her face and she suddenly had an idea of exactly how to bury any doubts once and for all. She knew what to do and exactly where to do it.

She held Destiny a little tighter and kissed her forehead. Faith closed her eyes. There were nothing but sweet dreams in this bedroom tonight.

* * *

Faith and Destiny explained to the realtor what they were trying to accomplish and he put together a deal to sell both of their properties while they made an offer on the building. The sellers accepted their bid and the realtor went to work selling their properties while they went through the closing process on the new home for Fields of Green.

They were putting the final touches on the flower beds of the massive project when Faith walked over to where Destiny was working in the rock garden. "Hey, babe," Faith said. "The fountain is working beautifully. It's better than I imagined."

"Oh, good, I'm finishing up a little design. What do you think?"

Faith looked over at the stacked rocks and smiled. "That looks great. Are we going to change the design when we mow and weed every week?"

"Of course," Destiny replied. "We have to keep it fresh."

"Maybe we should have rocks at the shop to practice with," Faith said. "Some of these designs are interesting, but hard to do."

Destiny stacked the last rock and looked up at Faith. "That's a great idea. It could be a stress reliever for us and our teams, too."

Faith tilted her head. "I don't know about that," she said warily. "They might want to throw the rocks at us instead of stacking them."

Destiny laughed. "You have a point." She got to her feet and looked around the garden. "I think it's finished."

"I'd like to walk around all three buildings one more time and be sure everything is as perfect as we can make it," Faith said.

"Okay."

"There are a couple of plants that don't look good at the back of the main building," Faith said. "Mark is going to change them out tomorrow and finish up with the mulch."

"We can do our final walk-through after that," Destiny said.

"How about we do it at sunset?" Faith's heart began to speed up at the thought of what she had planned tomorrow for Destiny. Once the idea came to her she'd asked Mark, Amy, and Monica to help her with the surprise.

"At sunset?" Destiny said, turning to Faith.

"Yeah," Faith said. "We love to watch the sunset together. Let's do it here."

"It can be our farewell to a job well done," Destiny said.

"Yep, we'll turn it over to the project manager the next day."

"You've got a date, babe." Destiny grinned and gave Faith a quick kiss.

Oh, this is going to be so much more than a date, my love.

33

Destiny opened her eyes and immediately knew it was going to be a great day. She'd woken up a couple of times throughout the night with Faith's arms around her and now her gentle breathing whispered in Destiny's ear.

Today they would do their final walk-through on the biggest project of both of their lives. It was easy to see that it was a success. They had imagined it, created it, planned it, and made it come to life, together. Faith had come across a building with land that was perfect to start their new company. They could afford it and all that was left to do was sign the papers and move their stuff.

The hurt and pain from the last three years of being apart was gone. They had found their way back to each other, learned the truth of their breakup, and recognized they both had issues, but wanted to grow together. Today, they were on the verge of realizing their biggest professional dream.

Destiny could tell Faith now trusted her in the way she couldn't when they were first together. Even though breaking up had broken Destiny's heart, Faith had put it back together. On top of that, Faith could now trust her own heart and that was invaluable. Destiny had watched Faith blossom into the person she always knew she could be.

Destiny had been trying to think of a way to show Faith that all the doubts between them were gone and that they should be living their lives together. An idea came to her and she smiled, looked over at Faith's peaceful face, and thought of who she needed to see to get this right.

Destiny gently kissed Faith's cheek and eased out of bed. She got to the bedroom door and stopped when she heard Faith's sleepy voice.

"Where are you going?" Faith groaned.

"To make you breakfast," Destiny said. "You can sleep a little longer." She grinned at Faith, who was looking at her. "I'd give you a kiss, but I know you're going to drag me back into that bed."

Faith chuckled. "So right."

Destiny went about making breakfast while Faith showered. They both planned to work at the site that morning, have lunch, then check in with other customers that afternoon. They would meet back at the site for the final walk-through later in the day.

The morning flew by while Destiny finished up in the rock garden. She'd made a circular design of rocks to show Faith that evening. For her it symbolized their lives together. The circle may have once been broken, but they put it back together and it was stronger than ever.

She walked over to the other garden where Faith was adjusting the fountain and whistled. "That looks beautiful, babe."

"Thanks," Faith replied, turning around to face her. "Is it time for lunch already?"

Until We Weren't:

"Yep," Destiny replied.

They sat down on the bench and Destiny handed her the lunch she'd packed for them this morning.

"Are you okay?" Faith asked, furrowing her brow.

Destiny looked up and smiled. "Yeah, why?"

"I don't know," Faith replied. "You seem distracted."

"I'm just looking forward to this evening," Destiny said. "Aren't you excited?"

"You have no idea." Faith grinned.

They finished lunch and Destiny kissed Faith goodbye. She got in her truck and drove to the one person who knew Faith as well as she did.

"What a nice surprise," Mrs. Baker said as Destiny sat down beside her. "I thought you'd be busy finishing up your big thing."

Destiny chuckled. "I was there all morning. Let me show you." She took out her phone and showed Mrs. Baker pictures of the gardens and the landscaping around the main building.

"That's an interesting design," Mrs. Baker commented when Destiny showed her the rock cairn.

"I did it for Faith," Destiny replied.

Mrs. Baker smiled. "She'll love it."

Destiny nodded and put her phone down. She looked at Mrs. Baker and took a deep breath.

"Okay," Mrs. Baker said. "Are you going to tell me why you're really here?"

Destiny's eyes widened and surprise covered her face.

"I can tell when something is on your mind and you need to talk," Mrs. Baker said.

Destiny nodded. "You're the closest thing to family that Faith has," she began. "My family loves her and we have good friends, but her family let her down over and over. She considers you her family."

"She's my family, too, and so are you," Mrs. Baker said, putting her hand over Destiny's.

"Our trust issues ran deep, but together we have rebuilt our relationship and become stronger. We are closer than we've ever been. On this big day when we finish this project and start our dream of working together, I want to take away any doubt that Faith could possibly have left that we're supposed to be together."

"Okay," Mrs. Baker said.

"After we do the final walk-through this evening, I want us to go back to the tiny house," Destiny said. She reached into her pocket and pulled out a ring. "I'm going to propose to her."

"Oh!" Mrs. Baker exclaimed.

"First, as Faith's family, would you give us your blessing?" Destiny asked.

Mrs. Baker laughed boisterously. "Give you my blessing! I've been trying to get you two back together this entire time. Of course you have my blessing!"

Destiny laughed and put her arms around the older woman. She pulled back to show Mrs. Baker the ring. "Do you think she'll like it?"

Mrs. Baker had tears in her eyes. "She considers that ring you gave her for her birthday almost like a wedding ring. I don't know if you've noticed how she plays with it on her finger. When she's happy or needs a little strength, she touches it or twirls it."

Destiny nodded. "I've noticed and it melts my heart."

"I think she will love this," Mrs. Baker stated. "When do you plan to pop the question?"

"Well, I could do it this evening when we walk through

her garden with the fountain or when I show her the rock cairn design," Destiny said. "But we've been our happiest at the tiny house, especially on her front porch where we talked. That's when I knew we had a future."

"I think the tiny house is the right place," Mrs. Baker said with a grin.

Destiny noticed a twinkle in Mrs. Baker's eye. "Is there something else you need to tell me?"

"Nope," Mrs. Baker said. "Wait, will you call me when it's done?"

Destiny gave her a big smile. "Of course we will."

She gave Mrs. Baker another hug and couldn't wait until this evening.

* * *

Destiny picked Faith up at her shop and drove them to the site.

"Are you ready?" Destiny asked once she'd parked.

Faith gave her a big smile. "I'm more than ready."

Destiny chuckled. "Just wait until after we've done our walk-through," she mumbled as she got out of the truck.

"What?" Faith asked.

"I'm ready to see it finished," Destiny said. Her heart was beating faster than it should and she had a nervous flutter in her stomach. She was excited and also anxious about proposing, but when she looked over at Faith she noticed her fidgeting rather nervously. "Are you okay, babe?"

Faith smiled and held out her hand to Destiny. "I'm a big ball of anticipation."

"It's okay, darlin'," Destiny said, taking her hand. "We're in this together."

"I wouldn't want to be anywhere else or doing this with anyone else," Faith said earnestly.

"Are you trying to make me cry?" Destiny took Faith's other hand and faced her.

"No. I love you so much and this is such a big day. It's like we're walking into our future."

Destiny leaned down and kissed Faith softly. "A bright future with an abundance of happy days, just like this one."

Faith nodded. "Let's see what we created."

"Why don't we walk around the main building and circle over to the fountain," Destiny suggested.

They stopped here and there to smooth soil around a plant or spread wood shavings evenly around a tree.

"I know they are still finishing out offices inside, but it's peaceful out here," Destiny commented.

"Just like we thought it would be." Faith smiled. "Would you like to sit with me a moment and listen to the soothing sounds of water?"

Destiny chuckled. "Why yes, I would."

They sat down on the bench and looked around the garden. "How did you do this?" Destiny said quietly. "We're in the middle of a busy industrial area, but you, my love, found a way to bring stillness and much needed calm to these lucky employees."

Faith shrugged. "I thought about how loud and stressful our jobs can be," she said. "I imagined where we'd like to take a break when we got off a lawnmower. I realize the people working here are staring at screens at a desk, but numbers, spreadsheets, data, and information can be noisy too. The soothing sounds of water can alleviate whatever the noise is in your head."

Destiny put her arm around Faith and pulled her close. "You are so smart and so right."

Faith chuckled. "We have another garden to see with another way to diminish stress and it was imagined by an equally smart person."

Destiny smiled. "Thank you. I have a little surprise for you at the rock cairn."

Faith's eyes widened and a strange look settled her face. "You do?"

"It's okay, babe," Destiny said, wrinkling her brow. "You'll like it."

"I'm sure I will."

They got up and walked to the back of the main building and paused at the little shack.

"Do you think they'll move this when they get through with all the construction?" Faith asked.

"I'm sure they will."

"That was some night," Faith said softly.

"It was the beginning of another chapter," Destiny said.

"I really like this part of the story," Faith said, leaning up and kissing Destiny.

"Me too."

As they approached the rock garden Faith bumped her shoulder to Destiny's. "When did you make me this surprise?"

"This morning," Destiny said. "It's a new design." She stopped and looked over at Faith before they walked into the garden. "Are you sure everything is okay?"

"Everything is perfect," Faith said. "After you."

Destiny walked up to the rock cairn and saw the circular design she'd so carefully constructed. She smiled and started to turn around to see Faith's reaction when she noticed something at the base of the structure.

Several small rocks were arranged on the ground to form the words *Marry Me.*

Destiny gasped and quickly turned around to find Faith on one knee smiling up at her. She gasped again and both hands flew to her chest and covered her heart.

Faith held out one hand and raised her eyebrows. "May I have your hand?"

Destiny nodded. She was so surprised she couldn't speak. Slowly, she lowered one of her hands and felt Faith grasp it between both of hers. One day when she looked back on this moment, Destiny would remember the silence. It was just the two of them in a love-filled haze.

"Des, you have saved me over and over," Faith said. "You showed me what trust and love not only look like, but how it feels. You saved me from ferocious dogs." She paused and grinned. "And you saved me by giving us another chance. It's my turn to save you." She took a deep breath and smiled. "You think you've got it all, but you need me to spice things up, to keep you guessing, and to keep things interesting."

"You have no idea," Destiny murmured.

"I've always loved you, but I commit to never letting anything come between us ever again. No secrets, unless it's a good surprise for you. If doubts ever creep in, I will tell you. If I'm afraid, I will tell you. But most of all, I'll tell you, show you, and share with you how much I love you every day."

"Oh, Faith," Destiny said, tears falling down her cheeks.

"You are my destiny," Faith said. "Will you marry me?"

Destiny sank to the ground in front of Faith and cradled her face between her hands. "Yes," she said through her tears. Then she pressed their lips together in a kiss of promise, new beginnings, and love.

34

Faith didn't know her heart could be this full. Her lips were pressed to Destiny's and she never wanted this kiss to end. She could feel Destiny's love, forgiveness, and relief that they were truly going to spend their lives together.

A noise in the distance brought Faith back to the realization they were kneeling in the rock garden at the site. She'd asked Mark to sneak to the rock garden and spell out *Marry Me* right before they started their final walk-through of the project. He, along with Monica, Amy, and most of their workers were in the parking lot waving, clapping, and hollering with happiness.

Destiny pulled away and widened her eyes. She looked over her shoulder and could see the commotion in the parking lot. "Is that—"

"Yep." Faith chuckled. "Here." She slid an engagement ring onto Destiny's finger. "If you don't like it we can get something else."

Destiny held her hand out and gazed at the diamond that sparkled in the fading sunlight. "It's beautiful. I love it."

"Oh, good."

Destiny stood up and pulled Faith up with her. "I can't believe this! I made this special design for you."

"Let me see," Faith said, looking at the rock formation. "Oh, babe. That's so cool! It's our love. From now on, it's an unbroken circle."

"You haven't seen it?"

"No," Faith said. "I had Mark come up here and place the rocks for me. I knew you'd done something special as a surprise and I wanted to see it with you."

"I don't think I've ever been so surprised as when I turned around and you were on one knee," Destiny said.

"I've told you, but I wanted to show you that I trust you. I trust us," Faith said. "What better way than getting married and committing to one another for life."

"We don't have to get married to do that," Destiny said.

Faith tilted her head. "You don't want to get married?"

"No, no," Destiny said. "I do! I don't want you to do this just for me."

"I want to marry you, Des."

Destiny giggled. "I want to marry you, too, babe."

They could hear horns honking in the parking lot and Faith laughed. "They're waiting on us. We're having a party at our karaoke bar to celebrate us and the project. Wait." Faith stopped. "We have to get a picture for Mrs. Baker. Smile!"

After the picture they hurried to the parking lot and received hugs from their friends and coworkers. Then they all piled into their vehicles and took off for the bar.

"We've got to call Mrs. Baker," Faith said, getting into the truck and pulling out her phone.

When the call connected, Faith exclaimed, "She said yes!"

Until We Weren't:

They could hear Mrs. Baker's laughter through the phone. "That's no surprise."

"I was surprised when I saw Faith on one knee!" Destiny said excitedly.

"I'm sure you were," Mrs. Baker replied.

"We're on our way to the bar, but we'll come by to see you tomorrow," Faith said.

"Oh, wait," Mrs. Baker said. "Destiny has something I asked her to show you at your house. You have time to swing by there, don't you?"

Faith looked over at Destiny and furrowed her brow. "Something for me?"

"Yeah," Destiny said, pulling the truck onto the street. "It won't take but a minute."

"Okay," Faith said.

Mrs. Baker chuckled. "Bye, girls. You were meant to be together."

"Bye," Destiny and Faith said in unison.

A few minutes later Destiny pulled around the shop to the tiny house and killed the engine.

Faith looked over at Destiny who was smiling and shaking her head. "What?" Faith asked.

"You want to marry me," Destiny said. She stared at the engagement ring that adorned her finger.

"I do." Faith grinned.

Destiny nodded. "Come with me."

They got out of the truck and Destiny led them over to the chairs in the area they designated as their front porch. The glow of the sun was still visible out in the field.

"With all the excitement we forgot about the sunset," Destiny said.

"It's beautiful," Faith replied. "It's like the sun knew we needed a special show tonight."

Destiny chuckled, put her arm around Faith's shoulders, and gazed out at the field as well.

"What are you supposed to show me?" Faith asked, turning to Destiny.

"Mrs. Baker was helping me out, so we'd have a reason to come here," Destiny explained. "You see, we really are on the same page, babe, because I planned to propose to you right here."

Faith gasped. "No way!"

Destiny nodded and laughed. "Yep."

"Oh, baby," Faith said, taking Destiny's face into her hands.

Destiny rested her forehead against Faith's and closed her eyes.

Faith pulled away and grinned. "Okay, then. Let's hear it."

"Hear what?"

"Let's hear your proposal," Faith said.

Destiny smiled and slowly sank down on one knee. She took Faith's hand. "I thought about proposing in one of the gardens at the site, but right here is where I got my life back. On this piece of ground we call a front porch, we sat here, drank beer, and shared our fears, our doubts, our pain, and opened our hearts." Tears stung the back of her eyes. "I never stopped loving you, but here is where my faith was rewarded. I may be your destiny, but you, Faith Fields, are my everything. I want to show you that you have my trust, babe. I commit to you now and always, but just for fun, will you marry me?"

"Just for fun?" Faith exclaimed with tears now in her eyes as well.

"I promise it'll never be boring." Destiny grinned.

Faith tilted her head. "I don't know. With all we've been through, maybe boring would be nice."

Destiny chuckled. "Are you going to answer my question?"

"I thought I already had," Faith said. "I told you I wanted to marry you."

Destiny raised her eyebrows and waited.

"Get up here," Faith said, pulling her to her feet. "Yes, my love, I will marry you."

Destiny softly brushed her lips against Faith's then pulled back. She reached in her pocket and pulled out the ring. "With this ring, I thee wed," she said as she slipped it on Faith's finger.

"Wow!" Faith exclaimed. "It's like the one I gave you."

"I know," Destiny replied. "I can't believe us."

Faith laughed. "You know who's laughing with us right now."

"Mrs. Baker," they said at the same time.

"She knew and didn't say a word to either one of us," Destiny said.

"You talked to her?"

Destiny nodded. "She's your family. I asked for her blessing."

Faith nodded. "I talked to your parents. They'll be at the bar."

Destiny wrapped her arms around Faith and stared into her bright blue eyes. "If we ever make it to the bar."

"I love you so much," Faith said.

Destiny replied by softly pressing her lips to Faith's. She could feel Faith's arms tighten around her, pulling her closer. Destiny deepened the kiss as soft moans provided the music to their dance of love.

Their love began as a newly planted garden with tender

roots trying to secure their hold. It was beautiful, but when the harshness of life sent them down different paths, on the outside, things withered. However, this love would not be buried. While they were apart their love remained. It grew, and overcame the darkness.

This current growing season brought about discovery, forgiveness, and hope. Their love's roots were strong and they knew that together they could withstand whatever life wanted to throw at them.

TEN YEARS LATER

"Be careful," Faith said. "Watch your step."

"I may be old, but I can still walk," Mrs. Baker said.

"I know you can, but I like to hold your hand." Faith guided the older woman to a chair on the back porch.

Once she was seated Mrs. Baker looked over at Destiny. "I know whose hand you like to hold."

Destiny chuckled. "We still hold hands all the time and I hope we never stop."

"You won't," Mrs. Baker said.

"Are you sure you didn't want to do something else for your birthday?" Faith asked.

"Nope," Mrs. Baker replied. "I love this backyard you two created behind your house. There's something new every time you bring me to visit."

"Yeah, but it's not every day a person turns one hundred years old!" Destiny said.

"I had a party at the retirement center and that's all I needed," Mrs. Baker said. "The few friends I have left and my family got to dote on me, but this is a real gift. You two mean more to me than you'll ever know. I don't plan on going anywhere anytime soon, but I think I can leave you two alone and you'll be all right."

"No we won't," Faith protested. "We need you!"

"I'm not going anywhere just yet," Mrs. Baker said with a smile.

"This is for you," Destiny said, handing Mrs. Baker a glass of wine. "And one for you, my love."

Faith took the glass. "Here's to you, Mrs. B. Happy birthday."

They clinked their glasses together and took a drink.

"Oh, that is good," Mrs. Baker said. "You're not drinking beer?"

"Not today," Faith replied. "We're celebrating with you."

"This is really nice." Destiny sat next to Faith on the small couch.

"What have you added to this beautiful garden?" Mrs. Baker asked. "Oh, look! There's a butterfly."

"Isn't it pretty?" Faith said. "The pink sorrels attract them."

"It reminds me of your wedding," Mrs. Baker said. "That was the best wedding I've ever been to."

Destiny laughed. "You only say that because you married us."

"That's not the only reason," Mrs. Baker replied. "Who gets married in a butterfly garden?"

Faith chuckled. "We did."

"Who has an old woman officiate the ceremony?" Mrs. Baker laughed.

"You had to be the one to do it," Destiny said.

"It was my honor." She smiled at them both. "I watched you two fall in love and even though you had your ups and downs your love remained steadfast. It's what got you through and always will."

"A constant reminder from a dear friend didn't hurt either," Faith said.

Mrs. Baker chuckled. "Your hearts knew the whole time. I just helped your heads along."

Faith looked over at Destiny and for a moment she lost her breath. She could see the strength of their love in those soft brown eyes, but she also saw the tenderness and warmth.

"I know that look," Mrs. Baker said, taking another sip of her wine.

"What look?" Destiny asked.

"You're thinking that this is one of the best moments of your life," she replied. "Like the day you proposed."

"That was such a surprise to us both," Faith said.

"Yeah," Destiny added. "You knew we were both planning to propose but you didn't tell either one of us."

Mrs. Baker chuckled. "Wasn't it a wonderful day? I'm sure you were thinking that was the best day of your life," she said.

"I remember thinking that," Faith said, taking Destiny's hand in hers.

"Until your wedding," Mrs. Baker said. "That was another best day."

"Oh, how it was." Destiny glanced at Faith with a sweet smile.

"That's the way it works. You take those best days and wrap yourself in happiness until the next best day comes along."

"Like today," Faith said.

"Like today." Mrs. Baker nodded. "Hey, I want you to build a little rock sculpture for me."

Destiny furrowed her brow. "A sculpture?"

"You know what I mean," Mrs. Baker said. "One of those rock designs you do together."

"Okay," Faith said.

"What are you waiting for?"

"Oh!" Faith exclaimed, getting up. "You mean now."

"Yep, both of you," Mrs. Baker said.

They walked over to the small rock garden in the corner of their backyard.

"Okay, this design tells the story of Destiny and Faith," Mrs. Baker began. "First, you need a big rock for the base. It's called trust. Faith, you start it."

Faith looked for a big rock with a flat surface on one side and set it in the middle of the space.

"Destiny, your rock is communication. It should be almost the same size and put it right next to trust."

"Yes ma'am," Destiny said. She carefully placed a another rock next to the first rock.

Faith smiled at Destiny and reached for her hand. "I know what comes next," she said, gazing into Destiny's eyes. "A whole lot of love."

"That's right!" Mrs. Baker exclaimed. "You know the story and how to keep it going!"

Faith and Destiny worked together stacking smaller rocks on top of the two large rocks at the base until they had quite a tower.

"What do you think?" Destiny asked as she stood up and gazed at their creation.

"More importantly, what do you think?" Mrs. Baker asked.

Faith put her arm around Destiny and looked over at Mrs. Baker. "I'm wrapping this happiness around us and will always remember this day as one of the best."

"I think it needs one more rock on top," Mrs. Baker said.

Until We Weren't:

Destiny handed Faith a small rock that was round on the top and flat on the bottom. Faith carefully set it on top of the others.

"Perfect," Mrs. Baker said. "That's my love that you'll always have in your hearts."

"Aww, Mrs. B," Faith said.

"I love to see what you two create together," Mrs. Baker said. "Like I've told you many times: you're meant to be."

Later that night Faith was lying in bed with her arms crossed under her head, staring at the ceiling.

"What are you thinking about?" Destiny asked as she slipped under the covers.

Faith released a contented breath and wrapped her arms around Destiny. "I was thinking about our rock sculpture, as Mrs. B called it."

Destiny chuckled and raised up, resting her head on her hand. "We've been married for ten years now and there have been so many best days. Maybe we should add a love rock every year to our stack."

"I love that idea," Faith said. Looking into Destiny's eyes suddenly caused her heart to overflow with love. Sometimes it could be a look, like right now, or a sweet word that made Faith lose her breath or her heart to melt.

"You're studying me with such intensity."

"I love looking into your eyes," Faith replied. "Sometimes it gives me comfort, sometimes it makes me hot, but right now you're making my heart overflow."

Destiny smiled. "I hope it's overflowing with love."

Faith nodded. "The best thing I ever did for myself was trust you, Destiny Green. It brought me all this love and happiness."

"It was the beginning of the story of Destiny and Faith."

"The never-ending story of Destiny and Faith," Faith corrected her.

"Are you ready to add another chapter?" Destiny asked, raising her brows.

Faith pulled her down until their lips met in a soft sensual kiss. The love overflowing in her heart had only one place to go and Destiny's heart was ready for it.

ABOUT THE AUTHOR

Jamey Moody is a bestselling author of sapphic contemporary romance. Her characters are strong women, living everyday lives with a few bumps in the road, but they get their happily ever afters.

Jamey lives in Texas with her adorable terrier Leo.

You can find Jamey's books on Amazon and on her website: jameymoody.com

Join her newsletter for latest book news and other fun. Join here.

Jamey loves to hear from readers. Email her at: jameymoodyauthor@gmail.com

On the next page is a list of Jamey's books with links that will take you to their page.

Jamey has included the first two chapters of See You Next Month which is an age gap, toaster oven, friends to lovers romance. When your client is a beach resort, visiting at Christmas can't be all bad. Kelsey and Isabella devise a unique marketing plan for the resort that has the new friends returning every month for a different kind of vacation. When sparks fly can they leave their hearts in paradise?

ALSO BY JAMEY MOODY

Stand Alones

Live This Love

One Little Yes

Who I Believe

* What Now

*See You Next Month

Until We Weren't: A Story of Destiny and Faith

The Your Way Series:

* Finding Home

*Finding Family

*Finding Forever

The Lovers Landing Series

*Where Secrets Are Safe

*No More Secrets

*And The Truth Is …

Instead Of Happy

The Second Chance Series

*The Woman at the Top of the Stairs

*The Woman Who Climbed A Mountain

*The Woman I Found In Me

Sloan Sisters' Romance Series

*CeCe Sloan is Swooning

*Cory Sloan is Swearing

*Cat Sloan is Swirling

Christmas Novellas

*It Takes A Miracle

The Great Christmas Tree Mystery

With One Look

*Also available as an audiobook

SEE YOU NEXT MONTH
CHAPTER 1

"Welcome to paradise," Kelsey Kenny muttered morosely as she stepped off the plane and walked through the long hallway into the airport. She looked around as people smiled at familiar faces or hugged. No one was there for her, so she strolled through the airport to baggage claim.

Passengers were already plucking pieces of luggage off the rotating table like they were precious prizes. Then, just as quickly, they turned to hurry out of the airport in search of their tropical vacation in paradise or perhaps some of them even lived here.

Ah, the Virgin Islands. Kelsey couldn't imagine living there—then again, she could work from anywhere.

Kelsey was in no hurry. Yes, she guessed this could be considered a vacation for her, but it simply didn't feel very festive. As she walked to the end of the baggage claim and found a place to wait, she spied her bright blue hard-sided suitcase beginning its trek around the sliding tabletop. She hadn't packed much, just a few swimsuits, some shorts, and a couple of cute dresses that she could dress up for dinner or dress down for a casual day at the resort.

A woman hurried towards where Kelsey stood. She was having trouble corralling her oversized purse and what looked like a computer satchel as she reached for one of the bags.

"Dammit," she huffed as the bag passed her by.

Kelsey watched this playing out and could see how frustrated the woman was, so she reached down and easily plucked the bag off the carousel.

"Here you go," Kelsey said as she rolled the heavy suitcase towards the woman.

The woman gasped. "Thank you so much! I missed it."

Kelsey smiled. "Glad I could help."

"I've got another one and you'd think they'd be together," the woman said, staring at the opening where the bags tumbled onto the table.

Kelsey smiled at the woman's Southern accent. It reminded her of syrup, sweet and slow. She turned back to the table only to realize she'd let her own bag pass by.

"Way to go, Kelsey," she mumbled.

"Excuse me?" the woman asked.

Kelsey chuckled. "I let my bag get by me. I'll just have to wait until it comes around again."

"Oh, I'm sorry."

"It's okay. I'm in no hurry."

The woman sighed. "I just want to get to my room. I hope there's a shuttle waiting outside."

Kelsey nodded and kept her eye on her bag as it came into view once again.

"Oh good, there's my other bag," the woman said happily.

A bag matching the suitcase Kelsey had taken off the

carousel for the woman was directly behind Kelsey's blue suitcase. This bag looked even larger than the first one. *She must be staying for several weeks*, Kelsey thought.

Kelsey reached for her bag and easily pulled it off the table. She could see the woman was having trouble lifting the large suitcase over the short rail, so Kelsey reached under the bag and gave it a push.

"Thank you!" the woman exclaimed. "I've done this before, but maybe I packed too much."

"You think," Kelsey said under her breath.

"I promise you, I handled both bags with no problems when I boarded in Charlotte. Just watch," the woman said.

Once she had both bags on their wheels and their handles pulled up, she slipped the satchel over one handle and her purse over the other. She rolled the bags away a short distance and spun each bag to do a little pirouette.

"See what I mean." She smiled and did a slight curtsey.

Kelsey chuckled. "You are skilled." She rolled her bag near the woman and smiled. "I can only manage one bag, so I have to cram everything inside."

The woman smiled. "I doubt that. I think you're just being nice."

Kelsey raised her eyebrows in surprise, and then smiled. "Let's see if we can find a shuttle."

They fell in step next to each other and rolled their bags the short distance to the exit. Outside, Kelsey looked both ways and then saw the shuttle for her resort.

"Thank God!" the woman exclaimed as she started towards the small bus. She turned back to Kelsey and smiled. "Thanks again for the help."

Kelsey returned her smile. "I think we may be going to the same resort." She nodded towards the bus and followed the woman.

"I'm going to The Coral Bay Resort," the woman said.

Kelsey nodded. "Me too. Let me get on the bus and I'll help you with your bags." She didn't wait for the woman to reply. Instead, she stepped onto the bus, smiled at the driver, and rolled her bag into the empty space in front of the first seat.

She turned back just as the woman was lifting her first bag onto the bus.

"Here, I've got it," the bus driver said, quickly getting up from his seat.

He took the first bag and rolled it in front of an empty seat then took the second bag and rolled it into the space across from where Kelsey had left her bag.

"Thank you," the woman said, taking her seat next to the bag.

Kelsey sat down and smiled.

The woman leaned over, extended her hand, and said, "I'm Isabella Burns."

At that moment the driver revved the bus and Kelsey barely heard the woman's name.

"I'm Kelsey Kenny." She took her hand and shook it.

"Thank you again for your help, Kelsey." Isabella smiled.

"You're welcome, Bella." Kelsey appreciated her nice, firm handshake.

The driver pulled away from the curb and Kelsey leaned back to glance out the window. What a beautiful place. If her girls didn't want to be with her at Christmas then surely this little piece of paradise would keep her from missing them.

She sighed and shook her head. It wasn't necessarily that her girls didn't want to be with her; they just wanted to do their own thing, which didn't include her. They knew she wanted to spend Christmas at a beach somewhere instead of skiing in the mountains like they'd always done in the past. But this wasn't what she'd had in mind; she wanted her daughters to be with her.

Kelsey had planned to stay home and work, but she knew the girls would feel guilty. When the opportunity arose to spend Christmas at one of her client's resorts, it seemed like a good idea. The folks at Coral Bay were so excited she was coming so that she could see and experience the resort at its best.

Once she was in her room, she'd give each of her daughters a call, and then try to enjoy the experience. She watched as the palm trees whizzed by.

Kelsey sighed, then glanced over at Isabella and saw her gazing out the window as well. She wondered if she was meeting her family here. Surely she wasn't traveling alone with all that luggage. Just then Isabella looked over at her and smiled.

"It's gorgeous," Isabella said, gesturing towards the window.

"Yeah, it is," Kelsey replied.

"It feels a little strange to be spending Christmas on a tropical island," Isabella remarked.

"It does to me, too," Kelsey agreed. "I noticed a Christmas tree in the airport, though."

"Oh, I missed that." Isabella chuckled. "I was hurrying to baggage claim. Maybe that's a sign I need to slow down and enjoy this beautiful paradise."

Kelsey nodded and smiled. Perhaps Isabella was right. It shouldn't be hard to enjoy these beautiful views, the crystal clear water, and island breeze. She'd wanted to spend Christmas at the beach and here she was, only minutes away.

This was an opportunity to get to know her client and

their product better, so it was a plus for her work life. As far as her personal life, she was at a beach resort on a tropical island. *Come on, Kelsey!* she chided herself.

"Are you okay?" Isabella asked, drawing Kelsey's attention back to her.

Kelsey grinned. "You're right. What's not to enjoy? Merry Christmas."

Isabella chuckled. "Merry Christmas to you, Kelsey."

The driver pulled up to the front door and Kelsey noticed Isabella stayed in her seat. She looked over at her and furrowed her brow. "Do you need any help?"

"With all the trouble my bags have caused since deplaning in St. Thomas, it's best for me to wait and let the other people get off first." Isabella chuckled.

"Are you sure? I don't mind helping you."

"I can get it," Isabella assured her. "I don't want to get in anyone's way."

Kelsey nodded. "It was nice meeting you."

"You too, Kelsey. Maybe I'll see you around."

"Maybe," Kelsey said, then exited the bus. At least Isabella would be a familiar face since she didn't know anyone else at Coral Bay.

"Can I help you with that?" an eager attendant asked her as he held open the front door to the reception area.

"No, but there's a woman on the bus with two large bags that could use your assistance," Kelsey said with a smile.

"I'm on it," the young man said, walking towards the bus.

Kelsey chuckled. She figured Isabella could handle her bags, but a little help was always nice.

"Welcome to Coral Bay," a woman with a cheerful smile said from behind the counter.

"Hi, I'm Kelsey Kenny. Carmen Oliver said to ask for her when I check in," Kelsey explained.

"Oh, Ms. Kenny, right this way."

Kelsey followed the woman down a hallway. There were a couple of meeting rooms on either side and executive offices at the end.

The desk clerk stopped in the doorway of a large office. "Carmen, this is Kelsey Kenny."

"Kelsey!" Carmen exclaimed, coming out from behind her desk. "You made it."

Kelsey shook Carmen's hand and smiled. "It's nice to meet you face to face."

"You as well. How was your trip?"

"It was uneventful, just the way I like it when I'm flying."

"Isn't that the truth? I have you all set up in one of the bungalows right on the water," Carmen said.

"Shouldn't you be using that for your paying guests?"

"You're a special guest. Let us spoil you a little. After all, it's Christmas."

"I can't wait to see everything. The pictures you've shared with me don't do it justice."

"I've told you to come see for yourself and I'm happy you finally have," Carmen said.

"I already have ideas for updates on the website," Kelsey said.

"Our website is as beautiful as our resort, but I trust you to make whatever changes it needs," Carmen said. "We've just gone through a branding change and thought it would be a good idea for you to meet the new team while you're here."

"That sounds great. I want Coral Bay to be successful and am happy to do anything I can to help," Kelsey said.

"I know you're a team player. That's why you've been our web designer all these years."

"You are a valued client," Kelsey said.

"That's enough business talk for today. Terese will take you to your bungalow so you can get settled in. I'd like to have a short meeting with you and the brand designer in the morning," Carmen said. "Don't worry, it won't be early. Everything moves a little slower on the islands."

"Sounds great. I'll see you in the morning," Kelsey said.

Terese, the desk clerk, took Kelsey's bag and she followed her out the back of the building down a path that went by an inviting swimming pool, and then opened up to the most beautiful beach.

"This is incredible," Kelsey said.

"I know. I've lived here all my life and the view never gets old," Terese said.

They left the path to walk over to a private bungalow. It had a small front deck with two chairs for lounging. Terese opened the front door and Kelsey was immediately drawn to the floor to ceiling windows that framed her own private view of the water.

Kelsey gasped. "This truly is paradise."

Terese chuckled. "You have a deck through those doors. Sapphire Beach runs along the entire resort. It's not too crowded this time of year, so it's kind of like a private beach for you, especially after sunset."

"Thank you, Terese," Kelsey said, reaching into her purse.

"Oh, no, Ms. Kenny. It's my pleasure," Terese said, holding up both hands.

"Will you at least call me Kelsey?"

Terese smiled. "I can do that. If you're hungry, I recommend the fine dining in the restaurant we passed when we exited the main building. The seafood is always fresh. If you need anything, please let me know."

"I can't imagine needing anything," Kelsey said, looking around the room.

"Enjoy your stay. I'm always nearby if you need anything." Terese laid the key card on the table and closed the door.

Kelsey opened the door onto her back deck and inhaled deeply. "Hello, paradise," she said with a touch of optimism in her voice.

CHAPTER 2

Isabella walked into her bungalow and gasped. "Wow, this is incredible."

"I'm glad you like it," Nadia said. "Where would you like me to leave your luggage?"

"Let's see," Isabella said, looking around the large room. "How about over there?"

Nadia rolled the bags in front of the closet. "Carmen has assigned me to be your assistant while you're here. If you need anything at all, simply call the front desk."

"Don't you get to go home at night?"

Nadia chuckled. "I'm here a lot, but yes, I go home at night. Someone will always be at reception if you need anything while I'm not here."

"Thank you," Isabella said. "Do you do this for all your guests?"

Nadia smiled. "Well, not everyone, but we try to be extra available to our guests in the bungalows since you're not in the main building of the resort."

"Carmen didn't have to do that for me. I'm supposed to be working," Isabella said.

"I hope you'll be able to enjoy the resort as well."

"Oh, I plan to," Isabella said. "Let me get something for you."

"No, ma'am. I'm here for you. It's all part of our service," Nadia said.

Isabella tilted her head. "Are you sure? I don't feel right not giving you something."

"Believe me, I'm glad to do it," Nadia said, walking towards the door. "All of our restaurants are exceptional. I suggest the fine dining restaurant tonight. The chef is always doing something special."

"Thanks for the suggestion."

"I'll see you later." Nadia left, quietly closing the door behind her.

Isabella turned back to the beautiful view out her back deck and took a deep breath.

This would be her first Christmas away from the boys and she wasn't handling it well. When her ex-husband told her he was taking them to New York for Christmas, she was upset. They had always spent Christmas at home in Charlotte. This was the second year they'd been divorced and it was his turn to have them for Christmas, so she couldn't really do anything about it.

Christmas wasn't the same without them. To keep from ruining Christmas for the people around her, she'd decided to work instead. A small smile played across her lips. It just so happened that her current client was a resort on St. Thomas in the Virgin Islands. Isabella had hoped the sun and sand would keep her mind off Christmas.

She planned to try to call the boys, but figured they'd be out doing something fun with her ex-husband's family. Isabella ambled over to the mini refrigerator and took out a bottle of water.

Once she opened the glass door onto the back deck, the rhythmic lapping of the waves called to her. She settled into one of the chaise lounges and drank deeply from the bottle.

Her thoughts drifted back to meeting Kelsey Kenny. Isabella furrowed her brow. *Did she call me Bella?* No one called her Bella and if they did, she usually corrected them. She tilted her head and smiled. There was no need to correct the kind woman. Isabella probably wouldn't see her again anyway. Just because they were staying at the same resort didn't mean their paths would cross. It was a big place.

When the attendant had appeared at the shuttle to help her with her luggage, she wondered if Kelsey had sent him her way once she'd gone inside the resort. Of course, the resort offered top-notch service, but she wouldn't be surprised if Kelsey had a hand in it.

Once she'd made it to the reception desk, she looked around and didn't see Kelsey anywhere. A few minutes later the resort's executive director, Carmen Oliver, appeared to welcome her and then Nadia led her to the bungalow, pointing out amenities along the way.

She wondered if Kelsey was traveling alone, just as she was. When they were on the drive from the airport to the resort, Isabella had glanced over at Kelsey as she gazed out the window. Something about the woman's face made Isabella think she wasn't exactly happy to be there.

Isabella sighed, closing her eyes and letting the island breeze waft over her travel weary body. She hopped up and decided to take a quick shower and change her clothes. Isabella didn't care for dining alone, but she was hungry and fresh seafood sounded delicious.

* * *

Kelsey strolled down the path back towards the main building. It was so peaceful and hard to believe there were so many other people at the resort. She walked past the bar and over to the entrance of the restaurant. Her eyes scanned the room, seeing mostly couples with a few families already seated and enjoying their meal.

She thought about going back to the bar and ordering dinner there.

"I knew it," a familiar voice said from behind her. "This place is full of couples and families."

Kelsey turned and looked right into Isabella's smiling face. "Hey," she said with a friendly smile.

"Shall we sit together? I hate eating alone," Isabella said.

"I do, too. I was about to go back to the bar," Kelsey said.

"Maybe we'll hit it after dinner." Isabella winked.

As they followed an attendant who took them to a table, Kelsey noticed Isabella's large purse on her shoulder. Kelsey smiled and couldn't keep from laughing as she remembered her looping the purse onto her bag and giving it a spin.

"What's funny?" Isabella asked as she sat down at the table for two. She hooked her purse over the chair.

"Your purse reminded me of your little dance with your luggage earlier today," Kelsey explained.

Isabella stared at Kelsey as she put the strap to her small crossbody bag, barely big enough to hold a phone and not much more, over the back of her chair.

Kelsey raised her eyebrows. "What?"

"You bring one bag and have a small purse and here I am with two large suitcases, my computer satchel, and a huge tote. Perhaps I could learn something from you."

Kelsey raised her eyebrows. "How long are you staying?"

"A week or so," Isabella said, resting her chin in her hand.

Kelsey laughed. "We'll see about that when you observe me repeating outfits later in the week."

"I don't know, the idea of not lugging all this around is appealing in this relaxed environment," Isabella said.

"The fewer things I have to carry with me, the better," Kelsey said as their server appeared with menus.

"Could you bring us two delicious fruity drinks fit for this paradise?" Isabella asked, looking over at Kelsey.

She nodded and the server disappeared to get their drinks, letting them peruse the menu.

"I have two boys," Isabella said, leaning over the small table. "I'm never without snacks or maybe a dinosaur or two in my purse."

Kelsey chuckled. "I remember those days."

Isabella studied Kelsey again and tilted her head. "Do you have kids?"

Kelsey nodded. "Two daughters, but they are in their twenties now."

"What!" Isabella exclaimed, surprised. "You must have been a teenager when you had them."

Kelsey thought for a moment. "My oldest, Dana, is twenty-four and Emma is twenty-two. Your comment made me realize that I was Dana's age when I had her."

"Really? I thought we were the same age," Isabella said.

"How old are your boys?"

"Wyatt, my oldest, is thirteen and Gus is ten," Isabella said.

"Oh, you're getting to the fun stuff then—teenagers," Kelsey said, widening her eyes. "I think you're a lot younger than I am."

Isabella shook her head. "I'm forty. That's not far behind forty-eight, but I swear, Kelsey, you don't look it."

Their server set two drinks down that were the color of

the sunset. Each had a skewer with a piece of pineapple and a cherry.

"Oh, these look delicious," Isabella said, holding up her glass. "To my first Christmas without my boys and no, I'm not taking it well."

Kelsey clinked her glass to Isabella's. "I get it. My girls didn't want to have Christmas with me."

They both sipped from their drinks and nodded in approval.

"What do you mean they didn't want to have Christmas with you?"

Kelsey paused. "Are you sure you want to hear this?"

"Yes, it might make me feel better about my situation."

"Okay, here goes. I'm from Denver. Dana is in nursing school and has been a patrol and rescue skier since she was a teenager. She stays on the mountain during the holidays, but usually makes it down for Christmas Day. Emma, my youngest, is in the last year of her political science degree and got the opportunity to go to California with her roommate whose mother happens to be a congresswoman. She's in heaven right now. So..." Kelsey paused to take another sip of her drink.

"So?"

"The girls know I've always wanted to spend Christmas at the beach. Be careful what you tell your kids," Kelsey said, leaning over the table. "They thought it would be a great idea for me to come on this beach getaway while they're doing their own thing for Christmas. I don't think either of them realized I wanted to spend Christmas at the beach as a family."

"Oh, okay. I'll remember that. Be specific," Isabella said, narrowing her eyes.

"Exactly." Kelsey nodded. "Now, what about you? You said this was your first Christmas without your boys?"

Just then their server came back to take their orders.

"Would you want to order the seafood sampler and split it?" Isabella asked. "We can try everything that way."

"That sounds good," Kelsey replied.

"And bring us another round of these drinks, please," Isabella said.

When the server left the table and after another sip of their drinks, Kelsey said, "Okay, Bella. It's your turn."

Isabella scoffed. "You called me Bella."

Kelsey furrowed her brow. "Isn't that your name?"

Isabella shrugged. "My name is Isabella."

Kelsey sighed. "I barely heard your name on the bus. The traffic was kind of loud until we left the airport. I'm sorry."

"It's okay. You can call me Bella. I kind of like it."

"Are you sure?"

Isabella nodded.

"I like your Southern accent," Kelsey said with a smile. "Now, about your boys?"

"I've been divorced for two years. We alternate holidays. I had the boys last Christmas and it's my ex-husband's turn. I didn't think it would be a big deal because we both live in Charlotte, but he decided to take them to New York to be with his family."

"I'm sorry. That must be hard," Kelsey said compassionately.

"I started to work over the holidays, but decided getting out of town would keep me from bringing my friends down. Can you imagine how awful it would be to spend Christmas with my friends and their kids? Anyway, I can work from anywhere, so here I am."

"So we're both single moms spending Christmas without our kids," Kelsey said with a frown.

"Yep. Hey wait, what about your girls' father?"

Kelsey raised her eyebrows and noticed their server coming towards their table. "That's a whole other story."

Isabella tilted her head and furrowed her brow.

Their server set the large platter of food in the middle of the table and gave them each a plate. Another server was right behind him with their second round of drinks. Once they had everything on the table and the servers were gone, Isabella raised her eyebrows.

"I'm all ears."

Get See You Next Month

Printed in Great Britain
by Amazon